# THE DEVIL'S MUSE

# THE DEVIL'S MUSE

## BILL LOEHFELM

SARAH CRICHTON BOOKS  FARRAR, STRAUS AND GIROUX  NEW YORK

Sarah Crichton Books
Farrar, Straus and Giroux
18 West 18th Street, New York 10011

Printed in the United States of America
First edition, 2017

Library of Congress Cataloging-in-Publication Data
Names: Loehfelm, Bill, author.
Title: The devil's muse / Bill Loehfelm.
Description: First edition. | New York : Sarah Crichton Books / Farrar, Straus
    and Giroux, 2017. | Series: Maureen Coughlin series ; 5
Identifiers: LCCN 2016044981 | ISBN 9780374279776 (hardback) |
    ISBN 9780374715632 (e-book)
Subjects: LCSH: Policewomen—Louisiana—New Orleans—Fiction. |
    BISAC: FICTION / Crime. | FICTION / Thrillers. | GSAFD: Suspense
    fiction. | Mystery fiction.
Classification: LCC PS3612.O36 D486 2017 | DDC 813/.6—dc23
LC record available at https://lccn.loc.gov/2016044981

Designed by Abby Kagan

Our books may be purchased in bulk for promotional, educational, or business
use. Please contact your local bookseller or the Macmillan Corporate and
Premium Sales Department at 1-800-221-7945, extension 5442, or by e-mail at
MacmillanSpecialMarkets@macmillan.com.

www.fsgbooks.com
www.twitter.com/fsgbooks • www.facebook.com/fsgbooks

10  9  8  7  6  5  4  3  2  1

*For Bill, Sr.*

I carry a madness, everywhere I go . . .

—OASIS, "Turn Up the Sun"

# THE DEVIL'S MUSE

# 1

On a misty Thursday night in New Orleans, Officer Maureen Coughlin stood in the middle of St. Charles Avenue, surrounded by fire.

Flames danced around her, throwing their fluid light against the steady darkness, igniting wavy golden glows on the hundreds of damp and screaming faces surrounding her and on the fluttering leaves of the ancient trees forming the canopy that yawned above her. The heat of the passing flames reddened her cheeks. She felt their warmth on her bare throat, and found it soothing. She breathed in the black smoke. A light sweat broke out across her hairline under her knit NOPD cap. She'd been cold for so long before the fire came that she sniffled despite the heat, and the tang of burning fuel stung her nostrils. She felt, for a moment, transported into a ghost story, one where *she* was the ghost, a blue specter floating weightless in a haunted Victorian parlor, with shades, spirits, and banshees suspended in the night air everywhere around her like the smoke from the fires, drifting to her like the heavy vapor of spilled propane.

Despite the march of the flames, she stayed unmoving in the street, her hands clasped behind her back, her feet spread on the pavement. She curled her toes, gripping the soles of her shoes, grounding herself on the avenue. Masked men danced around her on all sides. They carried the fire. They wore their knit hats and ball caps pulled low. Bandannas and towels covered their faces, only their glowing eyes and shining cheeks exposed. They waved and spun their burning torches in the night air above their heads, strutting, leaping, dancing, dipping their hips, arching their backs as they broke around her, a fluid, flaming wave breaking against a dark, damp rock. Thick drops of fire, like huge burning tears, tumbled from the torches, falling to the damp street, where they sputtered and died.

The people lining the street tossed sprays of coins at the fire-bearers, the flying money flickering like sparks in the light of the flames, the coins pinging and banging off the metal guards of the torches like baby gunshots. The men with the torches dipped and whirled, peeling the coins off the street with the long fingers of one hand, twirling their torches in the other.

They did this, these men, Maureen thought, for miles. She searched her brain for what they were called. One word, a French word, a New Orleans word one of her fellow cops had taught her as the other officers in the Sixth District tried to educate her in time for working her first Mardi Gras.

She found it. *Flambeaux.* That was it; that's the word. The men who marched with fire to light the parade were called the flambeaux. This was her first night parade that used them. The flambeaux were a superfluous, beloved tradition held over from the holiday's nineteenth-century roots, from when mule-drawn carts pulled the parade floats through the gas-lit streets. She was proud of herself for remembering this detail. She had plenty left to learn, that was for sure, but she was making progress. A tricky city, New Orleans, and she made you earn access to her intimacies.

The flambeaux moved on. The cold returned and thunder came to her now, tremors rolling down the avenue. She could feel the rumbling under her feet. A marching band powering her way, the drum corps beating out a heavy cadence to keep the marchers stepping in time. Those drums. She loved those drums. They were her new favorite thing about Mardi Gras. Even at a distance, now that was power. She would remain at her station in the street for them, too, and let the sound of the thunder envelop her like she had the warmth of the fire. The huge bass drums, carried high on the torsos of the teenage musicians who played them, would surround her after the rest of the band's sections had passed around her. The thick, pounding notes of the drums would vibrate deep in her chest, reaching all the way down to her heart, shaking her skeleton as if her ribs were the prongs of a tuning fork.

A few weeks ago, a fellow officer in her New Orleans police district, Louis Cordts, had tried framing what awaited them during the final days of Mardi Gras in terms that Maureen, a native New Yorker and rookie patrol officer working her first Mardi Gras season, might more easily understand:

"Well, imagine, like, a dozen Times Squares in NYC on New Year's Eve all lined up in a row, stacked like boxes one after the other. Okay? But instead of that happening for one night, that party lasts for six days. Now, imagine running big parades through the middle of that crowd every night. Huge parades with hundreds of riders that stretch for miles and take hours to roll. Except for the weekends, when the parades run all day, too. And remember drinking in the street is legal here. And barbecues and crawfish boils on the neutral ground, where the streetcars usually run. And beer kegs. They're okay, too. And tents. And couches. And remember that the riders on the floats throw things for the crowd to catch. Strands of plastic beads. Sometimes they light up. And toys. Stuffed animals, water guns, little Frisbees, it depends . . . Oh, and plastic go-cups, and these metal doubloons . . . Yeah, some of these floats, when we get to the big parades, like Muses, can have a hundred riders each. And then there's the kids in the crowd, yeah, they sit on top of these ladders with seats on them that their parents put on wheels, and then, oh, speaking of wheels . . . have you seen the Rolling Elvii? The Elvis impersonators on motor scooters? They'll come toward the beginning of the parades, them or maybe the Laissez

Boys, the guys in the smoking jackets that drive the motorized armchairs. They all usually come before the flambeaux . . . the flambeaux? The guys carrying the propane-powered torches? Yeah, like *fire* torches. Nobody told you about them? What about the Pink Pussyfooters? You heard about the Marching One Hundred, though, right? No? The Purple Knights? Greatest marching band in the world? You sure you've been here almost a whole year?"

Maureen had finally thrown her hands up in surrender. "I get it. I get it," she'd said, though she hadn't. She didn't want to tell Cordts he was only scaring her with every bizarre ritual he described.

"What I want to know is, what's our job during all this?" Maureen had asked. "Generally speaking."

"Generally speaking?" Cordts had said. He'd thought for a moment. "On the uptown part of the route where we'll be? Blood and bullets are what we worry about."

Maureen had laughed. "A bit dramatic, that. Don't you think?"

"Simply put," Cordts had continued, "we need to put an end to anything that can result in either of those two things. Preventive measures are best. A good night is when we see neither of those things."

"Oh, that's it?" Maureen had said, grinning at Cordts's attempt to impress her. "Just avoid bullets and blood? Yeah, what could possibly go wrong?"

"The shit you need to respond to," Cordts said, "it's like jazz or porn, trust me, you'll know it when you see it."

Though she'd always considered herself a woman of ample imagination, especially when it came to decadence, she hadn't realized how poorly she'd anticipated what she'd be dealing with until she had witnessed the rolling pageant of elaborately themed floats and costumed walking crews and proud and thunderous marching bands and more for the first time herself on a sunny Saturday afternoon.

Thousands of partying parade-goers jammed the wide, live-oak-lined blocks of St. Charles Avenue, which was the city's primary artery for Mardi Gras parades. The crowd stretched for miles in both directions, all of them revved up for Babylon, Chaos, and Muses, the Thursday-night trifecta of Mardi Gras parades kicking off the six-day bacchanal that was the run-up to Fat Tuesday. She'd worked the previous weekend's daytime parades, smaller and gentler undertakings compared with the rolling behemoths that were the super krewes, the first of which was this night's final parade, the Krewe of Muses.

After the first week of parades, she'd learned that when she worked the route sometimes she felt transported and romantic, as she had minutes ago amid the flambeaux or as she did awash in the drums; other times, like when she actually had to get somewhere or accomplish something in the middle of a rolling parade, she felt as if someone had filled the Superdome with people, poured in a million gallons of liquor, shaken the mix up good like a martini in a cocktail shaker, and dumped the contents into the streets of New Orleans. And then done it again ten more times.

Now, tonight, the heat of the torches gone by, in the pissing, noncommittal rain made worse by a spring cold snap, half a dozen parades under her belt, her feet and her back already sore, Maureen wasn't sure she understood the phenomenon any better. But at least she could work without her mouth hanging open like a tourist at the spectacle.

Her radio crackled over the sound of the band as the marchers flowed around her. She could only hear bits and pieces of the announcement over the music. She caught something about a disturbance in the crowd along the back of the parade route. She rose up on her toes trying to see the problem, peering as best she could over the heads of the crowd. Nothing yet that she could see. She settled back on her feet and rolled her shoulders, correcting her posture. She had a long night of standing ahead of her. She'd pay attention to the crowd and wait for whatever happened next. No reason to move just yet. If the trouble came to her, then she'd react . . .

She glanced at Cordts, one of the two other cops she was stationed with on this part of the route. Cordts, who'd stepped aside to the curb for the passing of the flambeaux, grinned and shrugged at her from a few feet away. He did a lot of that. He hadn't heard the full report either. Their third, Officer Wilburn, had wandered out of sight. He did that every now and again during the parades; he knew a lot of people in the neighborhood, and since he was a police officer, most of them fed him. He didn't like to share. But if they needed him, he probably wasn't too far away.

Maureen reached for her radio mic, thought about asking for more information or a repeat of the report, but the drums only got closer and louder, and the horns exploded into a song and the crowd roared at the rush of music. She clipped her mic back on her shoulder.

She would know the trouble, she figured, when it got to her. It wasn't like her to miss it, and it wasn't very often that trouble passed her by. Didn't take long for it to find her, either. Like beads tossed from a float, she always seemed to catch it as it went flying by, sometimes without even really trying.

# 2

"Pardon me, please," Maureen said over and over again, patting backs and shoulders with her gloved hands, gliding her way through the crowd, forcing a smile to her face, careful not to reveal that she was keeping a keen eye on that disturbance she'd now spotted approaching from only three blocks away and rushing closer.

"Stand aside, please," Maureen said, continuing to move through the crowd, syrupy as she could muster. "Stand aside for a minute, if you don't mind. Oh, what a cute baby . . . I hope you're old enough to be drinking that . . . Just need to get through here . . . Love that hat. It lights up? Amazing. Thanks."

She didn't need to hear the radio. She could see somebody charging right at her through the crowd. People leaped and stumbled aside in their efforts to avoid the man. Her first job, she knew, was to intercept this missile, and then to subdue it. From that point the mission became calm, control, and contain, she thought. Calm, control, and contain. And disarm, if necessary.

The parade route crowd was an organism, Maureen had been taught.

The NOPD officers stationed along the route functioned as the immune system, the white blood cells, the defense mechanism against chaos and breakdown. Protection against organ failure and death.

Maureen moved off the neutral ground, the grassy median dividing St. Charles where the streetcar tracks ran, and into the other side of the avenue. She watched a short, bony, brown-skinned man with an uneven afro sprinting down the middle of the road, the crowd parting around him. He was barefoot, running unaffected by the beads, bottles, beer cans, and other trash in the street. Not only was he shoeless, Maureen noticed, but he wore nothing on the rest of him but hot-pink zebra-print tights and a rapturous, orgasmic smile. As he ran, he smeared his face and bare chest with fistfuls of half-melted blue cotton candy.

Both he and a moving car, a pristine white SUV with tinted windows, arrived simultaneously at the intersection of St. Charles and Seventh Street. The SUV, which really should not have been there in the first place, was thankfully moving slowly, cautious of the abundant drunken foot traffic in the street. It rolled to a stop as the driver leaned hard on the horn. The bony man continued running right at the SUV, oblivious to its size and the blare of its horn, now loudly singing at the sky, "You and I we're gonna live for-evaaaaaaaaah."

He tripped, staggered, stumbled, then, as he regained his footing, startling Maureen, leaped into the air as if propelled from a diving board, launching himself onto the car as if belly flopping into a pool, landing with an audible *thunk* on the snowy expanse of the hood.

Maureen quickened her pace to a trot as she moved toward the intersection, calling into her radio for the closest officers to join her. The SUV's driver, who Maureen couldn't see behind the dark windows, punished the horn again.

The man remained sprawled facedown on the hood of the car, not moving, his breathing shallow and rapid. He'd smeared the hood and windshield with slimy blue cotton candy.

The driver's-side window rolled down, revealing a young white man, maybe twenty, wearing wraparound shades, a puffy shirt with lace cuffs, and a pirate hat, who sat wide-eyed and openmouthed, panting, his arms extended and his hands tight on the steering wheel. Maureen approached the vehicle, keeping a watchful eye on the man lying spread-eagle across the hood. Maureen wasn't sure he was conscious.

"I didn't hit him," the driver shouted. "I didn't. I swear. He came right at me. Out of nowhere. He's crazy. He's nuts."

"I know," Maureen said. He's high as a motherfucker is what he is, she thought. And so are you, though on something less than the cotton-candy kid here. "I saw. You're fine. I don't want you to worry." She peered into the backseat, didn't see anyone, but the driver had a passenger in the seat beside him. She said to the driver, "Do me a favor, sir, and remove your sunglasses." He didn't. She looked around him at his passenger. "And you, other sir, I need you to put out that cigarette."

"Why?" the passenger asked. "I'm just sitting here smoking. I just lit it. If he didn't do anything and he's driving I certainly didn't do anything as the passenger."

"Well," Maureen said, "let me see. For why, we could go with because that's a *joint*, and I'm a *cop*, and I don't want to see or smell that shit while we're dealing with our situation here and if you continue to irritate me I'll call my partners and we'll toss the whole car. Or we could go with because I fucking said so. Pick one, but put it out."

The passenger squinted at her. "Oh, shit, you're a cop. I'm sorry, Officer."

He looked around him, lost for what to do with the smoldering joint in his hand. He looked out the windshield, bouncing in his seat as if he had just then noticed the man draped across the hood. "Oh, shit. Dude, dude, dude, this guy, I bet he took that shit I was telling you about, bro. That zombie shit. They got it down in the Quarter. I'm telling you. I told you that shit was real. We gotta get some. *Look* at this guy."

"Fuck, dude," the driver snapped, "what is wrong with you?"

He snatched the joint from his friend's hand and tossed it over Maureen's shoulder. She watched it tumble through the air and land in the street, where someone walking by stepped on it. "Shit, sorry, Officer."

"Bro, you *owe* me for that," the passenger whined. "My brother's working in the CBD. I can't get any more tonight."

Maureen focused on the driver. "Sir, your sunglasses?"

"What? Oh, yeah." He slid off his shades. Under them he wore an eye patch that Maureen figured for part of the costume.

"Sir, what's your name?"

"Am I in trouble? Why am I in trouble? You said yourself I didn't hit this nut. My friend's an idiot. He didn't mean what he was saying."

"I want to know what to call you while we talk a minute," Maureen said. "That's all. No trouble."

"Rob. My name is Rob." He jerked his thumb over his shoulder. "That's Don."

"Rob, the parades are rolling. They've *been* rolling."

"I can *see* that," Rob said.

"And yet here you are," Maureen said, "trying to drive this behemoth down St. Charles."

Don gestured at the windshield. "This fucking guy. What a mess. He got some sticky shit all over your ride, bro. I don't even want to think what that is."

Rob swatted at Don with one hand, not even looking at him, trying to focus his one uncovered, bloodshot eye on Maureen.

"My point is," she said, "these streets are kind of closed, except for emergencies."

"I know," Rob said, "but I've got four cases, I mean, three, four bags of ice that we're trying to get back to Delachaise Street with, for the sausages. That we have."

Rob's friend snickered. "Dude. Snausages."

"I lock you up," Maureen said, looking around Rob at Don, "and it's Thursday when you get out. *Next* Thursday, Don. I don't care who your daddy is. I will fucking *lose* you for a week. Shut. The. Fuck. Up."

Don squirmed in his seat, looking away from Maureen, clutching at his crotch. "Bro, I gotta piss. Fuck."

"Holy shit, Officer, I'm so sorry," Rob said. "Don's a fucking retard. Seriously, it's, like, a medical condition. Our moms are best friends." He frowned. "How do you know Don's dad?"

"Okay, I don't know his father, I'm just guessing that . . ." She stopped. Was she really trying to explain herself to these two? She started again. "I know it's inconvenient, but I'm going to need you to remain in the vehicle and stay here for a few minutes. Turn the engine off, please. And put the emergency brake on for me, please."

"But I'm not in any trouble, right?" Rob asked. "My shit's gonna melt, though. Can I call my, uh, mom, and let her know I'm gonna be late with the ice?"

"No, no calling anyone," Maureen said. "I need you to be patient, and be quiet, while I deal with"—she gestured at the man draped over the hood of the car—"whatever this is."

"Yes, sir," Rob said.

Maureen walked to the front of the vehicle. She ordered the guy off the car. He did not move, did not acknowledge her. She tried it again, louder this time.

"Sir, you need to get off of the vehicle. Sir, I know you can hear me." She tapped the back of her gloved hand against his hip a couple of times. Up close, she noticed he was considerably younger than she'd thought. Couldn't have been more than a teenager. The kid was sickly thin, too, wasting away, bony at the knees, wrists, and ankles. "Sir? Sir. You are trying my patience here. We need to get this vehicle on its way."

Maureen noticed that several people were now watching the proceedings, some of them recording the scene with their phones and creeping ever closer as they did it. Getting themselves a dose of authentic Mardi Gras madness, she thought, to show the folks back home. She'd been warned to stay aware that recording devices were everywhere these days. Some she would see; others she would not, but they would be there. She had no desire to star in anyone's vacation videos. She turned her attention back to the kid in the pink tights. She saw that the strain of maintaining a grip on the hood of the car had turned his knuckles white. He couldn't hang on like that, she thought, if he really was unconscious. She was eager for more officers to arrive, not for help with the crazy kid, but with herding and distracting the curious onlookers.

"If you don't let go of the car," she said to the kid, trying not to glance at the cameras as she spoke, "I'm going to have to remove you from it. I will use physical force to do that."

She stepped back and waited a long moment, got no response. Rob pumped the horn again. Maureen raised her hands. "Knock that off. You are not helping."

He leaned out the window. "I'm sorry, but the third-grade bladder in here is gonna wet himself. I just detailed the car. Can he get out and walk?"

"He needs to hold it," Maureen shouted. Her patience with everyone, with the whole ridiculous scenario, was running out. "Sir," she said to the kid in the tights, "your present behavior makes you a danger to yourself and others." She waited again for a response. Nothing. "I know you can hear me."

She leaned in close to his ear. "I know you can hear me. Do not continue to test me." She thought she saw the slightest curl at the corner of his mouth. "All right, then. If that's how you want it."

She seized him hard by the waistband of his tights, determined to rip him off the car in one quick motion, like a Band-Aid. At her touch, the young man exploded to life, as if Maureen had jolted him with a cattle prod. He jumped to his feet, his head whipping around at her, bending over his shoulder at a frightening and unnatural angle, his eyes rolling back in his head like a shark's as he snapped his jaws at her, brown teeth clacking, as he tried to bite her face. She reared away from him as if from a rabid dog, bending far back, hanging on to his waistband with one hand, reaching for the pepper spray on her belt with her other. The man lurched away from her with surprising strength, breaking free of her grip.

She clenched her fists, fearing he'd leap on her, biting at her face again. But he seemed to forget she was there. He shook his rubbery limbs wildly, screaming as loud as he could and slapping the hood of the SUV. "You're killing me! You're killing me! You're killing me!"

Please, God, Maureen thought, don't let him piss himself.

Laughter and gasps erupted from the crowd.

The kid collapsed to the pavement, where, again, after a few twitches, the last gasps of a fish in a boat, he decided that he was unconscious.

Maureen looked at her hands. Her gloves were shiny with snot and rain and cotton candy. Only another few hours of this tonight, she thought. She wiped her gloves on her uniform pants. Maybe I won't dry-clean my uniforms after the holiday, she thought. Maybe I'll just fucking burn them.

The kid now lying at her feet didn't appear injured, but she was concerned about what bizarre drug he had taken. It was something powerful Maureen couldn't name, and she had a hard time recognizing its effects. This impressed and unnerved her, because there wasn't much she hadn't seen, or tried, at least before becoming a cop nearly a year ago. She couldn't decide what to do next.

Lying motionless in the street, the kid reminded her of a squashed roach, appendages sticking out in every direction, but not nearly as dead as it wanted you to believe. His hip bones protruded from the waistband of his tights. Maureen could see each of his ribs. She watched his lungs expand and contract as he took rapid, shallow breaths.

She tapped at the bottom of his bare foot with the toe of her boot. Nothing. No reaction.

So now what? She did not want to deal with arresting him, but she couldn't very well leave him lying in the middle of the street. He was blocking traffic, for one thing. She had to hand it to the kid. He was putting on quite a performance, playing possum and hoping, she guessed, that Maureen would lose interest in him if he lay there long enough on the cold wet pavement. And it just might work for him, she thought.

She sniffled, wiping her top lip with the back of her gloved hand. She flexed her fingers, trying to keep the blood in her hands moving. She sniffled again. She had tissues in her pocket but they were already wet. She tossed them in the street. No matter what she did, she couldn't stop her nose from running. She'd dressed like she'd been told, as the other cops had coached her: tights and an extra-long-sleeved T-shirt under her uniform, three pairs of socks, extra everything in plastic bags in a gym bag back in a patrol car that she'd lost track of an hour ago. The parades she'd worked the weekend before had rolled in beautiful early spring weather, sunny afternoons and cool but clear nights. Tonight was another story.

The temperature was fifty degrees, maybe, and dropping, and this kid wasn't even shivering. Despite the cold, his whole body was slick with a peculiar greasy sweat that was more than a cotton candy coating, as if he'd been dipped in cooking oil. Maybe she didn't need the extra clothes. Maybe she could do with a dose of whatever this kid had taken.

"Can I go now, *please?*" Rob asked, leaning his head out the window. "I'm sorry, uh, whatever." His face was chalk white. He's terrified, Maureen thought. He thinks I hit this guy with the Taser or something, and that I'm going to get him next.

"One more minute," Maureen said.

If she wasn't going to arrest the kid at her feet, then she really had no reason to detain these two idiots in the SUV. Neither of them should be driving, but there was nowhere to put the vehicle. Bringing out a tow truck would be a joke. They'd laugh at her if she called for one. And these piss-heads wouldn't get above five miles per hour. Delachaise Street, where they were headed, was less than a mile away. Once they were gone, maybe she could drag Druggy the Clown here out of the street and onto the neutral ground. Though without another cop around to bear witness, she was reluctant to put her hands on him again in front of the cameras.

She spoke into the radio mic on her shoulder. "Cordts, Wilburn, can I get an assist over here? One of you? St. Charles and Seventh, lake side."

# 3

Maureen sighed and looked over her shoulder, waiting for either Wilburn or Cordts to answer her or emerge from the crowd. She growled in frustration. Then she saw Cordts raise his hand above the crowd. In another few seconds he appeared.

He stopped dead in his tracks, shock freezing his face when he saw the sweaty clown at her feet. He locked eyes with her.

"Would you come over here and help me, please?" Maureen said.

Cordts shook off his shock and walked over to her, looking down at the kid in the street. "I have to admit," he said, "for a second there, I thought, well, Cogs has gone and done it, she's finally gone and killed somebody."

"That's a hell of a thing to say in front of people."

Cordts looked around. "Put your phones away, people, and live a little," he shouted. "There's a parade rolling. Greatest free show on earth. Go watch it." To Maureen's surprise, for the most part, his admonishments worked, and people wandered away, turning their attention back to the parade.

"Fucking sheep. Like they give a fuck about him." He looked around again. "Or us, for that matter." He checked his phone. "Why is this car here? Anyone trying to drive through this is a moron."

"That's exactly why this car is here," Maureen said.

Cordts shook his head. "Fucking useless white boys. What's the point of closing *some* of the streets if you're just . . . you know what, never mind. They gotta move."

"Yeah, I've been working on that."

He lifted his foot at the kid in the street. "So what's the story here? Nice pants." He nodded at the car. "They hit him?"

Rob started yelling. "I didn't hit nobody. He ran into me." He climbed out of the car. "Officer, ma'am, you saw, you saw the whole thing, you can't put this on me."

Maureen raised her hand. "Whoa, whoa, back in the car, please. You're fine, I got you covered. Back in the car, please."

"So the knuckleheads *didn't* hit him," Cordts said, "is the impression I'm getting."

"He came running up the street," Maureen said, "and threw himself on the car. He's super fucked up on God knows what."

"Happy fucking Mardi Gras," Cordts said. "So this has nothing to do with them."

Maureen walked over to the car. "You're not hurt?" Rob shook his head. "The car isn't damaged. You want to file any charges? We could charge him with assault or something. Attempted . . . whatever." Rob shook his head again. "Okay, then." Maureen turned back to Cordts. "Nope. We don't need them."

"Let's get rid of them," Cordts said, walking up to the driver's window and staring down Rob. "Look at me, junior." He made a V with his fingers, touched a fingertip under each of his eyes. "We see you. Okay? We *know*. And now you know we know, so keep it tight. You got me?"

"Holy shit," Don said. "Damn."

Rob looked like he might puke on himself in terror. "I got you, Officer."

"As long as we understand each other," Cordts said. With an exaggerated sweeping motion of his arm, he dismissed Rob and his friend. "Be on your way."

"If you could back up," Maureen said, rushing over to the car, "and drive around him, you can go." She forced a smile. "May as well avoid actually running him over."

Rob backed up, eased around the kid in the street, and pulled away, driving so slowly they could've walked where they were going faster.

Cordts walked up to Maureen. "We should get back to Wilburn. He gets surly with the tourists if we leave him alone too long."

"We gotta get this guy out of the street," Maureen said.

"I think I know what this is about," Cordts said. "Wilburn was telling me that Perez was telling him about some joker's been rampaging his way down the parade route, smashing shit up as he goes. I figured someone else would get him before he got to us."

"Which is probably what everybody thought," Maureen said. "Which is how he got this far down the route."

"He ran through the Hamburger and Seafood Company knocking shit off tables. Glasses, silverware. He flipped chairs. The bartender chased him out of the Columns Hotel with a paring knife. He has to be the guy who tackled the cotton candy vendor and punched a peanut guy a couple of blocks back. The cotton candy guy might need stitches."

"Wow. He covered a lot of ground."

"I know, right?" Cordts said, laughing. "An athlete, this one. I'll radio the EMTs about scooping this guy up." He shrugged. "I mean, we don't want him, right?" He paused to think. "He did make a mess and do property damage. I think the peanut guy is okay, but you never know." He smiled. "Hollander asked him if he felt like a salted peanut, but I don't think the guy got it. You'd think being a peanut guy he'd heard 'em all." He shrugged. "Figure him and the cotton candy guy, they're not gonna give up a night's work talking to us and filing charges over this, right? Stitches or not."

"Oh, hell no, we don't want him," Maureen said. "I'm not trying to get a unit over here. But what're we gonna do with him?"

"He *is* the very definition of drunk and disorderly." Cordts looked around, measuring the growing crowd. "It's gonna be a bitch getting him to the lockup van. It's like ten blocks away. Maybe we *can* sneak a unit through, toss him in the backseat."

"Of whose unit?" Maureen asked. "Who's gonna want in on this?"

"Good point," Cordts said.

"And if we do get him in a car, then what?" Maureen asked. "We drive him to the jail van, or to lockup ourselves?"

Cordts shook his head. "Then we're two short on the route. Who knows when we'd get back here? Sarge will never go for that. He'd want us to handle this ourselves."

Maureen gestured at the shirtless, shoeless kid now balled up on the wet pavement. "This here is *clearly* a medical situation. Clearly. Right? If the vendors or anyone from the restaurant want him later to press charges, we can find him at the hospital."

"No, you're right. You're right." Cordts spoke into his mic, requesting the EMTs. "He's obviously not well. Just look at those pants. What kind of choice is that? Let's get him outta the goddamn road for now, we'll deal with him later, if we have to." Cordts's radio crackled. He lowered his head to listen. "Oh, for fuck's sake."

"What?"

"Is he breathing?" Cordts asked in a huff.

Maureen checked. "He is."

"Is he bleeding?"

"He is not."

Cordts spoke into his mic, waited for a response. He shook his head at the one he got.

"EMS doesn't want him. They won't come get him with an ambulance. Best they'll do is send a bike."

"You're kidding. EMTs on *bikes* can't take him anywhere."

"They don't want to take a van out of service for something like this."

"That's bullshit," Maureen said. "It's their job."

"They're stationed on the river side of St. Charles," Cordts said. "Completely on the other side of the parade." He turned and pointed at a traffic light about half a mile up the avenue. "At St. Charles and Louisiana, by the Porta-Johns and the corn dog truck. If we bring him to them, they said, they'll take him to Touro."

"If we could get him to them," Maureen said, "we've pretty much carried him to Touro ourselves."

"I think that's what EMS is hoping for," Cordts said.

She was frustrated, but Maureen understood the predicament.

The EMTs would have to bring the ambulance across the parade route and maneuver through the crowd, then double back and do everything again once the clown was loaded in. Either that, or they'd have to take him to the medical complex in Mid-City, which *would* keep them out of service for far too long, cleaning up after a drug-induced vandalism spree. Bad things did happen along the parade route. Serious injuries, accidents. Life-threatening things.

Maureen didn't want to answer for costing their already thin resources a perfectly good ambulance when some bead-chasing kid got his leg run over by a float, or some drunk rider did a header onto the pavement. Taking another look at him, she noticed he had become more still, and his breathing was deeper and more rhythmic. Slower. Had this nutcase fallen asleep in the street? One good kick in the balls, she thought, and she'd be able to diagnose exactly where he was really at; she didn't need the EMTs for that. But the NOPD does *not* need, she thought, a viral video of me kicking somebody lying in the street.

"You ever seen anything like this?" Maureen asked.

"A Mardi Gras OD? Only every year. Surprised it took us this long to get one."

"But this weird?"

"The cotton candy facial is different, I guess." Cordts frowned, giving Maureen's question genuine consideration. "And that greasy sweat, like he got dipped in bacon grease. That's a new one. I mean, I don't know. I been at this six years. I don't remember every weirdo I've come across."

"If the EMTs don't take him," Maureen said, "what're we supposed to do with him? Leave him in the street? He's in the way and he's half-dressed and it's not getting any warmer out here."

"We could carry him across the way to the sidewalk," Cordts said. "Kind of lay him down gently in the roots of one of the oaks. Keeps him kind of out of the way of the traffic and the parade. He'd be sheltered by the tree if the rain picks up."

Maureen bent over, grabbing the man's ankles. "Fuck it. That'll have to do. You take his arms, I'll take his legs."

Cordts grabbed the kid's wrists and together they lifted him off the street. He weighed next to nothing, Maureen thought. She felt guilty for thinking about kicking him. This was not a healthy person, and no one was coming to help him tonight. There were no screams or spasms from him this time. She was willing to bet that he'd heard them talking. He knew they were about to leave him be.

A flurry of muffled pops punched through the crowd noise and the sounds of the passing parade. Maureen froze. Gunshots. And from not more than a few blocks away. No one in the crowd around her reacted. Had she made a mistake? Fireworks, then? She locked eyes with Cordts. Nope. Not fireworks. She wasn't wrong. She could tell by the look on his face. Without a word, they dropped the clown in the street and took off running toward the gunfire.

# 4

Maureen sprinted up Seventh Street, shouting into her radio, "Show Cordts and Coughlin responding to gunshots, heading north on foot up Seventh Street." Cordts ran hard at her heels.

Wilburn's voice crackled back to Maureen over her radio, reporting that he was trying to get an exact location for the shots fired, and promising to catch up. Maureen knew an NOPD unit was patrolling in the area, but Dispatch didn't know yet where to send them. As of that moment, no one knew exactly where the shooting had happened. She was glad there'd been no subsequent shots to direct her.

She and Cordts stopped running and tried to get their bearings. Latecomers to the parade rushed by them, headed for St. Charles, clutching everything from twelve-packs to screaming twins. Other people pulled rolling coolers, little red wagons, and crying children behind them, hustling for the relative safety of the parade route. They were spooked, Maureen saw, but they were not panicked, not fleeing for their lives. That told her that these people had heard the shots, but that the gunfire had come from a fair distance away.

She and Cordts were on the wrong street, of no use to anyone.

They stopped people going by, barking questions at them about the gunfire. No one had anything to offer. Most people shook their heads, not even speaking, refusing to meet Maureen's eyes. They didn't want to admit out loud, she could tell, to her or to themselves, the truth about what they'd heard. They pushed their strollers and towed their coolers and kids with their eyes cast down, their strides determined.

Anyone who was gracious enough to speak repeated the same thing, as if reading their lines from a cue card: "I'm sorry, Officers, I didn't hear anything. I didn't see anything."

Parade-goers continued flowing past her and Cordts, schooling fish headed downstream toward the big river of people on St. Charles Avenue, the authoritative rumbling of marching band drums adding a spring to their step. Nobody, Maureen noticed, had made an about-face and headed back to their car and away from the parade. And more was at work here than the unique New Orleans combination of enthusiasm and fatalism, Maureen knew. The parade-goers couldn't leave the area if they wanted to. There'd be no driving into or out of most of Uptown for another few hours. The parade had everyone boxed in together and they knew it.

Maureen could hear the throbbing drums moving away from her now. The echoes bouncing off the surrounding houses faded. Maybe that would help her find the right location. Wouldn't be long, though, before another band came marching up the street. This parade had been rolling awhile, she thought. Maybe they'd catch a break, and the end of Chaos was coming. She strained to hear shouting, screaming, or anything emanating from the scene of the shooting that might lead them in the right direction.

Maureen turned in a circle, her arms raised at her sides. *You,* she said to herself, cannot panic. We cannot have panic at the parade. Cordts hustled up to her.

"Where do you think?" he asked. "I'm stumped."

"I don't know," Maureen said. "You heard them, too. I'm not crazy."

"I heard them," Cordts said. "Wilburn heard them. All these people did. That was shots fired. This is happening." He turned in a circle. "Maybe more toward Downtown? Yeah, east, toward Downtown, I think."

"Fuck. Maybe we should split up."

Cordts tilted his head, listening to the radio chatter. "Or maybe we should wait for a definite location from Dispatch. We're not the only cops out here."

A tall, gray-bearded, bowlegged man in a Yankees cap, beads swinging around his neck, staggered up to them. He pointed behind him, toward Downtown, a bent cigarette burning between his swollen knuckles. "Washington and Baronne, by that bar over there. It's bad, Officers. I think maybe a kid got killed."

As they ran, Cordts called in their destination. Over the ecstatic cheers welcoming another float rolling up from St. Charles, Maureen heard a terrified woman screaming as loud as she could for someone, anyone to help her.

# 5

The screaming woman knelt in the center of the intersection of Baronne and Washington Avenue, outside a bar named Verret's. Blood stained her face and hands. She cradled a wounded man's head and shoulders in her lap. Every scream sent chills up the back of Maureen's neck. The man lying in her lap groped at the amoebic red stain spreading across his white T-shirt with a sleepy, limp hand. Maureen set her hand on her weapon, her palm slick inside her glove. Where's the gun that shot this guy? she thought. Where's the shooter? What are we walking into?

The bloodied woman was only one of several people crying out for help. They lay scattered in the street, like dolls dumped from a toy box by an angry child. On their backs, on their knees. Some were injured. Others were only confused and terrified. Everywhere Maureen looked, dark puddles spread across the wet pavement throughout the intersection like clouds in a black sky.

Maureen counted the possibilities: beer, wine, blood.

The air reeked of spilled booze and piss and smoke.

"What an absolute clusterfuck," she said. "Jesus Christ."

"We're gonna need some fucking help." Cordts keyed his mic. "This is Cordts. We found it. Intersection of Washington and Baronne. Multiple wounded. Multiple possible GSW. No sign of a shooter. We're securing the scene."

"The kid," Maureen said. "Where's this kid who got shot?"

She scanned the sprawled and wounded lying on the blacktop, searching for the dead child. She had to distinguish right now between the wounded and the merely frightened; the frightened had to wait. She focused her vision, looking for that child, and at the same time remaining alert for any continuing threat. She registered again that they had heard only the original set of shots.

"You see *anyone* with a gun?" Cordts asked. "Anyone who looks like a shooter? You see a gun anywhere?"

"I don't see anything but a big fucking mess," Maureen said. "I think the shooting is over. Where's that kid?"

Maureen turned around and looked down Washington Avenue toward the parade. She could see hundreds of hands rise in the air, a rock concert crowd, oblivious, as the glowing float rolled by, its ghostly masked riders tossing strands of beads into the air. Against that backdrop, she saw Wilburn jogging in their direction. Not quite the cavalry, but it was a start.

"Okay, listen to me," she said to Cordts, "I got these two in the intersection." She pulled on plastic gloves. "Get with Wilburn, try to make some sense of what's happening. Find out if that kid the guy was talking about is for real. We need to know who's been shot and who twisted their ankle and pissed their pants. We're gonna hafta direct EMS when they arrive. They're gonna have to prioritize."

Cordts rushed away to meet Wilburn, and Maureen moved to the woman in the intersection and knelt at her side. She had bright streaks of blood along her pale jaw from where she kept swiping at the strands of brown hair falling in her face. She had stopped screaming, and now shook with sobs, trying and failing to calm herself so she could comfort the man in her lap.

"Are you hurt?" Maureen asked to get the woman's attention. "Were you hit?"

"Of course he's hurt," the woman shouted. "Are you fucking blind? He's fucking shot."

"You," Maureen said. "I'm talking to you. Are you hurt?"

"No, no, no," the woman said. "Just him, they came after him."

The man licked his lips. His eyelids fluttered. He seemed aware of Maureen's presence. "It's okay, sir," she said. "Don't try to speak. More help is on the way."

His hand had stopped moving, lying like a dead thing on his chest. Judging by his wound, Maureen figured he'd taken at least one bullet, maybe two, high in the rib cage, under his armpit.

Maureen did not hear the telltale wet and sucking sound that indicated lung damage. More blood pooled underneath the man. He'd taken another bullet in the back of his leg, in the meat of his thigh. He'd been shot, Maureen noted, from behind. Remember that. *They came after him*, the woman had said. Maureen filed that away for later, too. The knees of his jeans were wet and dirty. She checked the palm of his limp hand, found it scraped. He had collapsed facedown and the woman had rolled him over. The bullet in his leg had not, thank God, hit the femoral artery. His pants were bloody, but Maureen saw no exit wound on the front of his thigh. That meant the bullet remained inside him, most likely moving every time he did.

Hang in there, Maureen thought. Hang in there. You lived this long. First, we have to do something about the bleeding.

She stood, placing herself at the center of a clock, trying to slow her breathing as she surveyed the scene. Fucking mayhem everywhere. She wiped her nose with the back of her wrist, careful of the blood on her hands. Other cops had arrived on foot from the parade route. They tended to the people in the street. That was good. We're gaining control of the situation, Maureen thought. She focused on finding one thing she needed at the moment, and that was help stopping the bleeding. There, at ten o'clock, standing outside the bar on the corner, hands over her mouth, was a bartender, Maureen identifying her by the white towel hanging from her belt.

"You," Maureen called out, pointing, striding in the direction of the bar. "Bartender. You run inside and get me bar towels." She clapped her hands. "Let's go."

She returned to the couple, kneeling again. "Miss, help is coming."

The woman turned, blinking at Maureen. "My God, they shot him. They fucking shot him. Oh my God. Where is the ambulance? Where are the medics?"

Maureen made eye contact with the woman, tried to hold her gaze. "Miss, EMS is almost here. We're gonna help you, both of you. Miss, what's your name?"

"What? Who? Me? Susan. My name is Susan."

The bartender appeared over Maureen's shoulder, extending a fistful of clean, fuzzy white towels. Maureen grabbed one, pressed it against the man's chest wound. She took the woman's hand, placed it over the towel. "Pressure here, Susan. Against his ribs. Keep pressure here."

The towel turned bloody quickly. These aren't wounds, though, Maureen thought, watching the redness spread, that should kill a man. We can't let him die. We can't leave him lying in the street like this. She clenched her teeth, moved Susan's hand, and placed a new towel over the first. She pressed Susan's hand again to the wound. "Pressure here. Don't worry, you can't press too hard. You won't make it worse. But let him breathe."

Having a task helped Susan focus. "Okay, okay, okay." She held the towels in place with both hands. Her face was the color of oyster shells.

Maureen tried using a towel to fashion a tourniquet for the man's leg. His thigh was too thick. She jammed a fistful of towels under his leg, guessing at where the wound might be. The man screamed in pain. Found it. She imagined the bullet moving around in his leg and chased the thought away. Squeezing his thigh didn't seem the best idea, but she wanted to keep as much of his blood as she could on the inside.

The bartender stood over them, at a loss for what to do.

Maureen was about to demand more towels, she didn't know what else to do, when two people in blue, a man and a woman, skidded up to her on their mountain bikes. EMTs. Thank fucking God. Not an ambulance, but better than her alone with a bunch of bar towels.

"What've we got?" the man asked, getting down on one knee. Maureen glanced at his name tag. Jewell. He pulled on latex gloves. Over his shoulder, the woman unpacked their gear from the bikes.

"Multiple GSW," Maureen said. "Chest, back of the leg. He's lost a good amount of blood."

Jewell leaned over the man in the street. "Sir? Sir? Can you hear me? We're going to help you out."

"He's in and out," Maureen said.

"Where are the rest of you?" Susan demanded. "Where is the ambulance? What is this? He needs an *ambulance*. You can't put him on a bicycle."

"There are more of you coming," Maureen said. "Right?"

"Of course, of course," Jewell said, nodding, his attention focused on the wounded man. "We were closest. We're quickest through the crowds. The ambulance is on its way." He looked at Susan. "They're minutes away. Tops. I promise."

Maureen stood, watching as two mounted police trotted up Washington Avenue, their horses' hooves clopping on the pavement. The horses snorted, alien and enormous, out of place standing in the middle of a city intersection, shaking their heads, jingling their bridles, as their riders reined them to a stop. The mounted officers, their faces impassive, surveyed the scene from under their rain-glistened helmets. Maureen knew they were assessing any possible threats, that they could see better than anyone on foot and so were watching the perimeter of the scene, but, to look at them, they seemed to be deciding if the plebian chaos at their feet was worthy of their attention.

We have bikes, we have horses, we have little red wagons, rolling coolers, and Mardi Gras floats, Maureen thought, but what we fucking need is an ambulance. Not a lot to ask for. She keyed the mic on her radio. "This is Coughlin. I'm on the scene. Repeating ambulance request. These guys on the bikes are not enough. We have multiple GSWs and other injured at Washington and Baronne. We need transport for the victims ASAP."

"On the way," came the response. "Offer whatever assistance possible until then."

"An ETA, maybe? People are getting panicked."

"ASAP."

Finally, she heard the sirens. About fucking time. "We're gonna need more than one."

"Any and all available units are on their way," Dispatch calmly told her. "We're doing the best we can."

At her feet, the two EMTs worked on the wounded man, talking calmly to each other, asking Susan questions about allergies, medical conditions. Susan sat in the wet street, knees drawn to her chest as she answered the questions, fighting back sobs.

Across the intersection, Maureen watched Cordts rise to his feet beside a green sedan punctured with bullet holes. He was pale and shaken, his back straight, his bright yellow vest smeared with blood. Maureen lost her breath when she saw what he held in his arms.

Cordts cradled a child, a young girl of nine or ten clad in black tights and matching fairy wings. She lay limp as a rag doll in Cordts's arms, her black wings crushed under her. Cordts leaned in and spoke to her, his head close to hers. She did not respond. One of her legs dangled blood-soaked and useless. A little red sneaker fell from her foot into the street, rolling then bouncing to a stop. From where she stood, Maureen could not see if the girl's eyes were open or closed, or if the girl was breathing. She could see the flashing lights of the ambulance rushing closer as it sped down Washington Avenue, the siren screaming louder and louder. C'mon, c'mon, c'mon, Maureen urged. Move faster. Everything needs to happen faster.

The girl's mother, a black-haired woman in black leggings and a purple-, green-, and gold-striped rugby jersey, was draped over Cordts's shoulder, grabbing at her daughter, trying to take the girl from his arms. Cordts saw Maureen watching him and called out to her for help. "Cogs!"

"We got this," Jewell said.

"Ten-four," his partner confirmed. "Go."

Maureen hustled over to Cordts.

He had turned his back to the mother once again, watching the ambulance approach, the girl in his arms not moving. It looked to Maureen like the girl was breathing, but she couldn't be certain wishful thinking wasn't playing tricks on her.

Wilburn stood a few feet away from them, his hands on the girl's father's arms, trying to talk him down. The father wore a floppy black-and-red jester hat that kept slipping down over his eyes. We gotta get these people outta here, Maureen thought. Wilburn looked ready to cuff the father. Cordts had started to hyperventilate.

"Ma'am, ma'am," Maureen said, rushing to the mother. The woman ignored her, repeating the girl's name over and over as she continued trying to reach around Cordts for her daughter. "Lyla, Lyla, honey, Mommy's here. Mommy's here."

"Ma'am," Maureen said. "The ambulance is here. Let the officer help Lyla."

Hearing her daughter's name struck the woman like an electric shock. She froze. Maureen took advantage of the moment and slipped between her and Cordts, freeing him to move with the girl toward the ambulance. The woman swung her fists, hitting Maureen on the arms, her eyes electric and wild, yelling, "She needs her mother."

She tried to move around Maureen. "Lyla, Lyla," she shouted again, loud and mournful. "Mommy's here. Mommy's here. You'll be okay."

Maureen could hear the guilt and the sheer terror fracturing the woman's voice. She kept her face turned away from the flying fists and grabbed the woman's shoulders, realizing she still wore the bloody gloves. The mother screamed, lunging after Cordts and her daughter. Maureen released her arms and grabbed her by the waist. The woman spun in Maureen's arms, breaking free, her face contorted in rage and agony. She brought her hand far back behind her, loading up for the slap she then delivered hard across Maureen's cheek. The crack was half as loud as a gunshot, the blow hard enough to stagger Maureen and set her eyes watering. She backed away, fists clenched at her sides.

"God. Damn."

The woman realized what she'd done. She staggered back, about to collapse. She covered her eyes with her shaking hands. "Oh, Christ, I'm sorry. I'm sorry. Please don't arrest me. My daughter needs me."

"Ma'am, Lyla needs you to calm down," Maureen said, blinking the tears from her eyes, her cheek hot and swelling on the outside, leaking blood on the inside. "Ma'am, Officer Cordts has taken Lyla to the ambulance. Once she is secured, you can go with her. But you have to let the professionals help her. And you have to calm down." She turned her head and spat blood into the street. "I know that's hard. Look at me. Look at me. If you can't stay calm and in control of yourself, I can't let you go in the ambulance with your daughter. That's the deal."

The ambulance hung a hard turn, bouncing up onto the sidewalk as the driver turned it around and slammed it to a stop. The EMTs cut the siren, left the lights flashing, and jumped out of the cab. They rushed to the back of the vehicle.

One of the medics flung open the doors, climbed inside, and started prepping the equipment. The other gently took Lyla from Cordts's arms and climbed into the back of the ambulance with her. As he worked to secure Lyla in the gurney, he pulled off her crumpled wings and tossed them aside. They fluttered out of the van into the night air. Cordts snatched them in one hand before they landed in the street. He stood there holding them.

"Are you with me?" Maureen asked the woman as they stood together, watching the action. The woman, biting her bottom lip, tears pouring from her eyes, nodded. "Okay, come with me." Maureen led her by the arm to the back of the ambulance.

An EMT helped the mother into the ambulance, talking to her quietly as he eased her onto the padded bench, careful to keep her where she could observe what was happening but couldn't reach her daughter and interfere with her treatment. He belted her into the seat, continuing to talk to her, his voice quiet and calm.

A few feet away, Wilburn managed the father as best he could, trying to calm and restrain him as he fought to climb into the ambulance with his wife and daughter.

"We'll get you there," Wilburn said, as he set his hands firmly on the man's arms, finally gaining the advantage and moving him away from the back of the ambulance. "We'll get you there."

"But I want to go, too," the father yelled. "Where are you taking them?"

"There's no room," Wilburn said. "Let them work, your wife will be with them. There's nothing you can do for her right this minute."

The second medic jumped down from the back of the ambulance.

Maureen could hear the first medic calling out as he worked on the girl, "Let's go, let's go, let's go."

The mother screamed.

"Jenny! Jennifer!" the father yelled to her. "Go with her. I'll be there. I'll be there."

"We're taking her to the UMC," the medic said to Maureen. He slammed the doors closed. Maureen grabbed him by the arm before he got away. He yanked free of her grip. "I gotta go, Officer. Now."

"We have more vics here," Maureen said. "At least one of them is pretty bad off. There are more of you coming, right?"

"Fucked if I know," the medic said. He shook his head as if to erase that last sentence. "I mean, I'm sure there are. I know there are. We'll come back if we have to. But right now, I have to go."

He ran to the driver's seat and climbed in the van. The sirens screamed to life, banshees freed from a grave.

The father yelped at the sound and lunged for the ambulance. This time Maureen helped hold him back, her hands on his shoulders. "Sir, sir? Look at me. Where is your car? Can you drive? Do you know where this hospital is? The new one, the UMC in Mid-City."

She asked him about his car to get him thinking about something else. She wanted to give him something to do, to focus on. But the truth was if he couldn't drive to the hospital, neither she nor any of the other cops could leave the scene to take him anywhere. The poor bastard was on his own from here. She wanted to, gently if she could, impress this upon him, but none of her questions registered. The man was growing more hysterical. Maureen caught herself wishing his wife had stayed behind to slap some sense into him. She could swing it, that's for sure.

"Let him go," Maureen said to Wilburn. "Just let him go."

They released him and stepped out of his way. He took off running up the middle of Washington Avenue after his daughter and his wife. His jester hat flopped and jingled as he ran right into the path of a second, oncoming ambulance that he somehow didn't see coming, despite the flashing lights and the raging sirens. The ambulance driver swerved hard to avoid running the man down, clipping two parked cars as it maneuvered, scraping their doors and smashing their side mirrors to pieces. Broken glass scattered in the street. The ambulance screeched to a halt.

"That's gonna cost the city," Wilburn said.

Cordts held the little girl's wings. "What do I do with these?"

Before she could answer Cordts, who did not look well, Maureen heard someone screaming, "What the fuck?" She turned. Shit. Susan. Maureen went to her.

Susan was livid, tears streaming down her cheeks. "The first one left. Now *they* crashed? Why is this taking so long? What is wrong with everybody?"

Maureen saw that the EMTs who'd arrived by bicycle continued working on the injured man. They had not paused or flinched at any of the crashing or screaming. That was until Susan grabbed the female EMT by the shoulder and started shaking her. "Why did they leave? Where are the rest of you? You're letting him die. Call somebody."

Maureen ran over. "Whoa, whoa." She ripped Susan's hands free of the EMT's jacket.

"Officer," the medic said. "I need to work in safety."

"I got it," Maureen replied. She turned to Susan. "Everything's gonna be fine. There's another ambulance here. Look."

"You let them leave without him?" Susan said, punching Maureen in the shoulder. Hard. "You let them leave. What the fuck? What the fuck is that?"

"There was a little girl," Maureen said, gritting her teeth. "She got shot, too." She turned, fighting the urge to rub her shoulder, gesturing to the second EMS crew, who were unloading the gurney from their ambulance. "Look, another crew is here. They'll take care of him."

Susan's face collapsed. "Oh my God. A little girl? Oh my God, is she okay?"

"She will be," Maureen said. Why not say that? Maybe she really would be. Susan had sunk to her knees and had started weeping again.

"Cogs! Yo, Cogs!"

Maureen turned. It was Wilburn. "I need some help over here!"

He knelt beside an older woman who was seated on the curb. Her chin was on her chest. Her gray and black hair flopped in front of her face like a mop. The shoulder of the woman's yellow leather coat glistened with what appeared to be blood. Wilburn was holding on to her other shoulder, trying to keep her from falling over into the gutter.

Goddamn it, Maureen thought. *Another one?*

The second ambulance crew approached, hauling their tackle box and gurney. Maureen tapped the female EMT on the shoulder. "Is he ready to move?"

"Definitely," she said. "The sooner the better."

"Pack it up," Maureen said. "We need y'all on that other corner. Go help Officer Wilburn. Let the other crew take this guy to the ER."

"Ten-four," the EMT said. She radioed for more backup. "How many GSWs do we have?"

"Three and counting," Maureen said. "Are there more of you on the way?"

"*Are there more of you?* We're making do with what we got." She turned to her partner. "Jewell, finish packing up and meet me at that corner." She took off, headed for the next victim.

"Wait," Susan said. "What's happening? Why is she leaving?"

Maureen got down on one knee beside Susan. She had to keep her cool. Susan couldn't attack anyone else. She glanced at the man, who, thank God, continued breathing. "Let's give the EMTs room to work. They're here to take him to the hospital."

She reached out, trying to help Susan to her feet. The woman pulled away, refusing to stand. Maureen didn't want to fight this woman so the EMTs could access the victim. She did not want to have to handcuff her.

"I'm not leaving him," Susan shouted. "I'm not leaving him lying here in the street."

"Neither are we." Maureen crouched beside Susan as the EMTs rolled up the stretcher. "See, Susan? The paramedics are here, and they're going to take care of him. He needs their help. He needs to go to the hospital." She draped her arm across the woman's shoulders and stood. As Maureen had hoped, Susan stood with her.

To the EMT she said, "Double GSW, maybe a triple, under the right armpit along the rib cage and the back of the right thigh, from what I could see."

"We'll take it from here, Officer."

The EMTs collapsed the stretcher to more easily load the man.

"I want to go," Susan said. Her breath was dense with beer. "I want to go with him."

Maureen glanced at the EMT, who gave the subtlest shake of the head, telling her they didn't want the drunk, hysterical girlfriend along. "If she's not family," the EMT said. "I'm sorry."

"What did he say?" Susan asked.

"He will go straight into surgery," Maureen told Susan. "Let the doctors work. Now and at the hospital. They'll only whisk him away from you at the emergency room. We'll make sure you get to him. He'll be okay." One lie after another. "He's holding up well."

The EMTs were already wheeling the man back to the ambulance.

Maureen felt Susan tense up, as if preparing to chase the gurney. Please God, Maureen thought, do not make me tackle this poor woman in the middle of the street. Susan didn't move.

Maureen put her arm around Susan again and guided her in the direction of the bar. Susan turned and watched the rolling stretcher over her shoulder. "Oh my God. This is awful."

"That's your boyfriend?" Maureen asked, careful to keep her references in the present tense.

Susan nodded.

"And what's his name?" His name would make him feel even more alive. "Cordell."

"He's going to be fine," Maureen said. "I've seen much, much worse. Cordell's in good hands." All of that, she thought, was true. For now.

# 6

Maureen led Susan up onto the sidewalk and to a long wooden bench outside the bar. The three drunk men sitting there sharing a joint quickly popped to their feet and moved away. The scent and smoke of the weed lingered. Maureen eased Susan onto the bench.

Susan leaned back against the building, her head hitting the wall with a thump, her bloody hands twitching in her lap. She was going into shock. She'd need medical attention soon, Maureen thought. The more time that passed, the worse this woman was going to feel. Getting useful information from her about the shooting would soon become impossible. Still, the woman needed a break. She deserved a chance to clean the blood off her skin and catch her breath.

"Susan, I want you to stay right here," Maureen said. "Breathe. Take slow, deep breaths. That's what you have to do right now." She thought of Cordell and Lyla. If they died, she'd be investigating homicides tonight. The longer she went without hearing about them, the better. "That's the trick, Susan. Keep breathing."

Maureen peered inside the packed bar.

Right inside the door, three skinny girls in gold tights and rainbow tutus draped themselves over the jukebox, hunting for more dance music. They were twenty-one, *maybe*. The bartender had returned to work back behind the bar with her two male cohorts, the three of them passing cans of beer and mixed drinks and draft beers in plastic cups over the bar as fast as they could pour them. Maureen watched the three of them work for a few seconds, catching her own breath. She thought of herself and Wilburn and Cordts as they worked the night's crime scene. They were not quite that smooth-moving a team. Not yet.

There wasn't a single useful witness in that bar. Maureen needed Susan to talk to her before the EMTs took her away.

Groaning, Susan lowered her head between her knees, her back shaking with the force of her weeping into her bloody hands. Maureen sighed and returned to the bench, sitting beside Susan and rubbing her back. This was, she thought, the part of the job she did the worst. Attending to the victims.

She spotted Wilburn standing not far away, his former charge in the yellow coat turned over to the care of EMS. He was lighting a cigarette in a pocket of darkness.

She called to him and waved him over.

"How's your vic holding up?" Maureen asked.

"Not too bad," Wilburn said. "Best shape of the three, I think. Winged in the shoulder. May have even been shrapnel that got her. The shooter did hit that car and at least one house while he was letting loose."

"I thought she'd be worse," Maureen said. "I saw the blood pouring down her coat."

Wilburn shook his head. "Wine. Someone else dumped a whole go-cup of red wine on her diving for cover." He shrugged. "The guy in the street, the one you had, he got the worst of it by far. You ask me, he was the target. Sure wasn't that little girl."

"We gotta get after the evidence," Maureen said. "People are trashing the scene."

Wilburn wiped his hand down his face. Maureen shared his apprehension. They were looking at a big job. They wouldn't get much help with it.

"It can wait," Wilburn said. "What're we gonna find? A few casings? They're not going anywhere. You know how these shootings go, there's never much left behind but the victims."

Maureen pointed across the street. "There's a crime camera right there."

"Twenty bucks says that piece of shit doesn't work."

"All the more reason the bullet casings are important," Maureen said. "We'll get serious shit, Mardi Gras or not, if we don't recover them. Maybe that crime camera doesn't work, but I promise you this bar has video over the front door, and that corner store has video. Maybe some of these houses around here. The clock is ticking on us. We need to leave everyone who's not a witness to the medics."

"The casings'll keep," Wilburn said. "I'm not sure we've found all the victims yet. And while the bullet casings help the DA, they don't help us catch who did this tonight. That's our main concern right now. He might not be done shooting people, and someone's gonna be coming after him for this right here. We don't know who did this yet, but somebody in the neighborhood does."

"Well, I don't hear any more screaming," Maureen said. "And I don't see anyone else who looks shot." Most of the people caught up in the panic were gone, she noticed. The intersection had largely cleared. Their chances of finding another witness in addition to Susan and the lady in the coat were shrinking.

"The shots seem so random," Maureen said. "The victims, too. That man, the little girl, and the woman, they weren't standing anywhere near one another. There could be bullets through windows. We're gonna have to check the whole block. Could be someone lying dead in their living room. We're gonna need more cops."

"There aren't a whole lot more available," Wilburn said.

"Where's Cordts?" Maureen said. "Let's put him to work. It'll do him good."

"Between you and me," Wilburn said, "he's somewhere up Baronne Street, puking his guts up in the dark."

"Seriously?" Maureen said. "We've worked worse scenes than this. No fatalities, even. I never figured him for squeamish."

"It's not the blood that gets him," Wilburn said. "He found the kid. Held her in his arms." He paused, as if weighing how much more to say. He looked away from Maureen. "He'll be fine. Probably. We're all exhausted already."

"What do you know about the little girl? How bad off was she?"

"Bullet through the calf," Wilburn said. "Cordts said it went clean through. She was conscious when she went in the ambulance, I know that much."

"Christ, she looked dead from where I stood," Maureen said.

"Nah. Tough little thing, that girl."

Maureen knew Wilburn was holding back on her about Cordts, though she didn't know why. She hadn't been worried about Cordts until that look away from Wilburn. Whatever his deal, whatever his secret, Cordts needed to be on the scene, working.

"Wilburn, listen to me. You know this investigation is on us. Me, you, Cordts, and maybe a couple other cops we can rustle up off the route. Everyone else is busy tonight, all night. We gotta figure out this one before that next one. They're contagious. You said it yourself. There are more little girls out here on the streets tonight, a lot more. They need our protection. They need us to do our jobs."

"The detective will be out here eventually," Wilburn said, looking around.

He was anxious to ditch this case, Maureen realized. Why?

"Maybe we should wait for him," Wilburn said.

"Yeah, he'll be here *eventually*," Maureen said. "But who knows when that is?" A single detective was on duty back at the station, working six-to-six. "Have you heard from Sarge?"

"Hardin's on his way," Wilburn said. "But he's coming from all the way up at where the parade turns at Napoleon."

"So it'll be a while," Maureen said. "Okay. No detective. No duty sergeant. This mess is ours exclusively for now." It was frustrating, and intimidating, she thought, but pretty damn exciting, too. She couldn't lose this chance to do some really good work. "Raise Cordts on the radio. Call him on his cell. Whatever you think is best, but get him back here. We need him."

She turned to Susan, set her hand on the woman's shoulder. "We're going to start the investigation with her. This woman is a real live witness. She was inches away. Susan? This is Officer Wilburn. He's gonna stay here with you for a minute while I talk to some folks inside the bar."

Susan didn't move or open her eyes.

"Make sure no one bothers her," Maureen said. "And that she doesn't wander off. I'll see if I can get something to clean her up."

Wilburn sat on the bench. He made no move for his radio or his phone. "Yeah, you got it, Cogs."

What was his fucking problem? Was it taking direction from a rookie? From a woman? She knew Wilburn. They worked together often. They'd never had this problem before. He was gonna have to man up. They could talk about his feelings later.

"When I get back," Maureen said, "you get a statement from your victim before she gets taken to the hospital."

"I've got time," Wilburn said. "We were lucky to get the two ambulances we got. It's gonna be a wait for the third. They know it's not life-threatening. She's not going anywhere anytime soon."

"Anything that woman might have seen," Maureen said. "It matters. Just get her to talk."

"Hey, Cogs?" Wilburn said, looking up at her from his seat. "I've been doing this a little while. Longer even than you. Longer than Cordts. I know how to take a statement."

Maureen raised her hands in apology. Better, she thought. Some life from him. "Roger that." She stood, wiping her hands on her pants. "Cordts. Get him back here."

"He'll turn up when he levels off," Wilburn said. "Maybe we should try to get him a clean vest." He looked at his own, at Maureen's. Both were streaked with blood. His face clouded over. "Maybe not. Fuck it. Too much has happened already."

"What is it?" Maureen asked. "What's wrong with him that you're not telling me?"

Wilburn shrugged. He paused. Maureen knew he had more to say, so she waited for it. "He wouldn't let go of those fairy wings. He was still carrying them around with him when he wandered off to puke."

# 7

Inside the raucous bar, Maureen yet again found herself shouldering her way through a crowd. A cop pushing her way through the jumble of drunks did nothing to dampen the party, which was finding its sea legs again after the bloody drama outside. Maureen could only imagine the electricity that the shooting had pumped into the night's festivities. How many of these people had already posted their pictures of the scene on their social media feeds. Their friends back at home would envy their brush with authentic New Orleans danger.

*Dude! What a way to kick off the night. The real New Orleans.* With hashtag *#imanasshole.*

The bar back, a skinny blue-haired kid in a black T-shirt, who looked about the age of the girls by the jukebox, collided with Maureen as he came around from behind the bar with his head down. He carried a dripping black bag of trash slung over each shoulder.

"What the fuck?" he said. Maureen saw him realize she was a cop.

"Shit. Sorry." He froze, the ropy muscles in his tattooed arms pulled taut by the weight of the trash bags. "Uh, can I help you?"

"I need the female bartender," Maureen said.

"Her name is Dakota." The kid turned his head as best he could to see over the trash bags, trying to yell over the jukebox music. "Dakota! Yo! Dee! Eyes slideways. Five-Oh wants you."

Maureen saw Dakota nod to show that she'd heard, but she didn't turn to look their way.

"I got it from here," she said. She stepped aside. "Please. You're working. Don't let me keep you."

The kid nodded his gratitude and waddled off under the weight of the trash. The dripping bags spilled bar juice on her boots. May as well burn them, too, when this weekend is over. She looked at her bloodstained vest. She hoped it cleaned up okay. Otherwise that was seventy bucks gone to hell. She was getting tired of waiting. "Miss! Dakota! Come see me, please."

Dakota held up a hand. She dug three High Lifes from the ice well behind her. Holding the bottles in one hand, she popped the tops with her opener and, turning, standing on her toes, the muscles in her thick thighs flexing, handed the bottles over the bar, taking a bill and ringing up the beers. She dropped the change in her tip bucket, wiped her hands on her ragged denim shorts. The crowd at the bar was three deep. People waved cash and credit cards in the air around her head. Dakota raised her hands at them in surrender, gesturing down the bar at Maureen and shrugging. Some people booed. Maureen figured the displeasure was directed more at her than at Dakota.

Dakota strode Maureen's way, rolling her shoulders and straightening her back, digging a crumpled pack of cigarettes from the pocket of her shorts. Broad shouldered and big chested, Dakota wore a tight, faded Sailor Jerry tank top. Colorful tattoos sleeved her muscled arms down to the backs of her hands. She stood maybe five feet tall in her knee-high cranberry-colored Doc Martens. A black, sweat-dampened bandanna held aloft her bright red hair, which was shaved at the temples and long at the top, and kept it from sticking to her forehead. Maureen was willing to wager Dakota's hair hadn't been washed in a while.

As Dakota lit a cigarette, Maureen noticed HOLD FAST tattooed across her knuckles. The lines at the corners of her eyes gave away the ten years she had on the rest of the bar staff, years you could see only close up.

"Sorry to pull you away from the crowd," Maureen said. "I know you're slammed. I only need a minute."

"Any excuse to grab a break," Dakota said. She dabbed with her pinkie at the thick red lipstick at the corners of her mouth. "But I'll tell you right now I didn't see the shooting. I was in here, and we were *six* deep at the bar when it happened. I mean, I barely even heard it."

"What about your bar back?" Maureen asked. "Or one of the other bartenders? Maybe somebody stepped outside for some air? To talk to a friend on the phone?"

"Officer, none of us has been out from behind this bar for anything but a piss for three hours."

"Except for you," Maureen said, "when you heard the shots."

"And even then," Dakota said, "I only ran outside 'cause someone came running in here saying there'd been a shooting outside. That was right before you came asking for the towels."

"So when you hear gunshots," Maureen said, "you run toward them?"

"You did."

"I wear a bulletproof vest."

"Not my first rodeo." Dakota shrugged. "I'm supposed to leave the guy bleeding in the street?"

"But you never went to him."

"I saw he wasn't alone," Dakota said. "And y'all came running quick. Props for that, by the way. I got responsibilities in here. Can't have the bar getting tore up. Registers, tip jars can't be left unattended. Though this time of year someone's just as liable to grab a bottle and run."

"You're the owner?"

"May as well be," Dakota said, exhaling smoke from the corner of her mouth, "the amount of time I'm spending here. I'm the manager. Such as it is. Not like it bumps up my hourly much. Or at all. I have an air mattress and a hot water bottle in the liquor closet. *Big* bottle of Advil." She sighed. "Every flock needs a shepherd."

"You'll have to call the owners," Maureen said. "They'll have to come down here. Tonight. I know it's a pain in the ass, but we're gonna need the security camera footage from outside. Probably inside, too."

"I'll call them," Dakota said. "When I can. But they're not around much over the holiday. No promises. They know my number, and they avoid answering if they can."

"Hence the hot water bottle and the air mattress."

"Yes, indeed. And they don't live in the neighborhood, so if I can reach them, who knows when they can get here? They might make you wait until next week, until after the holiday. Don't come after me if they blow you off, is what I'm saying."

"I get the point," Maureen said. She understood what Dakota was insinuating about the owners. The cops had time for nothing but Mardi Gras over the next few days, and plenty of people knew it. "Someone will come around looking for that video. Me or another cop. Probably a detective. Eventually. If not later tonight, next week, I guess." She hated the frustration she already heard in her own voice.

"Is he dead?" Dakota asked. "Cordell? He did not look good when I was out there."

"He was alive when they put him in the ambulance," Maureen said. "I think his chances are good."

Dakota's eyes watered, and she looked away from Maureen. "Susie and Cord, they're regulars here, and a sweet couple." She touched at her thick mascara with the tip of her pinkie. "I saw them putting someone else in an ambulance." She swallowed hard. "Looked like a kid."

"A little girl," Maureen said. "It looked like she was going to be okay. We're waiting on transport for one more victim. A woman was also injured. Not as bad as the others. Minor."

"Three people? Christ. There are some real fucking animals in this city. It's fucking Mardi Gras, for fuck's sake. They can't give it a break?

Used to be no one fucked with a parade. You know, *neutral* ground? Now, forget it. We get this shit every year."

"What shit is that?" Maureen asked. "You're here a lot. Maybe you heard something around the neighborhood, maybe Cordell got caught up in something? Susan seemed to think he was the target."

"I don't know what Susie is talking about with that. You might want to clarify that with her." Dakota shook her head. "As for the shit, you're a cop, you already *know* the kind of bullshit *I'm* talking about. The basic same old, same old. *New* New Orleans, my ass. This crew, that crew, who's beefing with who from week to week? Everything gotta be settled with a gun." She took a long drag on her cigarette. "The way everybody's fucking strapped, I guess we're lucky it's not worse."

"That's what we're trying to prevent," Maureen said. "Things getting worse."

"Good fucking luck with that," Dakota said. "My boyfriend, he never sneezes just once. There's always a second sneeze. Sometimes it comes quick, sometimes not, but there's always a follow-up. These shootings are like that. The next one is coming."

"Not if I can help it." Maureen couldn't help but smile. "You been at this a while."

Dakota chuckled. "You can tell? I've lived here a long time."

"It's my first Mardi Gras," Maureen said. "I'm kind of new in town."

"I can tell," Dakota said.

"I've got Susan sitting outside." Maureen dug into her pocket for some cash. "I need a couple bottles of water, maybe a few more towels. I want her to be able to rinse her hands." She shrugged. "The blood. I want her to be able to clean up some."

"Put your money away," Dakota said. She turned, put out her hand. "Darin," she shouted, "toss me a couple waters."

Darin dropped the liquor bottles in his hands back in the well, the drinks on the bar in front of him half-made. People bitched at him over the bar. He ignored them. He reached into a cooler behind him, backhanding two bottles of water to Dakota without even looking. Dakota caught one in each hand. She passed the bottles to Maureen. She opened a cabinet and grabbed more bar towels. "Owner's gonna shit himself over these towels. Guards them like gold. We can't get more until Monday at the earliest."

"He gives you shit," Maureen said, tucking the towels under her arm, "send him to the Sixth District, tell him to ask for Officer Coughlin. I'll be happy to discuss his priorities with him."

Dakota smiled. "Will do. Indeed." She stubbed out her cigarette in a plastic ashtray on the edge of the bar brimming with ashes and butts. "Coughlin. Okay. Good to know." She dug a tiny bottle of hand sanitizer from her pocket, rubbed some into her hands, then handed the bottle to Maureen. "Tell Susie, she needs anything, anything at all and she comes right to me. Drinks, cigarettes, she needs to beat the line for the bathroom, anything."

"I got it," Maureen said. "Thanks for your time. Go make your money."

Dakota dashed behind the bar and returned with a business card. She held it up, showing Maureen the front of it. "This is us. We don't answer the bar phone during the parades." She produced a pen from somewhere under her bandanna and scrawled a phone number on the back of the card. "This is my cell. I won't hear it, but I try to check it once an hour. If I can help with something, let me know. No promises, but I'll try. We love Cord and Susie."

Maureen tucked the card in her pocket. "Thank you for this."

"Go catch those motherfuckers who shot Cordell."

"Will do," Maureen said. "No staff leaves tonight without giving a statement to a cop."

"You kidding me?" Dakota said. "Y'all will be long gone before we will. Maybe I get home to get laid one night between now and Wednesday. Maybe."

# 8

Maureen exited the bar, stepping through the door into a white light so blinding it staggered her. She swore and raised her hands to shield her eyes. Squinting, she stepped aside, moving, her head turned to one side. A male voice apologized to her and the light moved away.

When she'd blinked away the spots in her eyes Maureen saw that the light emanated from atop a video camera perched atop the shoulder of a tall man in a flannel jacket. Even with the camera to his face, Maureen could see he had flowing black hair and a long, bushy beard. Another man stood beside him. This one was wide and compact, wearing a tight, short-sleeved checked shirt buttoned at the neck and a floppy, camouflage-patterned fishing hat. He held a long pole. At the end of the pole, dangling like a lure over Maureen's head, was a microphone. She saw that the cameraman had redirected the camera and its spotlight toward Susan, who seemed barely able to stay upright, slumped and exhausted against the building. The microphone swung that way as well.

Beside Susan sat a skeletal woman with white-blond hair colored hot pink where the tips touched her comic-book-enormous breasts. The same color, Maureen thought, as the OD's tights. The woman, shivering in the cold, her too-big black biker jacket shiny with the night's mist, leaned in close to Susan as she spoke to her in earnest tones, her painted-on eyebrows furrowed with concern about as authentic as her breasts.

"That blood on your face?" the pale woman said. "That's his? From when you tried to save him?"

"That's enough," Maureen said. "Stop this right now." Where was Wilburn, how had he let this happen? "What're you doing?" She made to move toward Susan, but someone stepped to her, purposely blocking her path.

"Excuse me," snapped another woman, this one about Maureen's height. She had wild, curly reddish-brown hair and dark, bloodshot eyes set far behind thick-framed glasses. She wore camouflage cargo pants low on her hips, ratty combat boots, and a puffy down vest over a long-sleeved Tipitina's T-shirt. She had a computer tablet tucked under one arm like a schoolbook. "Excuse me, Officer. You're in the shot. You can talk to me if you have questions."

"Who are you?" Maureen asked the woman, dumbfounded. She and this woman stood practically nose to nose. "And take a step back, please. You're way too close to me."

"I'm the producer here," the woman said. "And the director. Laine Daniels. I'm in charge here."

"The fuck you are," Maureen said. She set the water bottles and the towels down on the bench. "Get your camera crew and whatever *she* is and get the hell outta here. This is a crime scene. This woman is traumatized, and a witness to a terrible crime."

"This is a street corner bar," Daniels said. "This is a public space, we're on a public street, during one of the world's largest street party free-for-alls. I don't see any police tape anywhere. I see no directions or indications of a closed-off crime scene."

"Maybe the blood on this woman's face is enough for you?" Maureen said. "The blood in the street? How about that? Are you for real?"

"We're shooting here," Daniels said. "We have every right to shoot here."

Maureen laughed out loud at the woman's poor choice of words. "Excuse *me*. This is obviously an active crime scene and that's why you're here. Someone else was shooting here tonight, too. We're trying to conduct an investigation here—of a real shooting. The kind done with a gun. You need to leave that woman alone. She's a witness. We, the police, need to speak with her before anyone else."

Maureen leaned around Daniels, speaking to the woman in black leather. "Ma'am, get up from the bench and leave that woman alone. Get rid of that microphone." The blond scarecrow ignored her. Who got on TV with a nose like that? Maureen thought. "Stop talking to her. Now."

"We don't need your permission to talk to the public," Daniels said. "You've never seen news crews conducting interviews around the scene of a crime? I know you're not a fan, but check the Constitution."

"Holy. Shit." Maureen looked around. "A fan of who?"

"Thomas Jefferson? Heard of him?"

Where was fucking Wilburn? Maureen wondered again. He was probably walking the immediate neighborhood, she realized, looking for anyone else who might've caught a stray bullet. She hoped he came back empty-handed, at least when it came to there being any more victims. Bullets go places, she thought, and sometimes it's hard to tell where.

She surveyed the intersection. People heading for the parade route and visiting the corner store wandered through the crime scene. Laine Daniels was right, Maureen thought, up to a point. No one had strung tape. Only two other cops remained on the scene. Everyone else had either returned to their route assignments or was back on patrol in the neighborhood. The two guys left behind, Kornegay and Faye, stalked the intersection with their flashlights, heads down, placing a small bright orange plastic cone wherever they found a bullet casing. Maureen counted six cones. If there were that many, she thought, there would be more. She had a feeling the shooter had emptied his entire clip, or had come close. She checked her phone. Surely the detective on duty back at the district knew by now what had happened.

Why hadn't they heard from him? And where was the sergeant? Someone had to step up and put a tent over this circus. She didn't exactly have the authority to run the investigation.

Suddenly, Maureen found herself standing in the white light again. "Don't you *point* that fucking camera at me." The light moved away.

"Cortez," Daniels said, "you keep that camera pointed right here. Where *I* tell you. We talked about this."

Again Maureen was in the spotlight. "But you're not local news, are you? Local TV?"

"We are not," Daniels said. "We're not local. Or news."

"I live on the North Shore," Cortez mumbled. "Born and raised."

Hard as she was trying, Maureen couldn't ignore the fact that Cortez was filming her. The microphone hovered overhead on the very edge of her peripheral vision. She couldn't see it, and she couldn't not see it, either. She couldn't speak to Cortez without looking into the camera. She addressed him anyway, trying to look away from the lens and at the man. "This woman's boyfriend was shot in the street less than an hour ago. C'mon, dude. Be a human being."

"That's why we're talking to her," Daniels said. "She's a story."

"She's a person," Maureen said, trying to turn away from the camera and talk to Laine Daniels. "Ma'am, can't you interview her later? Christ, she still has his blood on her face. We, the police, need to talk to her."

"Exactly, you're not waiting until later," Laine said.

"We're not equals," Maureen said. "We can help catch the person who shot her boyfriend."

"You don't think we can?" Laine asked.

"Did you film the shooting?" Maureen asked.

"We got here after you," Laine said. "You were in the bar by the time we arrived."

"Then, no, I don't think you can help," Maureen said. "Who the fuck *are* you? What are you even doing in the middle of my crime scene, harassing the witnesses?"

"Who are you?" Laine asked. "Let's talk about you. This investigation seems very important to you. I hear a New York accent. I noticed you said 'my' crime scene. Are you a detective? I know everyone from every division is back in uniform for Mardi Gras."

"Don't try that shit on me. Pretending I'm a story." Maureen pointed over Laine's shoulder at the camera. "Get that thing off of me, I'm telling you. That microphone, too. Turn that off." She should walk away, that was the best remedy. But she needed to question Susan. And she didn't want to leave the poor woman to be picked over by these scavengers. She wanted to protect her. It took every ounce of strength she had not to threaten the camera crew with physical violence. She took a deep breath.

Be boring, she thought. If I can be boring, they'll move the camera.

The blond skeleton spoke. "Yo. If we're not shooting me, can I smoke a cigarette?"

"Just wait there, Donna. And don't smoke, I'm not doing your lipstick again."

"Hello?" Donna said. "I can do my own fucking lipstick, thank you."

"For the last time," Maureen said, "y'all are interfering with an in-progress police investigation. That is not within your rights. I will call over my supervisor. He's much larger and even less friendly than me."

Donna scoffed. "As if."

"You asked who we are," Laine said. "We're a video production company. Journalists. New York. Hollywood. You've heard of the *On Fire* documentary series. That's us. That's what we do, what *I* do."

"Yeah, you lost me," Maureen said.

"I live in the Bywater," the guy with the mic said. "My name is Larry. I just came to help out Cortez. I'm more of a music producer. Beats are really my thing."

"Larry, please," Laine said. "We talked about this. Not everyone wants to hear your résumé, especially while I'm paying you."

"Technically, Cortez is paying me."

"Out of what I'm paying him," Laine said. "Now, please, Larry, mind the levels and let me work."

"You need to leave our witness alone and go away," Maureen said. "I can't be clearer than that."

"We do real-life, street-level journalism," Laine said, ignoring her. "Gritty, real behind-the-scenes, in-the-dark-corners stuff. 'South Beach on Fire,' 'Spring Break on Fire.'" She waited for Maureen to acknowledge the titles. "'Burning Man on Fire.'"

"'Burning Man on Fire'?"

"You saw that one?" Laine was smiling now. "That was one of my best."

"'Burning Man on Fire,'" Maureen said. "That doesn't sound stupid to you?" Maureen chuckled. "I get it now. You're a reality TV show, like the desperate housewives of the Jersey Shore, that kind of thing. Like the tooth-less guys who catch fish with their hands." Laine's smile vanished. "Let me guess, we're doing 'Mardi Gras on Fire' right this very minute."

"You're one of the smart ones," Donna whined from the bench. "We get it. Congrats on your awesomeness. Laine, honey, this lady won't talk to me, I'm freezing my tits off, and I'm starting to nic fit. This sucks. Why is it raining?"

"There's a major fucking parade three blocks away," Maureen said. "Full-on, full-tilt Mardi Gras. Beads, bands, yelling and screaming under the live oaks. You're missing it."

"We got plenty of that." Laine made a sweeping gesture over the scene. "You're telling me this isn't authentic Mardi Gras right here? The masquer-ade that people not from around here never get to see? Tell me this isn't the *real* New Orleans. Tell me we're not behind the curtain right now. Christ, this poor woman, she has her boyfriend's blood on her *face*."

"So y'all have been out on the route since when?" Maureen asked. "For the whole night of parades?"

Laine hesitated, suspicious of the questions. "More or less. Until the shooting happened. When we heard about that, we left the route and came this way."

"Yeah, you know what," Maureen said, "I think I'm going to need that camera. You might have footage of the shooter. We won't know until we look."

"Nice try," Laine said, smiling. "We got here after, way after, the violence was over. I told you that. There's no way we caught the shooting on video, and you know it."

Donna stood, perfectly balanced on a pair of black spike-heeled boots. She zipped up her biker jacket with an angry flourish. "I'm freezing my *ass* off. I thought it was warm here. You told me this was the tropics. Practically the Caribbean, you said." She slid a long, thin white cigarette from a gold pack. "I'm getting a fucking drink. A big drink. *Inside.*"

Laine pressed the heel of a hand into her forehead. "Sweet Jesus. Can we try working like professionals here?"

"You know where to find me, bitches. Peace." Donna tottered by in her spike-heeled boots.

"Goddamn it, Donna."

"Whatevs."

The noise from inside the bar rushed out when Donna pulled the door open.

"Ever since that second goddamn sex tape she's been unmanageable," Laine said. She scratched her forehead. "I hired her because of the first one. That's what I get. I am reaping the whirlwind."

She turned back to Maureen. "Officer, the sheriff in Nevada tried this very same 'seize the evidence' routine on us. No dice. You want my footage? You get a court order. I promise you, TLC has more and better lawyers than the NOPD. And we both know nothing is happening in this town but Mardi Gras for the next week."

"We're gonna be on TLC?" Larry asked. "Holy shit. Yo, Cortez, I need more than a twenty bag from you if this shit's gonna be on cable."

"Holy shit, Larry, we're standing here with a *cop.*"

Maureen felt a twinge of sympathy for Laine. Wilburn and Cordts were far from perfect, but they were light-years ahead of Cortez and Larry.

Laine pulled a small bottle of Tylenol from her vest pocket. She shook out a handful and swallowed them dry. She turned to Cortez and Larry, her shoulders slumped. "Get the camera off your shoulder for ten minutes, Cortez. Let me know when that dim-bulb cooze reappears out of the bar. You know what? Fuck that. Larry, if she's not out in five, you go in and get her. I'm going to that store across the street for a forty-ounce."

Cortez turned off the spotlight and the camera, lowered it from his shoulder. He waved at Laine as she walked away. "Yeah, nothing for me, thanks. I'm good."

"Yeah, me, too," yelled Larry.

"She always like this?" Maureen asked Cortez.

"She used to be a journalist once," he said, "made a kind of famous documentary, I think. Won an award for it. Maybe. She was bragging on it when she interviewed me but I wasn't really listening. And I was high."

"What was the film about?" Maureen asked. "The documentary?"

Cortez shook his head. "She doesn't like to talk about it. No offense, my dad is a cop in Madisonville, and he doesn't like how we bug y'all, and I don't either, but Laine sees me talking to you without her around?" He shrugged and backed away from her. "It's bottom feeding, but it's a gig. And I need it. It's Mardi Gras. Gotta make that paper while I can."

# 9

With the camera crew dispersed, Maureen settled beside Susan on the bench. Neither of them said anything. She took a deep breath. She held it for half a minute, let it out slowly. Since the moment her butt had hit the bench she'd been fighting the urge to wilt from the heavy gravity of exhaustion. Where was the goddamn detective? There'd been no other calls for service that night. He or she, probably he, had literally nothing else to do. She hadn't checked who it was before taking her spot on the parade route. Not that it mattered. He or she would get here when they got here. Detectives did their own thing, even when it wasn't Mardi Gras.

Susan kept her eyes closed and leaned her head back against the building. As far as Maureen could tell, she had calmed. Her breathing was slow and deep. Her face looked jaundiced and wan, though, in the recessed yellow lights of the bar's awning. Tendrils of smoke rose from the cigarette burning between her fingers. The rain had stopped, Maureen noticed, but the temperature continued to drop. She shook off a chill. She needed to get moving. She worried she'd fall asleep if she loitered much longer.

Maureen looked around again for Cordts but didn't see him. She knew Wilburn hadn't reached out to him. She spotted Wilburn across the street, talking to the woman in the yellow coat who had suffered the shoulder injury. He sat beside her on the curb. Wilburn had his notebook on his knee and his pen in hand, writing as the woman spoke to him. She talked with one hand buried in her long hair, squeezing her scalp. The EMTs stared blank-faced down the block at the passing parade. The two bicycle EMTs sat with them. The four of them smoked cigarettes. The woman had her arm in a makeshift sling and her coat draped over her uninjured shoulder like a cape. Guess that wound is feeling okay, Maureen thought. That would be a good thing, since the third ambulance had never arrived.

"You hanging in there?" Maureen asked, turning to Susan. "I'm sorry those people with the camera bothered you. You're done with them."

"The blond one said she was a reporter."

"That's a stretch," Maureen said.

"They never even asked me my name." Susan spoke with her eyes closed. "I took something, by the way. While you were in the bar. A pill. I had it with me. It's pretty strong. I have a prescription. I hope you don't mind."

"You got a cotton candy fetish?"

Susan half opened one eye. "What?"

"Never mind," Maureen said. "Cop joke. A bad one. I got some towels here and some water. You'll want to clean up."

Susan collected herself, shifting forward on the bench, crossing her feet at the ankles. She opened her eyes, blinking. Maureen could see her struggling to remain present.

"Yeah, yeah, okay," Susan said. She tossed her cigarette in the gutter, frowning at the butt. "I don't even smoke. I don't even remember who gave me that." She swallowed hard, looking at her hands. "The blood is starting to dry. I want to see him."

"Hold out your hands," Maureen said.

Susan did it, her hands trembling again. She didn't even try to steady them. She tried to smile. "It's always so cold for Muses. Every year. It's like a curse. When can I go see Cordell?"

Maureen cracked open a water bottle, poured half of it over Susan's hands. She watched as Susan dried her hands with a bar towel, rivulets of bloody water running across the dirty sidewalk into the gutter. Her knuckles were red and raw.

"Dakota told me to tell you that if you need anything," Maureen said, "you go right to her."

"She's sweet," Susan said. "It's in my hair, isn't it?"

Maureen conjured a sympathetic grin. She'd had days when she'd been as bloody as Susan. Bloodier. Blood was stickier than you'd think, tacky like paste, and the smell lingered throughout the night no matter how long you stood under a hot shower. You woke up tasting it in the morning. Only sunlight seemed to cure it, and sometimes even that wasn't enough. She thought better of sharing her experience with Susan.

Maureen poured the rest of the water into a clean towel. "Lift your chin for me."

Susan raised her chin, averting her eyes as Maureen wiped at the bloodstains along her jawline. The red streaks, to Maureen's dismay, proved stubborn. She decided against grabbing Susan by the face. She wrinkled her nose and rubbed harder. Susan winced, clearing her throat. The towel Maureen used was cheap and the material was rough.

"I hate to ask you this," Maureen said as she worked at the stains. "But is there anything you can tell us about who did this? Dakota said you and Cordell live in the neighborhood. Anyone hassling you lately?"

"What?" Susan said, not looking at Maureen, jaw muscles tensing. "Because Dell's black, he's mixed up in some shit? That's what you're asking?"

It's not that he's black, Maureen wanted to say, it's that someone *shot* him. "Most people who get shot in this town, it's someone they know who did it."

"So it's Dell's fault he got shot?" Susan leaned away from the scrubbing, raising her hand to say "enough" and taking the towel from Maureen.

"You mentioned when I first arrived," Maureen said, "that you felt Dell had been targeted by whoever shot him. I'm wondering why you said that."

"I don't even remember saying that," Susan said. "And if I did, it's only because the shots were so close to us. Dell is from here, he's a music teacher, at two different middle schools. Charter schools, I'll have you know. He used to teach the *fifth grade* before that. He's not some gangster."

Maureen shook her head. "That's not what I'm saying. That's not what I meant. We want to catch who did this, as soon as possible. We need as much information as we can possibly get to do that. What did you see right before it happened? What did you hear? Maybe Dell pissed someone off by accident recently. He might not have even known he was doing it. Think back about the past couple of weeks. He take someone's parking space? Complain about someone's dog? Did he call us about a party, about one of his neighbors?"

"Seriously?"

"It doesn't take much," Maureen said. "Did Dell catch anyone's attention for the wrong reasons? For something both of y'all might've thought was silly?"

"Like for walking through a black neighborhood with a white girl on his arm?" Susan asked. "We've been dating for two years. I know all Dell's people. This isn't such a bad neighborhood. Thanks, Officer. Thanks for your help." She sounded more dismissive than grateful. She looked at the bloody towel in her hands, dropped it on the sidewalk. She swallowed hard, once then again. Maureen could tell she was trying to rein in her emotions. She wanted to help. Maureen gave her time, left a quiet void for Susan to fill.

"There was yelling," Susan said. She drew in a deep breath. "And then there were these explosions, the gunshots. They were so fucking loud. I can't believe I'm not deaf. I screamed and ducked and Dell, he was behind me, kind of, he always walks slower than me, I'm always waiting for him to catch up to me, and so the shots came and he just, he just . . . he grabbed me kind of around the waist then he crumpled into the street. The blood was pumping out of him so fast. And then everyone around us was screaming, people running everywhere. It was over as soon as it happened. Then Dell was bleeding in the street, and everyone was running *away* from us. Nobody would help us."

"So there was yelling," Maureen said firmly, redirecting Susan's thoughts away from Dell's blood, "right before the shots. Like *whoo-hoo* party yelling? Or more like an argument? A fight? Was it two people fighting? A group of people?"

Susan closed her eyes trying to remember what she'd heard. Maureen let her sit and think.

"Not a group of voices," Susan said. "It wasn't like that. One person. He yelled someone's name, or the name of something." She nodded her head, eyes closed, the memory clarifying as she let it come to her. "Yeah, now that I think of it, he could've been yelling at us, for our attention, or for Dell. There was music coming from the bar, but not too loud, like, yeah, someone yelled something from behind us, like an announcement." She sat up straight, eyes wide open, surprised at her recall. "Three-N-G, niggah! That was it. Three-N-G, niggah, then *bam, bam, bam*." She swallowed again.

"You're sure?" Maureen asked.

"There were more shots than that," Susan said. "A lot more than three. I'm not sure how many. Sounded like a hundred."

"You're sure about the words, what was said?" Maureen asked. She recognized 3NG as a shorter name for the Third and Galvez Boys, a long-standing gang of local drug dealers. And killers. Their name was a start. A good one. "Are you *sure* about that?"

"I'm sure," Susan said. "Yeah, yeah, the voice jumped out at us. Like a little dog barking real loud. I was thinking *what the fuck is his problem* when the gunshots started."

"You didn't turn to look at who was yelling at you?"

"I didn't know he was talking to us. Not at the time. I mean, we didn't really have time to, you know, process who he was talking to or what he meant. People yell weird shit to each other across the street and stuff all the time. He wasn't *that* close. He started shooting before I figured out he was talking to us. Maybe he wasn't. Maybe he was yelling just to yell."

Maureen scanned the intersection. Goddamn it, she thought. So someone had stood in the middle of the street and popped off a whole bunch of rounds in a crowded intersection. Somebody saw it. Multiple people had seen it, and they were gone, disappeared back into the crowd of parade-goers down on the route. Maureen glanced at Wilburn and the injured lady in the yellow coat. They continued talking. She and Susan could be enough. They might have to be.

"Is there anything you can tell us about his voice?" Maureen asked. "An accent? Anything? Did he say *anything* else?"

Susan sighed. "He sounded young. Like a kid, a teenager, maybe. It was kind of high-pitched."

"But the voice was male," Maureen said. "You're sure of that."

"Yeah." Susan shrugged. "Anyway, when this shit happens, is it ever a girl?" She patted the clean towels stacked next to her on the bench. "You know, I don't feel so good. I totally forgot I had like three beers before we left the house and then I took that pill. Maybe I'll try getting into the bath-room. They probably have hot water in there. I can clean up better."

"Right." Maureen stood. "Good idea."

She straightened and hitched up her gun belt. She knew that three beers and whatever pills Susan had taken—if she admitted to one she'd probably taken two or three—were going to knock the woman out of commission any minute now.

"Listen," Maureen said, "I'm gonna make sure you're looked after, that you get the information you need to get to Cordell. We have officers that spe-cialize in that, in taking care of people. You know, after." Of course, Mau-reen recalled, those officers were stationed on the parade route right now and unavailable until the parades had ended. "They'll probably find you at the hospital. Later. A detective might want to talk to you, as well."

"You're not one of those, I take it," Susan said, standing.

"A detective?" Maureen said. "Not yet."

"The caretakers, I meant. You're not one of those."

In Susan's now heavy-lidded eyes, Maureen could practically see the fuzzy gauze she'd hung between herself and her present environment. She probably *didn't* feel very good. She also probably did not want to be as high as she currently was and talking to cops. Or maybe she didn't care about that. Hard to blame her, considering what she'd been through that night.

"I'm not, in fact, one of those officers," Maureen said, smiling. "I'm surprised you noticed."

"I'm gonna go ahead inside," Susan said, gesturing toward the bar door, "and finish cleaning up."

"Please stay here around the bar," Maureen said. "We'll want to talk to you just a little bit more. And we want to make sure you know where Cordell is."

"Will do," Susan said.

"And if you see that skinny reporter," Maureen said to Susan, "don't talk to her, or any of the pople she's with."

"Sure." She went inside the bar.

Susan wasn't going to be worth a damn thing to them for the rest of the night, Maureen thought. She hated leaving her unattended without getting more information about the shooting. She had one good lead, the shouted gang name. Maybe there were more clues and leads to be mined. She had empathy for Susan for what her night had been like. She wasn't cold. She wasn't heartless. But the best way to prevent another shooting that night was to catch the guy who'd pulled the trigger in the first one.

The heart of 3NG territory was only blocks away. This was in fact the real estate of a rival gang—this was J-Street territory—which pointed to a gang dispute as the reason for the shooting. That was the first working theory, at least. She wasn't sure where Cordell fit into that mix. For now she was inclined to believe what Susan had told her about him, but Maureen was confident they could make quick work of a solid, simple lead.

# 10

Across the intersection, Maureen noticed Laine Daniels standing on the sidewalk outside the corner store, chattering into her phone between long pulls from a forty-ounce. Maureen heard Wilburn's voice crackle on her radio. She tilted her head to listen. Holy shit. He was calling in a description of the shooter. She looked over at him. He was triumphantly holding up his notepad, waving it at her as he talked. Yes. She raised her fists over her head. Damn it. Where was Cordts? They were solving this shit, in record time, the three of them, and he was missing it. They weren't even gonna need the detective.

When he'd finished on the radio, Wilburn walked over. Maureen slapped him hard on the chest when he arrived. Twice. "Look at this motherfucker here."

"How ya like me now?" Wilburn said. "I'm so bad I'm good. Check this out. That lady I was talking to, Doris Wilson, she lives a couple blocks from here, back in the neighborhood. She was heading for the bar for a drink to go before she met her grandkids at the parade when she caught fragments in the back, right under the shoulder. According to her, the little girl was on her father's shoulders when she got shot. He's six-three, she's all of three feet tall and *she* catches the bullet. Unreal. Then again, the shot missed his *face* by half a foot. Maybe. He dropped to the ground and shoved her under a car to protect her, but she'd already been shot. Insanity. No wonder he was so crazy."

Cordts wandered over at that moment. "Good get on the 'scrip, Wils. I heard it. We're gonna get this guy."

He had swapped out his bloody vest for a new one; Faye and Kornegay must've had a spare in their car. He looked hollowed out, as if something had sucked the electricity from him through the soles of his feet. He had the girl's black wings folded and tucked into his new vest.

"You all right, Cordts?" Maureen asked.

Cordts grinned. His face was as white as the belly of a fish. The wrinkles at the corners of his mouth were deep; his wet blue eyes quivered. He mimicked holding the girl in his arms. Dark spots of blood stained the sleeves of his uniform. He stared at his hands. "You wouldn't believe how light she was. She didn't weigh anything." He shrugged. "I just can't believe the bullet didn't do more damage than it did. So random. It was all so random. You'd think a bullet hitting someone that size would . . . you'd think that she'd . . ." He reached into his pocket and pulled out the little red sneaker that had fallen off the girl's foot. "And I've got this, too. I forgot to give it to her father before he left."

"Not your fault," Wilburn said. With narrow eyes and a tight mouth he studied Cordts. Maureen could tell he'd hoped for Cordts to be in better shape upon his return to the crime scene. "The father took off running. Things were chaotic."

"Yeah, I wonder if he ever got to the hospital," Cordts said. "They should be together, the three of them. The girl and her parents."

"Tell you what," Maureen said, flashing a wary glance at Wilburn. "Maybe we should lock up that shoe in one of the units. And those wings, too. We'll get everything back to her later." She reached out for the shoe and the wings.

"Right, right," Cordts said, but Maureen could tell her words hadn't registered. "Yeah, good idea." The wings stayed tucked in his vest. He stuffed the sneaker into his back pocket. "Oh, shit. I completely forgot." He pulled out a gun, not his department-issue Glock, but a small black automatic pistol, and showed it to Maureen and Wilburn, turning his wrist so they could get a look at it. "I found this. Forty-cal. Polymer. Lying right in the intersection." He shrugged, tucked it in the back of his pants. "I'm guessing the shooter tossed it when he ran."

"You think?" Maureen said. She looked at Wilburn. "Maybe we should bag that, Cordts?"

"Listen, Cogs, you got a cigarette?" Cordts said.

Maureen produced her pack and lit one for Cordts, passing it to him. His hand trembled as he took it from her. "Cordts, are you okay?" She realized she had no idea what she'd do or say if he admitted something was wrong.

"Crazy night" was all he said.

"The gun?" Maureen said. "We're gonna need it. We're gonna need to pull prints and such when we catch this guy."

"I'll take care of it," Cordts said. "Leave it to me."

Maureen held her breath, waiting for Wilburn to step in, to take her side. Other than the shooter himself, that gun was the most valuable thing they could possibly find. She turned to Wilburn, who raised a cautionary hand. "He's got it. He's fine."

The bar door opened behind them and everyone turned to look.

Donna staggered out, a melting Susan draped across her black leather shoulders like one of Dalí's watches. Maureen marveled at Donna's ability to balance on her impossibly high heels, top heavy as she was already, and now with a drunk hanging on her back.

Donna flipped her hair from her face, stray white strands sticking in her waxy red lipstick and her thick mascara. "Hey, Protect and Serve, can I get some help here?"

Maureen helped Donna ease Susan onto the bench, where she slumped like a blackout drunk, which, Maureen guessed, she pretty much was at this point. She'd cleaned the blood from her hands but not her hair.

"She was in the bathroom, crying," Donna said. "The other girls were scared of her."

"It was nice of you to look out for her."

"She was sitting on the floor," Donna said, "by the sink, under the sink, making these sad kitten noises." She freed her trapped hairs from her lips and her eyelashes, and steadied herself atop her heels.

"Her boyfriend did get shot tonight," Maureen said.

"The floor in there," Donna said. "It's filthy. Who runs that place? I wouldn't think you could fit a whole person under that sink. You can't fit more than three people in that whole bathroom. Does this city even *have* a health department?"

"Well, thanks for bringing her back outside," Maureen said.

"We're good for something, I guess," Donna said. "We evil TV people. I didn't see you rushing in to help her."

"I was just about to," Maureen said, wondering why she was defending herself to this plastic tart.

"I'm so sure you were. As if."

"How old are you?"

"What?" Donna said.

"Like I said, we're grateful to you."

"Whatevs. Do you know where Laine is? She has my per diem. I need to pay that chubby bitch of a bartender."

Maureen pointed across the street at Laine, who now stood talking to an enormous muscle-bound police officer. His coal-black bald head reflected the red neon letters of the corner store's OPEN sign. The officer leaned forward and down so he could better hear what Laine was telling him, his large hands clasped behind his back, his blue uniform straining against the thick muscles of his shoulders. Just like Sergeant Hardin, Maureen thought, to be out in his sleeves while the rest of us are bundled up. At least he'd finally arrived.

Hardin straightened and looked in their direction. Maureen liked Hardin. She'd crossed paths with him when he'd worked in the Quarter, and she had been pleased when he transferred from the Eighth District to the Sixth at the beginning of the year. "At least someone will finally put a tent over this circus."

"I guess we're going back to the parade?" Cordts said. He sounded disappointed.

"Fuck that," Maureen said. "I'm finding this shooter. We're on the trail. Who else is gonna do it? Korn and Faye? Please."

"Lookit fucking Laine," Donna said, chuckling. "For real, do you know anyone who still thinks drinking a forty looks gangsta? That girl was *meant* to be *behind* the camera. I mean, the hair alone, right? Tragic."

"You have nothing else to do right now?" Maureen asked. "Aren't y'all supposed to be making a TV show?"

"It's a Web-based documentary series," Donna said.

"Whatevs," Maureen replied.

"Do me a favor, Red," Donna said. "Tell Laine I went to the parade. No sense missing it."

"Excuse me?" Maureen said.

Donna lit another long white cigarette. "And tell that chiseled hunk of black marble, too. If he can find me in that crowd, I'll make him a star." She walked away in her spike-heeled boots down the middle of Washington Avenue, hips swinging, chest puffed out, already waving for beads with her free hand.

"Who was that?" Wilburn asked.

"Donna somebody. She's part of the *On Fire* crew."

"She famous?" Cordts asked. "She acts like it."

"She made a sex tape once," Maureen said. "Well, twice. The second one was the hit. That's what her producer told me."

"A sex tape," Wilburn said. "That doesn't exactly narrow it down. I didn't know you could even get famous for that anymore."

"They're annoying me, the TV people," Maureen said. "They're in the way. There's got to be a way to chase them."

"Freedom of the press," Wilburn said with a shrug. He took out his phone, started thumbing away. "You didn't get the memo? We're supposed to be extra helpful to any TV people out on the route. Every one of these dumb shows is a free fucking commercial for the city."

"'Mardi Gras on Fire'?" Maureen said. "These are the commercials we want? Interviews with murder witnesses? Blood in the streets?"

"I make these decisions?" Wilburn said with a shrug, focused on his phone. "I just work here. Be nice to TV, the bosses said. You were in the same meetings I was. You know what the brass wants, what the mayor wants."

"At least the holiday'll be over by the time it airs, right?" Maureen said. "They have to edit and stuff, right?"

Cordts shook his head. "I wouldn't be so sure about that."

"You're kidding me."

"This On Fire is a Web series," Wilburn said. "I googled the show. It's a YouTube channel." He shrugged. "They want, they can edit and upload their shit by morning, later tonight, if they want. All they need is a laptop."

"How do you know about this?" She thought about Donna's sex tape. "Maybe I don't want to know."

"My brother does stand-up comedy," Wilburn said. "He does all this shit. He's pretty funny. He's got a YouTube channel, too." He held out his phone to Maureen. "C'mon, Cogs, this isn't exactly NASA-grade technical shit."

She took the phone from him. He had Laine's YouTube channel pulled up on the screen. Sure enough, there was Donna talking to the camera, tits hanging out of some Mad Max–type outfit made out of a camouflage-print bikini and a singed and shredded potato sack. "Three hundred thousand people watched her Burning Man thing? Three hundred thousand? Holy shit. Joke's on me, I guess. What the fuck do I know?" She handed Wilburn back his phone. "There's money in this? We're in the wrong fucking business."

"You're telling me," Wilburn said. He looked across the street and put the phone back in his pocket. "Well, here comes Hardin. You can tell him yourself that Hollywood South with the tits is calling for him. I'm sure he'll be thrilled to hear it."

# 11

Hardin gathered Maureen, Wilburn, and Cordts around him in the street outside the bar. "Cordts, well done on recovering the weapon. Nice work, Wilburn, getting that description out. Nothing on it yet, but fingers crossed. Coughlin, I hear you've already corralled a couple of witnesses. Y'all are showing me something. Way to take control of the chaos. We're building a good case." He looked over his shoulder. "That TV lady is a trip."

"You should see the other one," Wilburn said. "And thanks."

"What else have you got for me?" Hardin asked.

"Cordts and I came down Baronne," Maureen said, "and Wilburn followed up Washington. Korn and Faye came up later, helped wrangle the bystanders. They helped contain the scene. Mounted came and went when they saw there was nothing left but mop-up duty. But none of us really focused on securing the scene, really locking it down. There's been foot traffic all through it. People were hurt and needed help."

"Y'all did fine," Hardin said. "Better than fine. Korn and Faye gave me the basics. Three shot, including a child, but no fatalities. Two of them at the hospital." He made the sign of the cross. "A fucking miracle. It's not good luck anytime three people get shot, but that none of them got dead? That's pretty fucking lucky." He looked at Maureen. "I hear you have a friend of the male vic?"

Maureen looked over her shoulder at Susan, now curled up asleep on the wooden bench. "Uh, yeah. His girlfriend."

"That's her?" Hardin asked, eyebrows high on his broad forehead.

Maureen took a deep breath, held it, her cheeks puffed out. "Yup. We kept her upright as long as we could." She looked at Wilburn, who tilted *his* head toward Cordts, who stood off to the side, smoking the burning filter of his cigarette, staring at the traffic light as if wondering what devil magic made it work. Not good, Maureen thought. Wherever Cordts had gone after putting that girl in the ambulance, he had yet to come all the way back. It was probably best Hardin didn't catch on. No sense ruining his good mood. She caught Wilburn's eye and looked at the store across the street.

"If you don't need us right this absolute second, Sarge," Wilburn said, catching the hint, "I'm gonna grab Cordts for a coffee run across the street." He reached out and touched Cordts on the elbow. "Hey, let's get a coffee. We got a long night ahead of us."

Cordts looked at Hardin. "Sarge? You need us right now?"

"Great idea," Hardin said. "While you're over there, double-check for me and make sure whoever's running that store tonight knows we want their video. Nothing gets erased. We should find out when the counter guys get off. We don't want them leaving without giving a statement." He paused. "You got that? You can handle that?"

"We got it," Wilburn said. "Simple police work. No worries."

"Handle that stuff," Hardin said, "and Coughlin here can fill me in on the rest from the scene, right?"

"I got you, Sarge," Maureen said. "Bring me one, would ya? Six sugars. And a pack of Spirits."

"You're good for it, right?" Wilburn said.

"I got it," Cordts said. "The yellow pack?"

"That's it," Maureen said. "Thank you, Officer Cordts."

Wilburn scratched at the space between his eyebrows with his middle finger before walking away with Cordts.

Maureen looked up at Hardin, who towered over her by a foot, maybe more.

Hardin tapped his chest. "What is that tucked inside Cordts's vest?"

"The girl who got shot," Maureen said, "she was wearing fairy wings. Cordts is hanging on to them for her. He has one of her sneakers, too, in his back pocket."

Hardin frowned, watching Wilburn and Cordts walk to the store. He let his misgivings go for the moment and turned back to Maureen. "Tell me about Sleeping Beauty, this other witness."

"Her name is Susan," Maureen said. "I'm sorry about the shape she's in. I think she's on medication. And she'd been drinking before everything started. That's what she told me. She gave us something good before we lost her, though."

"Which is?"

"Three-N-G."

"She named a shooter?" Hardin instinctively looked downtown, in the direction of the gang's territory. "She knew him from the gang?"

Maureen shook her head. "The shooter yelled it out, right before he pulled the trigger."

"She get any kind of look at him? Anything to confirm what Wilburn got?"

"That's a negative," Maureen said. "She said he sounded young, but that was the best we got from her. We know he shot from close range, but not close enough that he didn't hit a car and two other people."

"What do we know about her boyfriend? He roll with anybody?"

"That's the thing," Maureen said. "I haven't been able to confirm, naturally, but to hear Susan tell it? No way he, the victim—his name is Cordell—no way he's a gangbanger. He teaches music. He's ten or fifteen years older than any of those kids in that gang, any of the gangs. Susan and

Cordell, they're a longtime couple. They live in the neighborhood. The bartender inside said they're regulars. She knows them." She shrugged. "They sound like normal folks."

"What did the bartender see?"

"Nothing."

"They never do," Hardin said. "So was Cordell the target or not? He fail a gangbanger's cousin on his last report card?"

"Cordell was hit three times," Maureen said. "Susan told me the gunshots sounded like they were close, fired by someone coming at them from behind, which makes me think the shooter was definitely after him. And why announce gang affiliation for the whole street to hear unless you want the victim and/or the witnesses to know who got him? But what confuses me is the shooter throwing bullets all over the intersection. How many casings we find?"

"Ten," Hardin said. "So far."

"So why the wild spray?" Maureen asked. "Why the extra shots?"

Hardin turned, looking behind him at the intersection, dotted with the small orange plastic cones. Maureen studied the scene, trying to see whatever Hardin was seeing.

People walked along Washington Avenue, drifting around the ineffective streamers of yellow crime scene tape that Faye had halfheartedly strung in the last few minutes, probably on Hardin's orders. Passersby eyed the tape and the cones as if observing a bizarre art installation, the theme and meaning of which eluded them. The intersection seemed to Maureen like a movie set where the action had ended, or hadn't yet begun. Business remained brisk at the corner store, she noticed, with large groups of people strolling in then exiting swinging twelve-packs of beer, tearing open bags of chips, and banging fresh packs of cigarettes against their palms. What did she expect? That the neighborhood would clear out because there'd been a shooting near the parade route? Let the good times roll.

"You think Cordts is okay?" Maureen asked. "He seems in shock or something."

"Yeah, I think he's all right," Hardin said. "He's not a hundred percent, but we don't have the numbers to be sending people home."

"He's probably better off with us, anyway," Maureen said. "We don't want him sitting home alone with those fairy wings."

"Roger that."

"So if Cordell was the target," Maureen said, "for whatever reason, and the shooter got as close as Susan said, I'm wondering how Cordell's not dead with eight or ten bullets in him and how we have so much collateral damage."

"I'll show you," Hardin said. He took a step back from Maureen. He turned his back toward Downtown. That way he faced the same direction the shooter had likely been walking in when he had opened fire on Cordell. "Guy comes walking up Baronne Street and moves into the intersection, gun in his waistband, maybe his pocket. He's rushing, he's nervous. He's been following them, maybe for a couple of blocks, getting up the nerve. When he sees Cordell and Susan moving into the crowd, maybe heading for the bar"—Hardin raised his arm and made a pistol shape with his fingers—"he realizes he's losing his chance, he rushes after them, heads right for them, and he draws. He's got Cordell lined up at close range."

"Okay."

"But then," Hardin said, "this happens." He bent his knees, closed his eyes, and turned his head to the side. "Bang, bang, bang. Meanwhile Cordell has taken another couple steps."

"I think I got it," Maureen said. She copied Hardin's stance. "First couple shots hit Cordell, one on the back of the thigh, another two in the ribs, but as our shooter keeps firing, the gun barrel keeps jumping from the recoil. He loses control. His eyes are closed. One miss gets the little girl on her daddy's shoulders, he hits the car, throwing shrapnel in that lady, and so on."

Maureen lowered her arm, nodding her head as the thoughts clicked together. "It matches what Susan said. She talked about him sounding young. Wilburn's witness said he's young, too, probably a juvenile. So he's a kid, our shooter, and he's terrified of his own gun."

"I bet we'll find him with piss stains down the front of his pants," Hardin said. "And we *will* find him. Good thing he was so afraid. In a way. He probably put several rounds in a rooftop or in the sky that would've gone into more bystanders."

"Or into Cordell," Maureen said. "And then we'd have a homicide on our hands."

"That's what I'm thinking," Hardin said.

"A hit or a crime of opportunity?" Maureen asked.

"A bit of both," Hardin said. "I bet anything this kid was heading down to the route with that gun on him, or cruising the neighborhood looking for whoever he thought Cordell was. He's probably new to Three-N-G, looking to make his bones and an older member gave him a target, a job. Or maybe they don't want him and he's expendable. Our catch rate at these parade shootings is pretty good. Somehow the dopes who do these things forget they're boxed in and surrounded by cops.

"Maybe it's the first time he's ever carried a gun with the serious intent to use it. He's absolutely jacked up, on adrenaline, nerves, probably some other stuff, too, God knows what. He saw his chance to hit Cordell and blew his wad, totally lost it. Happens a lot on their first time. They go out in the East and out by the old amusement park where it's empty and practice shooting, like they're commandos or something, but they're never ready for the first time they pull that trigger in public, on a real person. Only the born killers don't shit themselves over the first time. This kid wasn't that. If our shooter was a born killer, Cordell would be dead and that lady wouldn't have seen a thing."

"As for talking to Cordell himself?" Maureen asked.

"That's not for us tonight," Hardin said. "The detective will get with him. Tomorrow, the next day, whenever he's well enough to talk. But if what his girl says about him is true, I don't see how he was the real target. Wrong place, wrong time for him, I'm afraid. Our shooter fucked up his homework is my best guess." He sighed. "Which means his own gang might be out to kill him now."

"Who's the detective on duty tonight?" Maureen asked. "He's got his work cut out for him."

"That's another thing I wanted to discuss with you," Hardin said.

"Don't even say it." Maureen raised her hands and backed away. "Don't even. I can't stand it."

"Indeed. It's Drayton. I'm sorry," Hardin said. "Get ready for a long fucking night."

"Why is it him again?" Maureen asked. "It was him last night, and the night before, and the night before that, too. He's like a curse."

"He volunteers for these shifts," Hardin said. "And the other dicks let him. No one else in Homicide wants to work the route with him. Would you? They're happy he's not back in uniform with them for the holiday. They're glad to get the break from him. So he takes the district guys' detective shifts, they get nights off during Mardi Gras, and he sits at the district for the night watching porn on his phone and racking up mad overtime. He knows he's not getting called out on the street for anything less than, well, anything less than what happened tonight. I don't think he ever even put his shoes on last night."

"So when he gets here," Maureen asked, "if he ever gets here, whose job will it be to catch him up on the fun we've had so far?"

"I wouldn't do you like that, Coughlin," Hardin said with a smile. "I know you and him have a history."

"He has a history with everyone," Maureen said. "It's not only me."

"I know that," Hardin said. "I'll handle Drayton when he gets here. And by the way, the party is just getting started. If Cordell was an accident, then whoever our real target was tonight remains a target. If this shooting is a gang thing, they *have* to get him now, tonight, which means Three-N-G is out there prowling the route, and strapped."

"I'm guessing," Maureen said, "that word is already circulating that Three-N-G is making a move on someone tonight. And I'm guessing the real target now knows he's in somebody's crosshairs, so he and his boys, they're strapped as well and looking to strike first. All of them and all of us, packed into this box together with about a hundred thousand of our closest friends."

Thousands of bodies, she thought, of every age and size, in every direction, on every street, each body with the potential to catch a bullet before the night was over. The thought made her sick. There was no way to protect them all, or even most of them. The high she'd felt about putting the case together evaporated. They were staring at gunfire ringing out and bodies dropping along St. Charles Avenue, at a potential slaughter that could make what had already happened tonight, Hardin's miracle of good bad luck, no more than a prelude rendered comical in its comparative insignificance. And the city would not cancel the parades. Not tonight. Not tomorrow or the next day. That simply wasn't a thing that happened. It was up to Maureen and her cohorts to prevent St. Charles Avenue from becoming a war zone for the next five days.

"We have got *our* fucking work cut out for *us* tonight," Hardin said. "You've heard people say Mardi Gras is a marathon, not a sprint? For us? Tonight? It's the hundred-yard dash. Nothing *but* a sprint. We're off to a good start, y'all have done good work, now let's keep the good times rolling. I'm optimistic."

Maureen's and Hardin's radios crackled at the same time. An announcement followed the static: "Be advised, possible shooting suspect spotted on Harmony Street, heading toward the lake, on foot."

"Oh, shit," Maureen said, turning, rising up on her toes, looking in every direction, her adrenaline spiked. "That's close. It's close." She saw Wilburn standing outside the grocery, chatting with Laine. She keyed her mic. "Dispatch, gimme a cross street. Harmony and what?"

The dispatcher continued her report, ignoring Maureen's request and repeating Wilburn's description: "African-American male, five-five. Slight build, red T-shirt, jeans or dark pants, white tennis shoes. Approach with caution. Suspect is considered armed and dangerous."

Cordts burst through the doors of the corner store and came running across the intersection, weaving through the passersby, a large coffee in each hand, the dark, steaming liquid sloshing over his wrist and hands as he ran. He didn't seem to mind. "Rabbit! Rabbit! Rabbit! Holy shit, let's go get him."

"Last spotted at Harmony and Danneel Streets," Dispatch finally said, "headed north on Harmony toward the lake."

Hardin turned to Maureen. "You're our best rabbit chaser. Get ready to run, Officer Coughlin. Down the hole you go."

# 12

Maureen ran the few blocks to the intersection of Harmony and Danneel at full speed. As she slowed to a jog she realized she was alone. She looked behind her down Harmony Street, back the way she'd run, hoping Cordts would somehow be catching up to her, but she saw no sign of him. No one had followed her. Who would? Who could keep up?

She eased down to what she hoped resembled a casual yet authoritative stride, trying to hide her labored effort to catch her breath. She thought of the pack of cigarettes Cordts had, hopefully, gotten her from the corner store. Her sprinting speed was as fast as ever. Her stamina, however, was suffering. On the other hand, nobody, she thought, but nobody, quit smoking *during* Mardi Gras. *Especially* not someone working it. She didn't need to be born-and-raised to know that was a fool's errand. Maybe for Ash Wednesday, though? Probably not.

Whatevs, as Donna would say. She had an eternity to go before she had to worry about Ash Wednesday.

Around her on the street, Maureen observed neighbors idling on their porches, smoking their own cigarettes, chatting quietly, and generally acting unconcerned by and uninterested in the young white girl police officer who had come sprinting down their street. At second glance, though, Maureen saw that the people were not as relaxed as they made out to be in front of her. They paced their yards and driveways and porches. Radios played hip-hop and brass band music, but the volume was set pretty low for a Mardi Gras street party. And nobody danced. Nobody was laughing. She knew that people not looking at her didn't mean they weren't watching her.

Inside one of the houses, a group of guys erupted into loud laughter, cranking up the music and, clapping in time, singing along loudly with an old Rebirth Brass Band song: *You don't wanna*, they sang, *you don't wanna, you don't wanna go to war.*

As she walked the block, eyes peeled for anyone hiding in the shadows, Maureen adjusted her gun belt, straightened her fluorescent vest. She took off her knit cap and wiped the sweat at her hairline with her uniform sleeve. Her nose was running again. She wiped it with the back of her glove, like a girl in a schoolyard. Nobody on the block was impressed with her; she knew that much already. She thought about lighting a cigarette.

A tentative voice called out to her from the front yard of one of the nearby houses. She stopped and turned.

A young woman in tight acid-washed jeans and a sky-blue puffy down jacket with a red Solo cup in one hand and a baby on her hip stood in the front yard of a faded double shotgun. She raised her red cup toward Downtown.

Maureen trotted over to her. "You saw something?"

The woman backed away, mute, again directing with her Solo cup, shaking her head, discouraging Maureen from coming nearer. A big man in a hoodie and baggy jeans stood over a smoking grill in the driveway, clutching a beer bottle in one hand and barbecue tongs in the other. Frowning, he followed the stunted conversation, head turning slowly from the girl to the cop and back again. Several friends hovered around him, leaning against a car in the driveway.

"Someone called us," Maureen said to the woman, "about someone we're looking for being right around here." She waited a moment. "Was it you?"

"I told you," the big man said to the woman, "take the baby inside. It's cold. We'll go down the parade after we eat. Muses ain't even rolling down here yet."

He continued staring down the young woman, who had not moved from the front yard and who stared right back at him, hard, her dimpled chin raised and stuck forward. She sipped from her cup and resettled the squirming child on her hip. The man rolled his bald head on his thick neck. They were having a fight, and it wasn't over yet. A couple of the man's friends suppressed grins, covering their mouths with the backs of their hands and rolling their eyes at Maureen. The bald man let out a heavy sigh.

He spoke to Maureen while looking at his girl. "The way she said, couple blocks, maybe. Whoever it was, though, they long gone now. Y'all are slow."

"So somebody came running this way?" Maureen asked. "A young guy, red T-shirt?"

How would this girl know, Maureen wondered, what the guy we're chasing looked like? How could she have called it in?

The man looked over his shoulder at his buddies. He turned his low-lidded gaze to Maureen. "You it? You what they could spare? We live the *other* side of St. Charles, they shooting people over there, twenty of y'all would be out here."

Maureen wasn't about to argue with him over the NOPD's allocation of resources. Essentially, he wasn't wrong. But she'd never convince him that during Mardi Gras there weren't enough cops for the white and wealthy neighborhoods on the other side of the parade route, either, no matter what the higher-ups said in public.

"Can you help me, please?" Maureen asked. She felt like the longer she stood there, the farther away the shooter got from her. "I don't have all night."

"I do," the man said. His buddies laughed. Maureen ignored them.

Maureen gestured at the woman and the child. "Sir. Seriously. It's Mardi Gras. There's kids everywhere out here. We got a shooter on the loose in the neighborhood. Your neighborhood. He shot a girl not much older than y'all's. There are kids everywhere tonight. You got nothing more productive to offer me than that?"

The man shrugged.

Frustrated, Maureen turned to leave, wondering again how they could know the description of the person the NOPD was looking for, and she realized something. The fight she'd interrupted, it wasn't a lovers' quarrel. It was a family spat between brother and sister.

"You know him," Maureen said.

The man flinched, as if a sore muscle had twitched in the small of his back, and she knew she was right. His friends studied their shoe tops.

"He came here to hide," Maureen said. "He told what he did and y'all sent him away. One of you called us about it." The woman hitched the baby higher on her hip then turned and headed into the house. Maureen took a shot, shouting to her. "His name?"

"Oh, shit," one of the man's friends mumbled. The group started breaking up, the men drifting around the parked car and up an alley along the side of the house, heading for the backyard.

The man turned the chicken and sausage on the grill, the fat falling from the meat into the fire popping and smoking. He shook his head, chuckling to himself. Maureen had known it was a ridiculous question with no chance of an answer when she had asked it. But she'd had to. She had to be able to tell her boss she'd tried. So he could tell his boss she'd tried. She realized as the grill smoke drifted to her that she was starving. *What I wouldn't give*, she thought, *to be at a parade party, drink in hand, food on the fire.*

The man looked up from his work and gestured with the tongs at the spot in the yard where the woman with the baby had stood. "If she says that boy run by, he run by. If she say he went that way, then that's the way he went. I don't argue with her. That's what she wanted to tell you. That's what we tellin' you now."

Maureen studied the house, looking for the numbers somewhere on the front of it. She couldn't find them. *I should get names*, she thought, and phone numbers, at least from the girl and her brother. She knew this conversation would be her only chance at that information.

Everyone here would eat and then they would scatter for the rest of the night, to the parade, later to friends and family, just in case the cops came back around later asking more questions. Then she remembered. Drayton was the detective tonight. Even if she could get that information, he'd never use it. He'd never come by this house. He'd never call. He'd never even try. He'd sit on it until after the holiday, when he'd get sent back to Homicide and the case would pass on to someone else who would put it at the bottom of their large pile of open cases.

Were they working a case on the other side of St. Charles, she thought, Drayton *have* to follow up over the next few days. The brass would make him. But not here. Not when no one had died. She needed to continue her pursuit of the shooter and she was losing ground on him, standing around. Making the arrest was her best chance at getting something meaningful done. Catch the shooter yourself, she thought, and what Drayton doesn't do doesn't matter.

"I appreciate your help," she told the man at the grill. "Have a good night."

He didn't even look at her, never mind speak to her again. She didn't blame him much. A cop was the worst kind of party crasher.

At a crisp jog, she turned around and headed back down Harmony, turning on Danneel Street toward Downtown, heading in the direction the young woman had indicated.

# 13

As she moved deeper into the neighborhood, Maureen noticed that, as if they'd been raptured, the partiers and parade-goers had vanished, sucked down to the route. Most of the houses around her now were dark and empty. Whoever wasn't down at the parade, Maureen figured, was, like Dakota and her crew, hard at work helping to throw the party. Nothing was coming over the radio. It wasn't out of the question, she thought, that the guy at the grill had been right. She might be the only cop out here chasing this guy. That thought made her want to be the one to catch him all the more. She turned in a circle to get her bearings. She considered calling in her location, but she had nothing to report.

It was a strange Mardi Gras phenomenon, how this happened, she thought, how you could wander into these pockets of dark and quiet while the whole city raged. These silent islands had a strange and powerful gravity. She wanted to linger, to hide. She felt like she was deep in the wings of the arena while a distant rock concert exploded on a stage at the other end of a long tunnel, the fans and the band oblivious to the bomb hidden in the building. She looked around again. She had the thought she'd been trying not to have since she took off running from outside the bar: that motherfucker could be anywhere by now.

Her radio stayed quiet.

The rain-dappled cars lining the curbs glowed in the streetlights, like she'd wandered into a slumbering herd of dark, wet beasts. The flickering blue-and-white ghost light of a television set illuminated the front window of one living room a few houses ahead. She could hear the murmur of the TV program. Canned laughter.

These neighborhood streets could be a maze. Getting turned around, getting disoriented, was easy, she thought, especially on foot at night. The houses, one shotgun double after another, they looked the same, presenting the same weathered working-class face made up from the same palette of washed-out primary colors. Street signs came and went: stolen or brought down by the weather and never replaced, turned in the wrong direction in order to make exactly what she was trying to do that much more difficult. On this side of St. Charles, the city didn't take the time or spend the money to tile the street names into the corners of intersections.

She checked the sky. She spotted the Coast Guard copter that kept a bird's-eye on the parade route. That was Homeland Security. That chopper wasn't engaged with police department pursuits. She stopped walking, set her hands on her hips, lowered her head, and listened to the neighborhood. She took deep breaths to quiet her pulse and calm down. A cold breeze from the direction of the parade route swept over her and she could, for a moment, hear delighted screaming and cheesy, bass-heavy pop music blaring from rattling speakers as a dance troupe moved along the route. Underneath the cheering and the music, ever-present as a heartbeat, she heard the rumble of the drums from another marching band making its way up the avenue.

Cold, tired, and hungry, she thought about going back to the crime scene, checking in with Hardin, talking to Wilburn and Cordts about getting back on the route. There were several hours of parade left to roll. Chaos would finish soon and then the night's main event: the Krewe of Muses. On the route she and Wilburn and Cordts and the others, they could watch the crowd, look for signs and signals, read the ripples and vibrations, let the crowd tell them, hopefully, what was coming next, or at least where it was happening. These empty streets were giving her nothing. She felt useless, wandering the streets like a redheaded Alice lost in some bizarro, broke-down, broke-ass working-class Wonderland. She reached for her cigarettes.

Her hand froze inside her jacket when she heard something moving nearby.

Not a noise floating her way from the route, or from a television inside one of the houses on the block, but a sound made by something alive and close to her, something or someone moving in the darkness. She turned her radio down and listened. There it was again. Rustling material. Clothing. The shifting of rubber soles on the pavement.

She lifted her head, squinting into the darkness, studying every shadow. Waiting for one of the shadows to move, to separate itself from the others.

She moved slowly and quietly out of the middle of the street, out of the glow of the streetlamps, making herself harder to see. She cursed her electric-yellow reflective vest. She didn't want to radio for backup. Not yet. Not until she knew what she had. And if she hadn't been spotted, she didn't want to surrender the element of surprise by making noise. She waited for her eyes to adjust to the greater darkness. She heard heavy breathing now. Whispers, maybe. Something, someone, was out there, moving in front of her on her right. There, she saw it.

Between two of the parked cars, there was definitely a shape, crouching in the dark.

She moved closer to the shape, easing her flashlight from her belt. She didn't turn it on. There was every chance he had seen her approaching.

Maybe he thought he held the advantage and planned to press it. She cursed her vest again. It made her an easy target.

She drew her weapon, holding it close to the flashlight. She'd use the beam to do more than aim. She recalled walking out of the bar right into Cortez and his blinding spotlight. She'd turn the flashlight on at the last possible moment. The bright beam in his eyes would give her the moments she needed to take charge of the situation.

Maureen heard breathing, grunting. Was he hurt? Was that why he had gone to that house for help and to hide? Wounded only made him more dangerous, not less.

She raised the flashlight and the gun, relaxed her knees into a better shooting stance. She clicked on the light, the bright beam splitting the darkness.

She shouted: "NOPD! Do not fucking move!"

Two confused pasty white faces, one male and one female, both barely twenty years old, stared back at her. The boy was raised up on his arms, his hands pressed flat against the hood of the car. He had a black feather boa wrapped around his neck. He turned his head away from the glare of Maureen's flashlight. The girl underneath him, bent over the hood of a parked car, covered her head with her skinny arms and started screaming. In her flashlight beam, Maureen could see the boy's white hips pressed up against the girl's ample, even whiter ass. "Are you kidding me?"

"We're not doing anything wrong," the guy shouted. He threw his hands in the air. "I know her. She's my girlfriend." He wore a rugby-style shirt with wide purple, green, and gold stripes, the same one as the mother of the girl who'd been shot.

As far as Maureen could tell the boy had not even withdrawn from his partner. Well, she'd told them not to move and they pretty much hadn't.

"Somebody called the cops?" the kid cried out. He clearly felt violated. "I can't believe somebody called the cops. What the fuck? There's *nobody* around here. We walked for *blocks* to find a private spot."

He stood there with his hands up, the black feathers of his boa fluttering in the cold breeze, waiting for Maureen to tell him what to do.

The girl underneath him, who wore heart-shaped, red-glittered antennae on her head and had her purple, ruffled, sock-hop-type skirt tossed over her back, started slapping at him as best she could from the awkward position she was in. Maureen thought of Rob in the SUV slapping at his passenger and she tried not to laugh. The girl's antennae bounced and waved as she swung her hand at her boyfriend. She wore a toy ring on her slapping hand that blinked red, yellow, and white, like the lights of a teeny-tiny ambulance.

"Get off, get off, get off me. Dennis! Oh my *God*."

Hearing his name brought rugby boy halfway back to his senses. Letting his oversized shirt drop over his newly exposed privates, he stepped back from the girl, who slid down the hood of the car to the street, hoping to disappear, Maureen figured, right through the wet pavement and from the face of the earth. Maureen, doing her best not to laugh at the poor girl's agony, could see only her waving antennae above the front of the car. "Miss, are you okay?"

No answer. "Miss?"

"I'm *fine*. Oh. My. God. I am going to *die*. This is so harassment."

"Sir, pull up your pants, please. Please. Right now."

He set to it, giving Maureen one more unwelcome glimpse of a Mardi Gras full moon.

"Be glad the camera crew didn't follow me," Maureen said.

The girl shot up from between the cars, adjusting her skirt. "*What?*"

Maureen raised her hands in a placating gesture. "Never mind. Listen to me. Y'all need to leave the area. Right away. We're searching the neighborhood for a dangerous person. It's not a good time to be creeping around in the dark. Go back to the parade."

"Holy shit, Tanner," the boy said, "we were totally just *doing it* in the middle of a *manhunt*. Fuckin' A. That's hot." He dug into his pants for his phone.

Maureen put her face in her hands. She wished for some of Laine Daniels's Tylenol. Or something stronger.

"Don't say my *name*, you asshole," Tanner said, slapping at him again from her improved, upright angle, her antennae waving, her ambulance ring blinking. Dennis's phone clattered to the street. Tanner raised her hands and leaned away from him, her mouth contorted in disgust. "I'm going to *kill* you, Dennis. Are you still hard? In front of a cop? Gross. You are so gross. What is wrong with me?"

"You can't say that in front of a cop," Dennis said, "that you're going to kill me." He looked at Maureen, fixing his shirt to make sure it covered his crotch. "Right, Officer? Right? Were you serious about the camera crew? Where are they at?"

"Would you two get the fuck out of here?" Maureen said.

"You don't have to be mean to him," Tanner said. "We weren't doing anything wrong. And I didn't mean it. I'm not going to literally kill him. Of course not."

"GO!" Maureen shouted, pointing in the direction of the parade. "GO NOW!"

"Bring the beer," Tanner said, pouting and strutting away, antennae bouncing.

Dutifully, Dennis snatched up the half-empty twelve-pack and trailed after Tanner, his boozy, horny gaze fixated on her plump, swaying, purple-satin-and-lace-draped bottom. Please lead him the hell away from here, Maureen thought. She clicked off her flashlight. She rubbed her temples. I'm going to be seeing these two all weekend, she thought, I can feel it. Fucking like rabbits. Speaking of rabbits. She looked around. Nothing was coming over the radio.

"Fuck this." She reached for her cigarettes.

Then she heard a distinct metallic ringing she'd known her whole life, a sound that she'd made herself plenty of times. Someone jamming the toe of his sneaker into a chain-link fence. To make quick work of jumping that fence. She peered again into the shadows. She saw him. Climbing clumsily over the top of a fence four houses behind her. She heard his sneakers slap the sidewalk.

She shouted, "Stop! Police!" But he didn't listen, like she'd known he wouldn't. He took off running. Maureen took off after him, back at full speed.

# 14

They'd only covered a single block before they both realized Maureen would catch him, and catch him quickly. So he broke left down a side street, turning back toward the parade. Oh, no, no, no, Maureen thought, no way am I letting him run into that crowd. Now she really had to chase him down. She feared losing him in the chaos of the parade route. That was surely what *he* was hoping.

She saw him hesitate and almost skid to a stop at an intersection, dropping one hand to the street to right himself. "Stop right there," she yelled. "Stop!" She pointed at him as she ran, as if there was anyone else she could be talking to. "Stop fucking running! Get on the ground!"

She was almost close enough to tackle him. She braced herself for the impact. He slipped away from her and ran up the nearest driveway.

Instead of jumping the fence into the backyard, he dropped to his belly and crawled underneath the raised house.

Maureen stopped at the foot of the driveway, panting. She read the house numbers from above the front door so she could report the address. "You motherfucker. I got you now."

She hit the mic on her radio and called in her location. Almost immediately she heard sirens a few blocks away. Less than a minute later she heard Hardin's request go out over the radio for the K-9 unit to meet her. She retreated to the sidewalk, breathing heavily, pacing, squatting, shining her flashlight everywhere the suspect could pop out from under the house. She had a feeling he was done running, though. If he had the energy for it, he would've leaped the fence and kept going. He was digging in now. He was tired and scared. No way, though, was she going under there after him. She would wait him out. She would wait for the dogs.

She continued pacing the sidewalk. "Young man, if you are armed," she called out, "you need to say so. Things don't need to escalate." She got no answer. She hadn't really expected one. "Come out from under the house. Slowly. You don't, you're gonna wish you had." As if there were any other way to do it than slow, she thought. "Come out with your hands where I can see them." Again, she got no answer. Surely, she would've heard him scramble away if he'd popped out on another side of the house. She continued stalking the perimeter of the property. No fucking way she was losing him now.

Across New Orleans, many houses stood atop short brick or concrete pillars, raised two or three feet off the ground as protection against the flooding that could plague the city during the heavy rains of summer. She'd heard of suspects diving into these crawl spaces to hide from the cops. Thing was, most suspects chose this tactic only when there were no cops watching them do it. A hiding place isn't worth shit if the person you're hiding from sees you climbing into it. Tonight marked the first time a suspect she was actively chasing had used this particular evasive tactic on her. She knew full well how it was handled. The K-9 unit. Most of the crooks in the city knew that, too. They hated the dogs. Feared them much more than human police officers. Maureen couldn't understand why the petty-criminal class continued subjecting themselves to arrest by canine by trying the crawl space trick. It didn't work for attics, either.

Thinking you could outsmart, outlast, or outrun the human cops was one thing. But nobody ever escaped the dogs. Part of her hoped tonight didn't get to that. Talk about escalating things. She thought maybe she could keep trying to coax the guy out from under the house by reminding him about what came next. And, honestly, she could get uncomfortable with how much some of her fellow cops enjoyed watching the dogs work. And then she recalled that this guy had shot a little girl. And a teacher. And a grandmother.

Well, if, she thought, and it was a big if, she had the right guy trapped under that house. Everything they wanted to accomplish that night required getting the right guy. Maureen hoped she hadn't been sent on a goose chase by a resentful ex-girlfriend. She doubted it. If that girl was trying to set up an innocent man, she would have given Maureen much more than a gesture made with a plastic cup; she'd have given a name.

Maureen moved up the driveway and squatted where the kid had dived under the house, shining her light into the crawl space. The flashlight beam caught a bright pair of eyes that flashed at her. A filthy feral cat hid under the house, hissing and baring its fangs at the intrusion. She spotted a couple more grungy cats deeper under the house, the three felines glaring at her like they were a punk band she'd caught shooting up in an alley. "Oh, my little friends, you're not going to like the dogs, either."

The cats, Maureen thought, would have the sense to get out from under the house when the dogs arrived. Her suspect, she feared, would have no such sense. She could see him. She saw the top of his head, the shoulders of his red T-shirt. His arms were out at his sides. She could kind of see his hands, not as well as she would've liked. The kid kept his face turned away from her, as if as long as he couldn't see her, she wasn't there, and this situation wasn't happening. He was acting, she thought, like a child. Like the terrified child Hardin had described to her. She wanted to be sympathetic, but he was scared and cornered. Sympathy was dangerous.

"Let me see your hands," she instructed. "Raise them off the ground, wiggle your fingers."

The porch light came on, illuminating the driveway. Maureen stood. "Shit."

The front door flew open. "What is going *on* out here?" A middle-aged woman dressed in black sweats and fuzzy pink slippers stormed out the door. She had a hammer in one hand. "What are you *doing* out here?"

"NOPD, ma'am," Maureen said.

"I can *see* that. And you can call me Ms. Cleo."

Maureen didn't know what the woman had heard. She didn't want to frighten her. "Ms. Cleo, there's been an incident in the neighborhood."

"It's Mardi Gras," the woman said. "Whole damn neighborhood is an incident."

"I know that, ma'am, Ms. Cleo," Maureen said, feeling dumber and more flustered by the second. Why was it nobody gave a shit that she was a cop? And you can call me Officer Coughlin, she wanted to say. But why make things any more hostile than they already were? "We've been pursuing a suspect through the neighborhood—"

"A suspect in what?"

At that moment, two NOPD Explorers skidded to a stop at opposite ends of the block, their blue lights flashing. Maureen could hear the squawking of the truck's radios as an officer climbed out of each one, slamming the doors behind them. One of them was Cordts. The other was a very large officer who, unfortunately, wasn't Hardin.

"Ms. Cleo," Maureen said to the woman, "maybe you could put the hammer down."

# 15

"Where is this motherfucker?" the large cop shouted.

He was tall and built like a defensive lineman, wide shoulders, narrow waist, thick thighs, six-four and two-twenty easy, which made him almost of Hardin's stature. He walked with a conspicuous limp that was not part of his natural gait. Maureen couldn't see his face, but she recognized his form, and his temper. Officer Jay Morello. Biggest gym rat in the Sixth District. Well, the second biggest now that Hardin had moved uptown. The problem with Morello, Maureen thought, was that while he had biceps comparable to Hardin's, he did not have any of the sergeant's wisdom or patience. Nearing twenty years on the job, he was usually lazy and indifferent, which meant he got pissed when he had to exert himself. She'd never seen it, but she'd heard that if properly provoked he went from zero to beat-down in under six seconds. She had a bad feeling about why he was limping.

"Coughlin," Morello yelled. "Where *is* that motherfucker? I don't see him. You better be right, he better be here."

"What is *his* problem?" Ms. Cleo asked. "Does he not see me standing right here?"

"There was a shooting not long ago," Maureen said, "a few blocks farther uptown. Right off the parade route. We think our suspect is hiding under your house."

"Why would you think that?"

"Because I chased him under there."

Maureen could see the woman wondering why anyone would run from her. Running from Morello made sense, but *her*? "There's a man with a gun," Ms. Cleo said, "*under* my house?"

"We think we have his gun," Maureen said. "We recovered it at the scene, but we can't say for sure. I can see him under there but he won't talk to me."

"You think . . ." The woman hooked the hammer over the porch railing and pressed the heels of her hands into her eyes. "You don't even know if he has a gun." She threw her hands in the air. "So am I a hostage now?"

"I don't think he's a threat to you," Maureen said.

Morello again: "Coughlin, where is this piece of shit?"

"I wasn't talking about the boy under my house being a threat to me," Ms. Cleo said, raising her chin at Morello. "I'm not worried about him."

"He's under the house?" Morello said. "Nice."

"I never mentioned anything about a boy," Maureen said. "Did you see him go under there?"

"Don't try that on me," Ms. Cleo said. "One, two, three cops and more on the way, I'm sure. Who else could be under my house but some young black boy? Who else would y'all chase like this?"

"He shot three people," Morello said. "A little girl, a teacher, and a lady who looks a lot like you. So, yeah, we chasin' him."

Maureen felt for the lady. The woman was as weary as she was aggravated. Five more days of Mardi Gras and half the city was already exhausted, she thought. Are we going to make it?

"Goddamn it," Ms. Cleo said. "This is my one night off. I have to be back at that goddamn hotel for the next four goddamn days and now I gotta deal with you all? I *hate* Mardi Gras! Next year, I'm leaving town!"

"We'll do the best we can," Maureen said, "to get out of your hair as soon as possible. With as little drama as possible. For safety's sake, it's probably best if you stay inside until we can give the all clear."

"I don't even care," the woman said. "There's an old cat or two lives under there sometimes, when the weather gets bad and raw, like tonight. Try not to hurt her. Some of them's older than you are, Officer." She looked at Morello. "And don't think I won't be paying attention to what's going on out here from inside the house."

Before Maureen could reassure her that they'd be careful of the cat, the woman went back inside, turning off the porch light and slamming the door behind her.

"Thanks for nothing, lady," Cordts said, appearing beside Maureen out of thin air, like a ghost. "It's not like we could've used that light. People, you know?"

"That's what you have to offer?" Maureen said, snapping at him then regretting it.

Speaking of ghosts, she thought, Cordts remained awfully sallow. She'd met a few officers who could steel themselves against anything, no matter how bloody or brutal, unless it happened to a child. Cordts was looking like one of those officers. He no longer had the wings tucked in his vest. Maureen was tempted to ask about them, but decided against raising the subject.

Cordts gestured at the house. Maureen could see his temper rising. "I'm just saying. She wants us out of here ASAP and she goes and makes our job that much more difficult. Does she even *know* what this punk did? What we want him for? Why we chased him under her house in the first place?" He took a deep breath, rolled his shoulders. "Not very thoughtful of her, is all I'm saying. Not proactive. Not good community involvement."

"Should you be out here?" she asked, trying to make it sound like a joke. He didn't seem to get it. "Do you need to sit down?"

"Why are you asking me that?" Cordts said.

Maureen considered asking him to wait in the truck until she could figure out what to do with him. She didn't know what she'd do if he said no, so she didn't ask. Hopefully Wilburn was on his way and could offer help.

"Hey, I have some bad news," Cordts said.

Maureen was worried that the little girl had died. "Spit it out."

"I'm pretty sure the TV crew found out where we are. I think they heard Hardin calling out the dogs, so to speak."

Maureen looked around her. No sign of "Mardi Gras on Fire" yet. Morello limped past her up the driveway. She trotted after him, Cordts at her heels.

"I can't get him to talk to me," Maureen said.

Morello scoffed at her. "And why do you give a fuck what he's got to *say*? I'll tell you what he'll say, save you the trouble. He'll say he didn't do it. Same thing they all say."

Morello lowered himself to the ground, getting on his hands and knees in the driveway. He shined his flashlight into the crawl space. "There he is, that rat fucker. Yeah, that's our guy. He matches the description. We got your punk ass. You hear me? We got you, bitch."

Maureen got down on her hands and knees beside Morello, peering under the house. He was really going to do it, wasn't he? Morello was going to make her feel sorry for this kid. He was going to make her protect him. The suspect had moved even deeper under the house.

"Yeah, you stay right there, rat fucker," Morello said. "Stay right there. We got something for you. Oh yeah, we do." He pushed himself to his hands and knees then struggled to his feet. "I thought these punks all talked to each other in lockup. I thought word gets around. How can he not know what comes next? Another stupid motherfucker."

"What's with the limp?" Cordts asked, unwrapping a piece of gum. He threw the wrapper in the street and it blew away in the breeze. Cordts didn't chew the gum as much as grind it hard between his back teeth. Maureen watched the muscles in his face tense and flex. He compressed

THE DEVIL'S MUSE    101

his jaw like he was fighting against something ugly crawling up his throat and out of his mouth.

"That piece of shit," Morello said, "I'm out of the car, it's parked and I'm just checking the backstreets behind the parade, and I spot him a few blocks from here, toward Downtown, in the Muses, by the dairy, looking all shifty and shit, and, plus, he matches the 'scrip to a T. Well, he sees me see him and instead of doing the right thing and stopping where I spot him, like I fucking *told* him, he rabbits. Trust me, I did it right. I gave him his chance to come quietly. But he decided different.

"I chased him for four blocks, both of us going full out, when I slip in this puddle of puke some drunk left behind and twist my fucking knee going down. It's already swelling like a fucking grapefruit. Anyway, down there by Erato and Thalia the parade crowd is even denser than up here, it just gets worse and worse as you head for Lee Circle, and down that way, there's five of us on every block, so he can't run down there, right? So he doubles back this way, I guess," turning to Maureen, "and runs right into you."

"Maybe you should get off that knee," Maureen said. "The cold and wet can't be helping it any."

"And do what?" Morello asked. "Sit in the truck and watch y'all have all the fun? Go to the nurse's office until my mommy can come pick me up? Fuck that."

"Forget I said anything," Maureen said. "Fuck you and your knee, Morello."

"Hey, hey, same team here, people," Cordts said.

Maureen and Morello laughed at him. Cordts leaned down to peer under the house, his thumbs hooked in his gun belt. A twitch had his left eye jumping at the corner. "Him. He's the problem. Him."

Morello winced as he set more weight on his knee. Maureen saw his eyes water. He drew a sharp breath.

"I swear to Christ," he said, "if this piece of shit costs me my Mardi Gras OT, I'm gonna wear his spine around my neck like fucking blinky beads. I'll fucking kill him."

Okay, Maureen thought, it was past time to get that kid out from under the house and get rid of him. "You know, I could fit under there. I could go get him. He's no bigger than I am."

"Oh, fuck that," Morello said. "Don't even get your pretty face dirty."

He pointed down the street. Another Explorer pulled around his, bumping up on the sidewalk, and approached the house. Maureen read the large red letters painted along the back doors: CANINE UNIT.

# 16

"I'm so gonna enjoy this," Morello said. "Long as that rat fucker doesn't ruin it and crawl out on his own. They think sometimes the canine unit won't actually come. Like we don't really have one."

"We didn't for a while," Cordts said. "After the storm."

"We do now," Morello said. "That's all that matters."

Maureen heard Cordts say, "Remember that bad news I mentioned." He sucked his teeth, slapped his forehead. "Shit, I think I was supposed to pick up Wilburn before I drove over here. I heard you got this kid, I got excited."

Looking like a mini-parade of five, with their bright spotlight leading the way, the camera crew from "Mardi Gras on Fire" marched up the block. They even had their own police escort. Wilburn. Chatting up Laine Daniels as they walked.

"Fuck me," Maureen said. The presence of the camera crew changed things.

The NOPD was about to send two big dogs under that house, Maureen thought, to drag that boy out from underneath it with their teeth. She didn't exactly feel bad for the kid. He'd fare better with the dogs than he would with Morello, and he had most likely shot three people. But there would be vicious growling and loud barking for everyone to see. Then there would be screaming. There might be blood. From the sound of it, there would be cheering from Morello. And the whole sordid mess would be caught on camera. It would be gripping TV, or Internet video or whatever, Maureen knew, and it would also make the NOPD look like a bunch of savages in front of the entire world.

Nobody but "Mardi Gras on Fire" comes out a winner here, Maureen thought.

She racked her brain for a better way to do things. She had nothing. Maybe, if she was careful, she could keep herself off camera.

She watched as the canine officer, a dark-haired woman not much older or bigger than Maureen whose name tag read MORRISON, opened the back of the Explorer and led the dogs as they jumped down into the street. They were, Maureen had to admit, gorgeous, noble animals—tall, powerful, bright-eyed, black-haired shepherds—the best-looking cops she had ever seen, and she found herself much more concerned about their safety than that of the young man under the house.

The TV crew was only half a block away. There was no way they were getting that kid out before the crew arrived with the camera rolling. It was probably rolling as they made their approach.

"Give me half a minute," Maureen said. She walked up the driveway. Morello stopped her. "What're you doing?"

"Let's give him one more chance to come out," Maureen said.

"Fuck him," Morello said. "He had his chance to cooperate and then some. Don't wear yourself out on this asshole, Coughlin."

She glanced at the camera crew. "You see what I'm talking about. I'm not talking about protecting him. I want to protect us from them."

Maureen walked to the house. She got down on her hands and knees. She flashed her light under the house, trying to get the kid's attention.

"Listen to me, very carefully. The canine officer is here. The dogs are ready. This is your last chance to come out."

The kid yelled something, but Maureen couldn't tell what it was he'd said. His voice was muffled in the dirt.

"Enough," Morello said. "You gave him more than he deserved, Cogs, I'll back you on that. You've done it by the book. You're a good cop, but you can't reason with stupid."

Maureen and Morello backed out of the driveway. Maureen looked at the dogs. She gave Morrison a shrug. "I tried."

"You did," Morrison said.

Using a raised hand, she made the dogs sit. They watched her intently. Maureen figured she could set off a mat of firecrackers and it wouldn't break their focus. I wish I could concentrate like that, Maureen thought, on anything.

Morrison shouted a single command. *"Blaffen!"*

The dogs jumped to their feet, erupting into an explosion of barks and snarls so savage and wild that Maureen nearly jumped out of her boots. Her knees went watery and the hair on her arms stood straight up. The dogs, however, did not move from their handler's side. They raised their ruckus where they stood. Morello laughed and cheered.

From under the house came a panicked yelling, barely audible over the dogs. Maureen could hear Morello's celebration turn into disappointed swearing. She got Morrison's attention and drew her finger across her throat. The officer raised her hand again and the dogs went silent and sat, their pink tongues lolling out over their white teeth. The handler fed them each a treat.

The kid's pleading voice grew louder as he crawled their way, desperate to get out from under the house rather than have the dogs sent in after him.

"That was amazing," Maureen said. "What did you say to them?"

"'Speak,'" Morrison said. "They're Belgian. They get their commands in Dutch." The canine officer surveyed the surroundings, obviously proud of commanding the most efficient, most effective, best-behaved, and most handsome cops on the scene. "I haven't had to send them into that muck once since I taught them that trick."

"And where is the fucking fun in that?" Morello asked.

Morrison ignored him. "I think they know they don't have to get baths if they don't go under the house." The dogs sat at her feet, panting, pleased with themselves. "So they put extra effort into their performance."

"They scared the *shit* out of me," Maureen said. "Damn."

Morrison scratched one then the other behind the ears. "Don't think they don't know it." She opened the back of the truck. The dogs jumped into the Explorer. "They love what they do. Shepherds love to have jobs. Like people, they want work to do."

She walked to the tailgate, scratched the dogs behind their ears again, one dog with each hand. "All right, ladies." She closed the tailgate, turned, and smiled at Maureen. "I'll wait here until he's all the way out. Y'all stay safe. Happy Mardi Gras."

# 17

Maureen walked back up the driveway and, crouched, watched the kid crawl toward them. He couldn't get out from under that house fast enough.

"You run again," she shouted to the kid as he got close, "and *we're* not chasing you. This time, we take the leash off the dogs."

The kid was out of breath, panting. He was filthy. "I'm coming. I'm coming. No dogs. Please, no dogs."

Maureen saw two green eyes glinting in her flashlight beam from deep under the house, and bared white fangs. The others had vanished but the first cat had stood its ground. Good for you, old girl.

Behind her in the street, Maureen could hear Laine shouting orders to her crew. Thankfully, her instructions were mostly for them to stay out of the way of the police. Fucking up an important arrest with your dopey camera crew was not a good career move.

The porch light came back on. Ms. Cleo walked outside again, a full wineglass in her hand this time instead of a hammer. She seemed more relaxed. "Are y'all *still* out here?" The spotlight hit her. She pointed at Cortez. "Oh, no, don't you point that thing at me."

Maureen watched as the filthy kid dragged himself out from under her house. He never even got to his feet, collapsing facedown in the driveway. She could see his ribs heaving. He laced his fingers behind his head without being told, his hands and arms trembling from effort or fear or both. Maureen could see he was defeated. He wasn't a threat to them anymore, if he ever had been. She was glad Morrison had shown him mercy.

But damn, she thought, raising the back of her hand to her nose, taking a step back, if the kid didn't have a sour, eye-watering stink coming off him. Cat piss, Maureen guessed. The kid had crawled right through one big litter box. She hoped that was it. Please tell me this kid didn't shit himself when those dogs went off, she thought.

"Five officers and two wild dogs for one skinny black boy," Ms. Cleo said. "My tax dollars at work. The *new* New Orleans, my ass." She waved her finger at the camera crew. "Put *that* in your news report."

"Let me remind you that he shot people," Morello said, "which was what started this whole episode, but we can leave him here with you if you want. You can feed him hot soup. He can tell you his troubles. Maybe you can help him get a scholarship."

"That's gonna sound so great on TV," Cordts said.

"Fuck you, beanpole."

"That, too," Cordts said. He stepped toward the kid, toed his shoulder. He folded a fresh stick of gum into his mouth, mashed it in his teeth. "You shoot those people, you shoot that precious little girl?"

"I didn't shoot nobody," the kid said into the pavement. "What little girl? Why is this on TV? I can't see nothing down here."

"You shut the fuck up," Morello said. "Nobody's gonna be on TV. Especially not your sorry ass." He touched the kid with the toe of his shoe. "Those dogs make you dump in your drawers? I hope so. It's Mardi Gras, you gonna jail in those drawers till Ash Wednesday." He turned and stalked toward the camera crew. "None of this is being recorded. Right? Right? Because that would be stupid."

Cortez, terrified, lowered the camera and backed away from Morello. Maureen thought Larry might throw the mic down in the street and take off running. He and Cortez looked to Laine for direction. Laine, to her credit, stood her physical ground, but she didn't argue with or contradict Morello either. She didn't say anything.

Maureen felt resentment and envy rising inside her as she watched the same fake television crew that had sassed her earlier outside the bar acquiesce to Morello's threatening attitude and imposing physical presence. What I wouldn't give, she thought, oh, the damage I could do, with another foot of height and another hundred pounds of muscle.

To Maureen's surprise, while Cortez, Larry, and Laine hung fire, Donna decided to act up. She puffed out her chest and cocked a hip, an exaggerated version of the "Hey, big boy, buy me a drink" stance. Yet her attitude radiated more defiance, Maureen saw, than seduction.

"Maybe we can do an interview," Donna said to Morello, craning her neck to look him in the face. "You know. Later. Just you and me. Off camera. When things have calmed down. I want your side of the story."

Morello turned his back on the camera crew without a word, walking toward the stoop. Maureen couldn't be sure if Donna's attitude had thrown him off his game, or if he had lost interest in the video camera.

"Goddamn," he said, covering his nose. "You got bodies under this house, lady?"

Ms. Cleo, one eyebrow arched, stared at Morello a long time before going back into the house without a word.

"She's got more than one cat under there," Maureen said. "I know that much."

"I think she likes me," Morello said. He turned to Maureen. "It's my natural charm. You need someone to do follow-up with her, you let me know."

"I'm in charge now?" Maureen said. "When did that happen? Can I count on you for help here, Cordts?"

"I suppose." He sighed.

"What?" Maureen asked. "You bored?"

"Somebody needs to search this motherfucker," Morello said, trying not to laugh. "I know we got his gun, but he's got something down the back of his pants."

"I didn't shit myself," the kid said. "It's them cats. They killed things. I think there's dead things under there."

"Maybe this nice lady will let us hose you down," Morello said.

"Has anyone called Drayton?" Maureen asked, growing exasperated. "Or Hardin?" She hated bringing the detective into this, but that was her job. They'd caught the suspect, now the detective would talk to him.

"He said call him back," Morello said. "I called him when we were waiting for the kid to come out from under the house. Right after the dogs. Sounded like he was at a party. I wouldn't hold my breath waiting for him to get here. 'Specially when he finds out the kid shit himself."

"I didn't shit myself," the kid said. "There's something dead under there. I told you."

"Sure you didn't," Morello said. "I ain't putting him in my car, I know that."

He walked away, laughing.

Maureen felt someone creeping up behind her. She turned. "Hey, Wilburn. Look who showed up. Thanks for nothing. Why you sneaking up on me, for chrissakes, like a fucking specter?"

"I have some bad news," Wilburn said, mumbling.

Maureen nodded at the camera crew. "I saw. Cordts told me they were coming."

"No," Wilburn said. "Not them. Worse than that."

"I already know," Maureen said, "that Drayton caught the shooting. We're gonna be here all night and we'll get fuck-all done. I already know these things." She brushed her nose with the back of her wrist. She looked at the camera crew. "Does he know about them? Drayton's *such* a fucking peacock. He's gonna love them. Shit. It could be a real problem."

"You know what, though?" she said. "Maybe we could use them to get him out here. We could get Laine to play it up, like he's the star. She'll get good footage. He gets a look at Donna, he'll come running." She shook her head. "Drayton is such a pig. That lounge-singer haircut. Maybe we should send him a photo of Donna."

She could tell Wilburn wasn't interested in this latest turn of events, or her opinions about Drayton's haircut. Whatever news he carried had him distracted and distraught.

"Drayton is terrible news for everyone, as usual," Wilburn said. "Well, except for the shooter. But it's not what I came here to tell you."

"Well?" Maureen asked, pulling her gloves tight, grabbing her cuffs from her belt. They couldn't leave this kid lying in the driveway for the night. They had to conduct as much of an investigation as they could manage. They needed to know the story behind the shooting to know how much danger the parade route was in that night. "Out with it," she said to Wilburn. "I got work to do."

"You know what?" he said. "I can wait until after you're done with the arrest. Maybe that's better."

"Now. Now is better. You're miserable."

"Yeah, I don't know."

Maureen had an awful thought. She looked around for Cordts, spotted him standing by his car, texting on his phone. She didn't want to speak too loudly and draw his attention. She whispered, "The little girl died. Holy shit. That's it, isn't it?"

"No, no," Wilburn said, matching her whisper. "This has nothing to do with her."

Maureen sighed with relief. "See? Suddenly this bad news is good news. It's all in how you look at it."

"If you say so," Wilburn said. "Well, remember that kid in the pink pants?"

"How can I not?" Maureen said.

"Yeah, well." Wilburn looked over one shoulder then the other, before telling Maureen, in another sinister, conspiratorial whisper, "He's dead."

# 18

"What do you mean he's dead?" Maureen asked.

"What, they didn't cover that at the academy?" Wilburn hissed. "And keep your voice down. You know they have a microphone to go with that camera. He's dead. Expired. *Morte.*"

"Y'all killed somebody," the kid said, panic in his voice. "I hear y'all talking. Y'all killed somebody and are coverin' it up. Hey! TV people!"

"Who's dead?" Cordts asked, walking over, dropping his phone in his pocket, the corner of his left eye twitching. "I thought there were no fatalities."

"Now you wanna talk," Maureen said to the kid at her feet. "Well, now you can shut up. The only one around here tryin' to kill people is you."

"I didn't do nothin'," the kid said. "I ain't killed nobody."

"We'll see about that," Maureen said.

"Who's dead?" Cordts asked again, raising his voice. He spat his gum into the street. "Wilburn? Who's fucking dead?"

"I'll tell you who's dead," the kid shouted. "The person you cops killed, that's who. They gonna kill me next."

"You might not be wrong," Cordts said, raising his foot like he was going to step on the kid's neck.

"Cordts, don't worry about it," Wilburn said sharply, raising a cautioning hand. He reminded Maureen of Morrison and her dogs. "Listen to me, Cordts. It's not the girl; it's something else. Keep cool. Don't listen to this jerk-off."

Maureen turned to see the camera crew inching closer. She pointed at them. "And the TV people need to stay right where they are. Far away."

"We're on the *Internet*," Donna shouted, stamping her foot. "Get it right." But they stayed put. Maureen was sure the camera was rolling. She wasn't sure there was anything she could do about it.

"Can we get a move on here?" Wilburn asked. "We really need to get back to, you know, that other thing."

"The parade route," Cordts said. "You know. The parade."

Letting loose a big sigh, holding her breath against the stench, Maureen got down on one knee beside the kid. One at a time, she cuffed his hands behind his back. His pants were filthy from crawling around under the house, as was the rest of him, but as far as she could tell, he wasn't lying about not shitting his pants. Thank the Lord for small favors, she thought. Didn't make him stink any less.

Using the cuffs, she brought him up onto his knees then onto his feet. She moved him forward, braced him up against the house, her hand pressing hard on the space between his shoulder blades. She turned out the kid's pockets and patted him down, Cordts positioned himself right behind her, keeping careful watch.

"He's clean," Maureen said. "Well, he's unarmed. He's a long way from clean."

"Roger that," Cordts said.

"He's got absolutely nothing on him," Maureen said. "No wallet, no cash. Not even a phone." She poked the kid in the back, hard. "Why is that? Where you going, what are you doing that you don't need a phone, cash, cards, keys?"

"I got robbed," the kid said, his head lowered. "Early tonight. I did. That's why I was where I was when that other cop started chasing me. I figured whoever took me off might've tossed my shit in the street."

"What shit? Like your library card?" Cordts asked. "You're not carrying anything on you because you knew you might get picked up tonight. Because you went out to shoot somebody in a neighborhood filled with innocent bystanders. Because you know you have a record and figured you'd stick us with some fake name when we nailed you."

"Whatever," the kid said. "Fuck you, man. You got an active imagination."

"You got that right," Cordts said. "You don't even know."

"Yeah, you got robbed," Maureen said, moving between Cordts and the suspect. She didn't like being as close as she was to either of them. "Right. So that's why you took off running as soon as you saw a cop? Because *you're* the victim. Nice try."

"What? You got to be playin'," the kid said. "What makes you think I'd come to y'all 'bout *any*thing?" He tossed his head at Cordts, then in the general direction of Morello. "This one here, the big one over there, look how they doin' me. With no proof that I done anything."

"You should've stayed home tonight," Cordts said. "You *really* should've just stayed fucking home."

Maureen turned the kid around, studied his dirty, angry face. There was something familiar about him. "Tell me about this robbery, then."

He turned away from her, suddenly reticent, averting his eyes. And, looking him in the face for the first time that night, she knew why he wouldn't look at her. She knew him. He was young, maybe even younger than Susan and Hardin had suggested he would be. He was in his mid-teens at best. That didn't mean she hadn't run into him before. Or even arrested him. She had a face in mind, one that used to be more fleshed out, with lingering baby fat. One she hadn't seen since the fall.

"You ran," Maureen said, "because you know Officer Morello. You recognized him and you were afraid he'd recognize you."

THE DEVIL'S MUSE 115

The kid hesitated, his mouth half-open as he struggled to decide what to say next. "Look, he started chasing me before I started running, you see what I'm sayin'? Like, he saw me standing there doin' nothin' and jumped outta the car and started running at me, yelling, so I ran, 'cause he was chasing me." He would not look at Maureen, no matter how hard she tried to catch his eyes. "You see what I'm saying? I wasn't doing nothin'. He *started* it. He's a big dude, and, yeah, he's got a rep. People in the streets know him. I was scared, all right? It was just me and him on that street. Everyone else was at the parade. Who knows what he was gonna do? That don't mean I *did* nothin'."

"But what about me?" Maureen asked. "Maybe I buy that you're scared of Morello, maybe, but then why run from me? I'm not nearly his size. I don't have his rep."

"You still a cop, though," the kid said. "And, honestly, you getting a rep, too."

"That's not it. That's not why you ran from me."

"Yeah it is," the kid said. "I mean, c'mon, you're asking why I ran from the cops? Y'all are *cops*."

"I know you," Maureen said. "That's why you ran."

"The fuck you do," the kid said.

"You're Todd Curtis. Todd Goodwin Curtis," she said, feeling surer with each passing moment. She knew this kid. He was fifteen years old. And he was a hard-core criminal. Maybe even a killer. "You used to run with Marques and Mike-Mike. They called you Goody."

"Whatever," the kid said. "I don't know no Goody. Punk-ass name like that. Fuck you."

"I thought you blew town," Maureen said, "right after Mike-Mike turned up dead in the trunk of that car." She felt silly now for any sympathy she'd felt for him. The detective in charge of Mike-Mike's case had pondered Goody's role in putting Mike-Mike in that trunk, and in dumping the body. Maureen felt a surge of confidence that they had the right person for the shooting. "Came back for the holidays, did you? No good parades in Baton Rouge?"

"Fuck Baton Rouge and fuck you. You making shit up now."

"No, fuck you," Maureen said. She could feel the kid shutting down; that reaction, and the virulent, ramped-up hostility he showed, told her she was right about his identity. "You know what, Goody? You're going back in the system. You're gonna be somebody else's problem for the next week. Welcome home and happy Mardi Gras. You have the right to remain silent, anything you say can and will be held against you—"

Morello came hobbling over, stopping her. "Whoa, whoa, hold up."

She looked over her shoulder at Morello. "And what's your problem? I'm making the arrest here."

"Don't bother with that yet," Morello said. He put his hand on her shoulder. "Hang tight for a minute."

"Excuse me?" Maureen said, turning to glare at Morello's hand. To her surprise, he removed it. "We got a witness from the scene of the shooting who'll say he did it. Wilburn has the contact info. He matches the description. The witness can make an ID tonight. We have the gun. An eyewitness and the weapon is a pretty damn good starting point. It's certainly enough for an arrest. I know this kid. He's got a sheet. A long and nasty juvie sheet. Assaults, armed robbery."

"She don't know nothin'," Goody said. "She lies."

"It's not about that," Morello said. "I believe you that this kid's a punk. Let's not rush things. He goes in a car until we figure out what to do with him."

"There's nothing *to* do with him," Maureen said, "other than arrest him. You hear me? The *only* thing to do with him is arrest him."

"I think you're misunderstanding what I'm trying to tell you," Morello said. "We're going to detain him on suspicion for Drayton to question. That's what we're going to do. That means your job here is done."

He spoke as calmly as he had at any point that night, as if Maureen was the one with the two-hundred-pound frame and the violent temper. The change in tone was so profound it made Maureen suspicious of his motives. She checked to see if they were being filmed. Didn't appear so. The crew seemed oddly distracted, in fact. Laine stood away from the rest of them, thumbing her phone. Here was the big arrest after the shooting, and they'd let themselves be bullied out of filming it.

Granted, the bust lacked for drama, but wasn't this moment what they'd hopped on the bandwagon hoping to capture? "This detention-without-arrest order comes from Hardin?"

"Not directly," Morello said. "I didn't consult him on it. That's not really a necessary step. He knows what's up."

"Does he know we caught this kid or does he think we're chasing him around the neighborhood?"

"Doesn't matter," Morello said. "This isn't Hardin's call."

"But it's yours?"

"Not technically. But I am senior officer on the scene."

"Until Drayton gets here," Maureen said. "You're telling me that Drayton doesn't want him arrested, either?"

"Why don't you turn the suspect over to me?" Morello asked. "I can handle it from here. You can step out of it. Go back to the route. It might be quite a while before Drayton gets here."

"Yeah, I don't know about that. Maybe I'll wait for Drayton, too."

"Everybody knows you and Drayton don't like each other," Morello said. "Let me save you the trouble of dealing with him."

"I know y'all is doin' me dirty," Goody said. He started yelling to the woman in the house that he was getting killed. "Lady! Hey, lady in that house. They gonna do me! They gonna do me out here!"

"I'm gonna punch you in the fucking head," Morello said, as calmly as he spoke to Maureen. "That's what I'm gonna fucking do."

"You don't shut up," Maureen said, shaking Goody by the cuffs, "and I'll feed you to him. You'll be wishing for the dogs." She grabbed the kid by the arm, turned him to face her. "I know your name. I know the kind of shit you get up to. No more of this robbery bullshit. No more fairy tales. What are you doing out tonight?"

"Fucking Mardi Gras," Goody said, shrugging as best he could. "Same as everyone else. Everybody out tonight."

"Why'd you shoot that guy?"

Goody laughed at her. "I didn't shoot nobody, and can't nobody prove I did."

He'd been emboldened, Maureen could tell, by the dissent over how to handle him. She wanted to ask him why he'd run to that house on Harmony Street, but doing so would give away that the girl had called the cops on him, and then pointed Maureen in the right direction after he'd run from her and her brother.

"Don't make the mistake of underestimating me," she said to him. She wasn't going to argue with Morello in front of a suspect. She had to give way to him, but she didn't have to give Morello exactly what he wanted. She called Cordts over to her.

"Would you do me a favor?" she asked him. "Take Mr. Curtis to one of the units, please. Hook him up in the backseat and stay with him there until we can all get on the same page about how to process him."

Morello set his hands on his hips and stared down at the sidewalk, but he didn't interfere as Cordts led the suspect away. "You need to hear me on this, Coughlin. You really do. We have a certain way of handling things like this."

"You need to hear me," Maureen said. "This kid is young but he's dangerous. I know him. If we have a chance to get him off the streets, out of the life he's living, we have to make sure that happens. He can't walk free later because the PD finds out you beat information out of him."

Morello laughed at her, disgusted and dismissive. "This thinking you know everything about everybody, that you got it all figured. It's going to hurt you. It already is."

"Cogs, you need to help me deal with this other thing back on the avenue," Wilburn said, rocking on his heels. "Time is of the essence. Let Cordts and Morello handle things here."

"Going by what you told me," Maureen said, "time is the one thing we do have. Now with this case here, there may be other shooting targets on the route, questioning this kid here is where the clock is ticking. We don't have time to waste waiting for Drayton."

"Do yourself a favor, Coughlin," Morello said. "Go with Wilburn."

"You misunderstand me, Cogs," Wilburn said.

"Contrary to your previous sarcasm," Maureen said to him, "I understand 'dead' just fine."

"The dead guy is not who I'm worried about," Wilburn said.

"Who's dead?" Morello asked.

"Nobody," Maureen said. Shit, she thought, lowering her head, listen to me. I don't know who he was, but he wasn't nobody. "Don't worry about it. It doesn't involve the shooting."

"That's easy," Morello said. "Peace out. I got work to do. I'll let you know how it goes."

He limped away in the direction of the NOPD Explorer at the end of the block where Goody now sat in the backseat, his hands cuffed behind his back, one leg inside the car, one leg hanging loose out the open door. Cordts stood beside him, ignoring him, arms crossed, leaning on the car, smoking a cigarette and staring up at the sky. Let it go, Maureen thought. Whatever Morello is up to, let him do it. Let it go. But she couldn't. She couldn't let him poach her bust like this. She ran after him.

"Morello, c'mon, it's my collar," she said, walking alongside him. "Make sure Drayton knows that."

"We both know he doesn't give a fuck," Morello said. "We know, your fellow officers of the Sixth District. What do you care about Drayton? You're done here, Coughlin. Be glad, the fun part of this case is over. It's nothing but bullshit from here."

Morello kept walking, turning away from her, using his huge shoulders to block her out. Had she the size of Morello, Maureen thought, or Hardin, she could plant herself between him and the car and let things play out like they would between men. Instead, here she was wheedling, nagging, nipping at his heels like an attention-starved puppy . . . at least his limp let her chase him at a quick walk.

"I want to talk to him," she said. "A couple more questions. Drayton won't ask the right ones, the ones that'll help us tonight. We both know that."

Morello stopped, and despite the pressure it put on his knee, rose to his full height in front of Maureen, stepping fully into the big-dog role. "The detective will question the suspect any way he sees fit."

"But it's Drayton. He'll blow it. You know he will."

"Doesn't matter," Morello said.

Maureen decided to try a different tactic. "Look, I know this kid. That's to our advantage."

"I don't know about that," Morello said. "He doesn't like you very much. He hasn't been very receptive to your previous inquisitions. I think your work here is done. Leave Goody with me"—he leaned close to her—"and go someplace else. Trust me on this. I'm actually looking out for you here."

"You can't knock him around," Maureen said, taking a step closer to Morello. "Just because of what happened to your knee. We need that kid."

"Smarten up," Morello said. "I heard you were better than this. You don't trust me, fine. I'll let the insult pass. I'm nice like that. Cordts is here with me. You trust him. For the last time, leave Goody here with me and go about your business. Maybe, just maybe, the rest of us know what we're doing."

He turned from her again and walked away. Maureen watched him, her face burning, feeling as if something important had eluded her, or had been hidden from her.

# 19

From Wilburn, over her shoulder, "Coughlin, can we go now? We need to deal with this."

"Yeah, yeah. Morello can't get rid of me fast enough, anyway."

"And you want to know why," Wilburn said. "I understood that, but forget it. We got other problems."

"That's the message I'm getting." Maureen checked on the camera crew. They were collecting their gear, looking ready to get on the move again. "Oh, for fuck's sake."

"Morello told them earlier they have to split," Wilburn said.

"They can't come with us," Maureen said. "They can't. We can't let them know about this. We don't want them shooting video of a dead body on the parade route."

"Coughlin, they're the ones who found him," Wilburn said. "Well, Donna did. Remember when she left the bar, went back down to the route? There were twenty people standing around him, she said. She called Laine and Laine told me. I went down there with them to check it out. It's true."

"You let them film a fucking corpse in the middle of St. Charles Avenue?" Maureen asked. "What the fuck is wrong with you?"

"I had to control the scene, protect the body," Wilburn said. "I couldn't control the camera crew at the same time. You and Cordts were here, dealing with this. Our area of the route has been unmanned since the shooting."

"There were no other cops on the route nearby?"

"Not close enough to help me immediately," Wilburn said. "I didn't want to broadcast it over the radio and across the route, you know? That I was babysitting a dead body? That there *was* a dead body on the route. I'm not sure how many people really believed he was dead. I saw no reason to convince anybody."

"But Hardin knows about it, I take it."

"It was Hardin who sent me here to get you," Wilburn said. "He knows you were the last person to handle that kid. He wants to talk to you about it. He's trying to keep everything quiet as possible, and he wanted me to warn you about what you're walking into."

"Me and Cordts, *together*," Maureen said. "The two of us. We tried to move him out of the road, then the gunshots went off. He was alive when we left him. I saw him breathing. Holy shit, I can't believe Hardin is going to put this on us. Wait, warn me about what?"

"I'm sure that kid was alive when you left him," Wilburn said. "I am. But that's not what people are saying. People are saying you tased him to get him off the car and did nothing for him after that. That you stood around telling jokes. They say there's video of it."

Maureen's jaw dropped open. "I did no such thing. There can't be video because none of it happened. It's ridiculous."

"It's what people are saying," Wilburn said.

"What people?"

"The people on the route," Wilburn said. "The people Donna talked to."

"Goddamn it, Wils! Why is she talking to anybody other than us about a *dead body*?" She started pacing in circles. Maureen couldn't believe the pink-tights kid had died. What *had* he been on? What had she missed? She couldn't think. "Can't we get control of *anything* out here?"

"It's Mardi Gras," Wilburn said. He threw his hands in the air, waved his arms in the direction of St. Charles. "It's the parade route. What do you want me to do? Donna found him. We're lucky she told Laine instead of walking away. Who knows when, and how, we would've found out then. We're lucky Laine did us the courtesy of telling me as soon as she heard."

"Remind me to get Laine a medal," Maureen said, "for telling the cops about a dead body in the street before putting it on her TV show."

"Actually, it's a Web-based series," Donna said, walking over.

Maureen screamed at her. "I don't fucking care!"

"This," Donna said, backing away. "This right here? This is why nobody likes the police. You try to help and this is what you get."

"Look, now you know what people are saying," Wilburn said. "That'll help. You can think about what you want to say to Hardin in response. Maybe you can get out ahead of it, as much as you can."

"Get out ahead of it?" Maureen asked. "Get out ahead of it? A kid wearing nothing but zebra-print tights, slathered in cotton candy, dies in the middle of the parade route, and people think I *killed* him? How does one get out ahead of that?" She could hear the hysteria ringing in her own voice. She sounded crazed. She realized the camera's spotlight was on her. Maureen raised her hand, pointing into the light but staring at her feet, trying to hide her face, like that mattered now. She was not handling her first Mardi Gras very well.

"I swear to Christ," she said, "if you are filming this I will fucking kill you." The light stayed on. Maureen didn't move; she kept her feet planted where they were, for fear that if she even flinched she'd lose control of herself and attack Cortez. "I will beat you to death with that fucking camera." She pointed at Larry. "You don't wanna know what happens to the microphone. You don't."

"Cortez," she heard Laine say, "lower the camera. Kill it." And the light went out. "Larry, you, too."

"Thank you," Maureen said. "I appreciate that." She realized she was sweating, breathing heavily. She waited a long moment before she spoke again, not looking at anyone. "You can delete that last bit, right?"

"We edit," Laine said, "before we post anything."

Maureen heard something come over Wilburn's radio that he greeted with "Oh, shit."

"What?" she asked. "What now?"

Next came a loud cackle from a block away that she knew could only be from Morello. Why was everything that happened to her so hilarious to him? She turned to see him hobbling her way, a big smile on his face. "Coughlin! Holy shit. You are in some trouble now."

She turned to Wilburn. "What is it?"

"You didn't hear that? The, uh, the secret is out, I guess."

Maureen checked her radio. She hadn't turned it back up after turning the volume down to listen for the kid in the street before the foot chase. That chase felt like it had happened three nights ago. "Mine was off. Damn it."

Morello limped closer. He was shaking his head, chuckling to himself. "I just got a text from one of the guys on the route. You tased some drunk homeless guy on the route and *left* him there? You're never boring, Cogs, I'll give you that. Holy shit."

"So much for getting out ahead of it," Maureen said.

"And then he *dies*?" Morello said, laughing. "You have the *worst* fucking luck."

"Who is saying these things?" Maureen asked. "None of that happened."

"Hardin is waiting for you on the parade route now," Wilburn said, "with the body and the EMTs. You need to go to him. I think they're picking it up now. I guess they didn't want to bring the coroner's truck to the parade route. Makes sense."

"I guess not," Maureen said. She hitched up her gun belt, rage and frustration burning in her chest. She adjusted her knit cap. "Guess I'll go see my sergeant, then. Back to the route it is." She turned to Wilburn. "Give me a head start before you follow with these guys and that goddamn camera? Please? And check in on Cordts before you go, will you? I'm worried about him."

"You should really get going," Wilburn said. "Hardin doesn't like waiting around."

Without another word, Maureen headed off down the street, toward the lights and noise and chaos of the parade route. She could hear Morello yelling at her as she walked away. She could hear the amusement in his voice. Please don't ever let me be like that, she thought. A shooting, a death on the parade route, chaos everywhere, and he struts and laughs at everything around him like none of it means a thing to him, like none of it touches him. Please, she thought, don't ever let me be like that.

"Wait, wait a minute, Coughlin," Morello shouted. "I didn't get a chance to say good-bye." He raised his camera phone. "Let me get one last good look at you before you go." He snapped a picture. "Happy fucking Mardi Gras."

# 20

Maureen walked back toward Hardin on the open side of St. Charles, brooding about what she would tell him.

He would know better, Hardin would, than to think she and Cordts had straight-up shirked their duties, that they'd been indifferent to a dying man. He'd know there were mitigating factors. And it was easy enough to verify she had never fired her Taser. But she wanted to know what had happened after they left to pursue the gunshots.

For the life of her, she couldn't recall any indication that would've shown the kid was in mortal danger. She had trusted her training as a police officer, and she'd trusted her real life experience from before she was a cop. She had witnessed ODs before, fatal and not, both as a cop and as a civilian. Sure she was tired and impatient from being overworked during Mardi Gras, but not enough to overlook signs the kid was about to die. Sure, the kid had been very, very high. Lots of people, in fact, most people who got really fucking high didn't die. It nagged at her, too, that she hadn't pegged what drugs he'd been on. She knew her street drugs, again from both her previous civilian career as a cocktail waitress and her current career in the police department. If she'd been able to suss out what the kid had taken, maybe she would've known he was in grave danger. Maybe they would've acted differently before the gunshots, insisted on EMTs coming to help.

Cordts hadn't predicted a dire outcome for the kid, either. Not that she was looking to shift blame, but he had six years on the job. She could claim deference to his experience, if that wasn't too much like throwing him under the bus. Cordts had a good rep in the district as a solid guy. He was goofy to the point of being annoying sometimes, but he was not a fuckup by any stretch. She'd heard nothing but good things about him. His backing up her story would carry weight with Hardin. That was a positive. She hoped Cordts would remember things the way she did. Who could tell what he was going to say, though, the way he'd started acting since the shooting? Maybe having Goody in cuffs would calm him down. Maureen hoped so. His support might turn out to be the sum total of good things she had going for her right now, especially if civilians were making statements. As much as the police relied on witnesses, like they were doing tonight with the shooting, civilians were unreliable. Not only did they completely miss shit that happened right in front of them, but more than half the time they saw things that had never happened.

That Hardin had asked only for her and not for Cordts, too, when he knew they were together, told Maureen that he wanted to speak with them separately. She wouldn't get a chance to talk to Cordts and square their stories before Hardin got to him. Cordts should've been the *first* person she went to when she heard the news about the death. She knew how cops—how she—questioned suspects. One of the most effective strategies was pitting them against each other. Getting them to sell each other out. She didn't want to go through that. Maybe her mistake would work in her favor. Maybe she and Cordts would look less guilty because they hadn't conferred.

She stopped walking. "We're not guilty of anything. We didn't do anything wrong. Remember that. We didn't do anything wrong." She continued on, repeating the words to herself. She didn't want to meet Hardin looking or feeling guilty.

As she walked, bunches of beads splashed in the street around her as the riders on the last of the Krewe of Chaos floats overshot their targets in the crowd. She'd heard the masks they wore and the lights on the floats made the riders nearly blind to the crowd, like performers on a lighted stage in a dark theater. The colorful, tangled strands of plastic beads made a sound like water balloons exploding as they hit the pavement. Sometimes packs of kids darted into the street after them, but mostly the piles were left on the wet asphalt, like rotten, valueless fruit fallen from the bead-strewn tree branches over her head. Maureen knew that later that night, after the parades and the street parties had ended and before the sanitation crews raked the streets, before the street-sweeping machines scoured and sprayed, scavengers toting big plastic bags and pulling wagons would scour the avenue for abandoned and broken strands of beads in the low branches of the trees, the trampled grass of the neutral ground, and the gutters and potholes of the avenue, like divers searching the ocean floor for treasure spilled from a shipwreck.

She was fascinated by the elaborate and self-sustaining ecosystem that existed on the parade route. She wasn't sure what the bead collectors did with their gatherings, if they hoarded them in closets or attics, if they sold them or recycled them. She had seen one man out every night, late, pulling his plastic-laden wagon along the street. Every night he wore the jersey of a different football team, though never the Saints. He seemed slow, or off in a quiet, harmless way. Clean and well fed enough that she could tell someone looked after him. She wondered what he did with the pounds and pounds of beads he collected after every night's parades. She imagined him lying atop a mountain of plastic trinkets, like Scrooge McDuck in his vault full of money, waving his arms and legs, like someone making snow angels. She wondered what he did the rest of the year, when it wasn't Mardi Gras. Tourists bought, wore, and threw beads around the French Quarter year-round. Maybe he shifted his efforts down there. Or did he have other things he collected? Did he hibernate? Taking his rest on Ash Wednesday and reemerging on Twelfth Night to begin his scavenging again.

Maybe there was money in it, this bead scavenging. Might want to look into that, she thought as she approached the intersection where her night had gone downhill.

She might be looking for a new way to make a living real soon.

# 21

As Maureen approached the intersection where the Kid had died, she saw that the crowd along the route had grown even denser, the people packed closer together than she had seen at any of the previous parades. The air around her warmed. She could *feel* the collected body heat.

Muses, the night's biggest parade, the main attraction, was on its way up the avenue, rolling at full steam right on the heels of Chaos, and the manic energy on the streets had increased tenfold. The opening acts had come and gone and the headliner, the real rock-'n'-roll star, was hitting the stage. Rotating spotlights bathed the huge glowing white balloon bearing the blue-lettered "Muses" logo that fronted the parade. Rolling cannons exploded, scaring the heart out of Maureen, shooting fluttering clouds of purple, green, and gold confetti into the broad, sweeping beams of the spotlights. The crowd roared and raised their faces and hands to the tumbling slips of paper like nomads lost in the desert greeting a long-awaited rain.

People packed the neutral ground, shoulder to shoulder, everyone drinking, smoking, eating, laughing, and dancing. Everyone got bumped and jostled and poked and stepped on while they did their thing. Drinks got spilled, food got dropped, chairs got toppled, and any and all personal space that had been carved out on the neutral ground was invaded—by friends, family, and complete strangers.

Maureen couldn't help but be impressed, both with the sheer turnout for a nighttime block party in truly shitty weather and with the way the crowd, despite the increase in its size and its sheer frenzied power, for the most part policed itself. That was a very good thing. Even if the NOPD weren't as depleted as it currently was, there was no such thing as enough cops to control an environment like a Mardi Gras parade. Too many moving parts, too much space, too many people. She couldn't stop imagining and dreading what prolific mayhem would ensue if someone with a weapon opened fire on a crowd like this. The stampede would do more damage than the bullets. She hoped that with Goody caught and secured, they'd seen the last of the night's gun violence. She hoped Morello knew what he was doing. She realized she had no real reason to think he didn't. She knew the face he presented on the street, and knew next to nothing about what he hid behind it and how he really operated.

"You were able to get him out of here pretty quickly," Maureen said to Hardin as he approached her out of the crowd. She had to raise her voice over the din of the surrounding throng. Hardin didn't come across as very angry to her. She reminded herself that the surface impression didn't matter; he wouldn't show how he felt in public.

"I'm sure you heard," Maureen said, wanting to lead with good news, "that we caught that runner. We have him hooked up. Morello and Cordts are with him, waiting on Drayton."

"Cordts doing okay?" Hardin asked.

"Of course," Maureen lied. Nervous as Cordts had made her tonight, she couldn't sell him out to their superior. Not when she needed him on her side. Once these reports about her and the John Doe got cleared up, if Cordts stayed dangerously weird, she'd come back to Hardin.

"We were lucky to get an ambulance over here," Hardin said, "considering we had two out of service because of the shooting, to get that John Doe off the route that fast, though I wish we'd been the first to find him. That really would have been better."

"I'm sorry about that," Maureen said. "I wish we had seen it coming. We didn't know it was going to go that bad. We didn't think his life was in danger. You know that, right?"

Waiting for a reply, she saw that Hardin was looking at something behind her. She turned and saw Laine and her crew gathered around the tangled roots of a big live oak, like a pack of jackals. Cortez had the camera on his shoulder, pointed right at them. Fuck these people, Maureen thought. They could be doing some real good, keeping everybody honest while that kid cuffed in the back of a patrol car waited on the detective. Instead, they wanted their money shot, the one where the rookie cop got her skinny ass busted in the street by her tall, strapping superior officer. Ignore them, she thought. Just ignore them.

"Crowd doesn't seem very spooked," she said.

"There was no blood," Hardin said. "No visible signs of violence on the kid. To look at him, he may as well have been passed out. The EMTs did a hell of a job playing it cool." Hardin shrugged. "I don't know how many of these people believed he was dead. They've probably convinced themselves by now that those gunshots up the way were firecrackers. You and I, though, Coughlin, we do not have the luxury of these delusions, Mardi Gras or not."

He gestured at the parade-goers. "There's not much else for these people to do, anyway. And no matter what they believe, dead or alive, gunshots or fireworks, the parade's not stopping, and no one's getting out of the neighborhood for hours. We're stuck here together." He raised his chin at the passing parade. "And there are plenty of distractions, of course."

A woman came striding toward them, yelling at them as she approached. She kicked beer cans out of her way as she marched closer. She was about Maureen's height. Her corn-silk hair was done up in short pigtails. She wore an old leather pilot's helmet and aviator goggles with big round lenses. A blue-and-white-checked dress with a puffy skirt and sleeves, black-and-white-striped tights, and fingerless leather gloves completed the ensemble. She had a hand-rolled cigarette burning in one hand. The woman reminded Maureen of a steampunk biplane-pilot Dorothy who'd never made it back to Kansas from Oz and instead buzzed the Emerald City in a sputtering Sopwith Camel. Maureen noticed a frail bug-eyed dog peeking its quivering head out of her shoulder bag.

Maureen set her hands on her hips. This oughtta be good.

"She's the one," the woman yelled. She was speaking to Hardin and pointing quite emphatically at Maureen. "She's the one I was telling you about."

This, then, Maureen thought, is the "people" that Wilburn was talking about. One angry woman with a camera in her phone.

"Philippa," Hardin said, "we spoke about your tone. Professional respect, please."

Maureen watched Hardin. Since avoiding the general public is not an option in this line of work, she thought, I really need to learn how to talk like that.

Philippa walked right up to Hardin, stood toe to toe with him, red cheeks flaming, blue eyes blazing, unchastened by his size and authority. She looked like a toy come to life next to Hardin's bulk. The dog burrowed deeper into the shoulder bag. That dog, Maureen thought, is the smartest creature I've met all night.

"I'm glad you're finally listening to me," Philippa said. She stuck her cigarette between her lips and began thumbing away at a cell phone she seemed to have had up her sleeve. She raised the phone, attempting to take a photo of Maureen.

"Hey, no way," Maureen shouted, moving out of what she guessed was the picture frame. Philippa followed her with the phone. "Don't do that." Everyone with a fucking camera, she thought. Is this what it's like to be famous? Or notorious? "This isn't *The Hunger Games*, everyone doesn't need to see everything."

Hardin reached out a big hand and blocked Philippa's shot. "You're making a mistake."

"You're interfering with freedom of the press," Philippa shot back. "And my First Amendment rights."

"I told you," Hardin said to her. He took a deep breath. Maureen marveled at his patience. "A smartphone and a Twitter account don't make you the press."

"It makes you a clown at a parade," Maureen said. "An angry clown with a frightened dog."

"No need to provoke," Hardin said.

"I don't need corporate lame-stream media creds to have First Amendment rights. I have my platform, and I have my rights."

"My officer has rights, too," Hardin said. "You're making serious accusations. And I did not bring her here to answer to you."

"She's the one who that other officer was talking about," Philippa said. "He *said* he'd been waiting for her to kill someone. He said it. I *heard* it. Lots of people heard it."

"You heard him say it?" Maureen asked. She stepped closer to Philippa. She couldn't imagine that she would not have noticed her hanging around on the route earlier, when she was first dealing with the kid. Maureen had made sure to stay aware of the crowd. The lady plain stood out; Maureen would've noticed her. "I don't remember you. You weren't there."

"I have three people who heard him say it," Philippa said, shaking her phone. "I recorded their statements."

"But you didn't hear it yourself," Maureen said, "did you? You didn't see anything, either. You wandered across after the action was over with your phone and your leather helmet looking for trouble. So people would pay attention to your shitty blog."

Philippa would not look at or speak to Maureen. She would only address Hardin. "That other officer said that it was about time she killed someone." She held up her phone again. Maureen wanted to snatch it from her and shove it down her throat. "It's a matter of record."

"What record?" Maureen said. She turned to Hardin. "It was a joke. Ask Cordts. He was making a joke." She pointed to the camera crew under the tree. "This is them. I bet Laine set this up. They're filming this whole thing.

You in on this gag, Philippa? I warn you, working for Laine doesn't pay that well."

"Police brutality may be a joke to you," the woman said, finally rounding on Maureen, presenting physically as if she and Hardin were a unified front, "but it's not to the people of color in this city. I have photos of the body. You can't hide this. You can't make him disappear, that poor boy."

"I'll know that poor boy's name before you do," Maureen said.

"We've had enough of your blue privilege and your blue cone of silence."

"We? Who's this 'we'? You're whiter than I am," Maureen said. "What's that accent? Midwest, isn't it? Do you even live here?"

"Officer Coughlin," Hardin said. "I'm not asking you to respond to these accusations. In fact, I'd prefer you didn't. Philippa, we've said what we're going to say on this matter. My officer and I have other matters to attend to."

The woman thumbed madly away at her phone, shaking her head, speaking her words as she typed them. "I am *witnessing* the NOPD cover up a police killing. This is going viral. This is huge. We're changing the paradigm in real time."

"Are you serious?" Maureen asked.

Was this woman turning her into an Internet villain right before her eyes? Maureen wondered. She'd had such a hard time taking this self-serving woman as a real threat, but she'd dabbled enough in social media to know the basics of how the Web worked, namely how fast things could spread across it. She knew the Web was a magpie economy, that the dull truth didn't matter compared with shiny provocation; it was like her standing next to Morello. Who did people listen to, no matter which of them was telling the truth? Nobody vetted the value of what made the rounds, or the veracity of who was doing the talking. And who could tell anymore if a person had ten, had a thousand, had ten thousand people who listened to them?

She'd never have guessed in a million years that three hundred thousand people would watch Laine's trumped-up home movies about Burning Man. She was weak in the knees with relief that Hardin had stopped the photo from being taken. But really, what could she do if Philippa decided to take another one, later, from a distance? She could say anything she wanted about Maureen and no one could stop her. She knew how women fared on the Web. New Orleans was a small city. In no time at all, like before Muses was over, a lot of people, including people on the route, would know exactly what cop Philippa was talking about. She turned to Hardin. "Sarge? Can she do this?"

There was fear in her voice, and she *hated* that Philippa could hear it. That was, of course, if the woman could stop talking long enough to listen to anyone.

"You can try to continue this pattern of harassment," Philippa said, "but I wouldn't advise it." She stuffed her phone in her bag. "People listen to me." The dog yipped at his master's hand.

Maureen hoped Philippa would race off down the road to the next stop in her digital revolution, bored by Hardin's polite stonewalling, but instead the woman produced a pink business card. Again with the business cards, Maureen thought. The parade had stalled. The balloon had gone by, but none of the floats had arrived. Marchers carrying huge fiber-optic butterflies danced in the street, waving the glowing wings of their insects overhead. Stilt walkers and unicycle riders did acrobatic tricks in the street waiting for the sign to keep marching. These delays happened a lot with the big parades, Maureen understood that, but the break meant that several people from the crowd had turned to watch the Philippa show. Why *should* Philippa go anywhere, Maureen considered, when she was the center of attention right here? Maureen looked at the card. First you want to attack me and ruin my life, she thought, now you want my attention. Fuck it, she thought. She took the card. She had to admit she was curious about how far this woman took her act. She read a false name and a Twitter handle: Philippa Marlowe, @JaneDoeJustice. How exciting. How brave. How very original.

"Philippa Marlowe," Maureen said. "Cute."

"So you've seen the films," Philippa said, unable to mask the surprise in her voice over Maureen getting the reference.

"I've read the books," Maureen said. She handed the card back to the woman.

"I have plenty," Philippa said. "Keep it."

"Consider it recycling," Maureen said. She noticed the ground around them was littered with trampled pink cards that had been dropped among the rest of the trash. Apparently, Jane Doe Justice was having trouble rallying people to her cause. Judging by the litter, the difficulty was not due to lack of effort. Like Hardin had said, distractions were everywhere. Maureen found herself actually feeling sad for Philippa. Fighting Mardi Gras for attention was probably a pretty lonely business.

Hardin had turned to chat with someone in the crowd, which Maureen knew was his way of turning the situation over to her. He knew she needed practice when it came to working on de-escalation and dealing one-on-one with people who needed a pair of ears more than they needed a pair of handcuffs. Maureen considered taking a less adversarial approach.

"I have the information memorized," she said. "You made it easy to remember. That was smart. And the cards are not free to make. I know that. You must go through a lot of them."

"Don't patronize me. I have a master's degree." Philippa took the card, dropped it in her bag. Her dog ate it. "Queso!" she scolded. The dog growled. She lit another cigarette. "Now he'll be pooping pink." She'd pulled the cigarette from a tarnished silver case. Maureen recognized the acrid smell of a discount brand. The hand-rolled had probably been bummed off someone else.

"If I told you," Maureen said, "that I didn't kill that kid, that I tried to help him, would you report that, too? To your followers or friends or whatever. Or does that not serve your story?"

"I didn't see that part of it."

"Oh, I know that." Maureen tried to smile, and knew she did a terrible job of it. "C'mon, you didn't see any of it. You're missing a big part of the story. You know, the truth. Find me on the route tomorrow, maybe I'll tell it to you."

"I'll be out here tomorrow," Philippa said, "and we'll see how my story matches yours. I'm not letting this go."

"I'm looking forward to it," Maureen said.

"We have our eye on you. All of you. We're everywhere. All over the route. Y'all are accountable now."

"Consider us warned," Maureen said. "You know what? I want one of those cards." She put out her hand. "Give me one before you go."

Philippa tried to hide her smile, and handed over another pink card.

"Enjoy the parade," Maureen said.

Philippa's phone rang. She answered the call, backing away from Maureen and Hardin, covering her mouth as she talked so they couldn't read her lips.

What was it like, Maureen wondered, to think of yourself as so brave and important? To think everyone was so interested in what you had to say. Or maybe, she reconsidered, Philippa felt the exact opposite of brave and important, and hence the act. Maybe Philippa spent her time chasing whatever the Internet told her was brave, important, and interesting.

"Seriously," Maureen said, turning to Hardin, "is Red Baron Barbie gonna make my life hell? Can she do that? With a cell phone?"

"I looked her up on the Web after the first time I talked to her," Hardin said. "While I was waiting for you. From what I can tell, despite what she says, nobody listens to her there, either. I think we'll survive Jane Doe's justice." He smiled. "Didn't kill you, did it, being nice to her."

"It did not. I know my bedside manner needs work." She turned and stared down Laine and her crew. "Them, on the other hand, I refuse to like."

Cortez had the camera pointed right at her, but they made no move to follow her. She wasn't sure the camera was even on. She thought of waving, or of flipping them the bird, but she did neither. Right then, she didn't need any more enemies than she already had.

"Take a walk with me," Hardin said.

# 22

The crowd parted quickly around Hardin. He moved with the heft and authority of a tanker on the Mississippi. Maureen felt small, trailing in his wake.
He didn't have to ask anyone to step aside for him. Nonetheless he repeated, "Excuse me," calm and steady, as he moved through the closely
gathered people. Maureen mumbled the same as she walked behind him.

The parade was still stalled, and in the break the riverside lanes of
St. Charles had filled with people. Mostly little people. Very excited little
people gone insane on sugar, lights, sound, and general overstimulation.

Adults moved along the edges of the street, talking, texting, and taking
pictures, their go-cups from last year's parades in one hand, their Mardi
Gras–only cigarettes hidden behind their backs in the other. Out in the
street, dozens of kids made use of the free toys they'd accumulated during
Babylon and Chaos. High-bouncing Super Balls, mini-footballs, and small
Frisbees soared through the air and bounced in the street. Kids popped paper
snappers at one another's feet. Maureen found it remarkable how well the
kids got along. They couldn't possibly all know one another, yet they

integrated effortlessly for the night, for the occasion, their games and groups forming and dissolving with equal ease and quickness, without reason or rancor. When an overthrown flying disk disappeared into the crowd, a mini-football instantly popped out to take its place and the games continued; the good times rolled on.

As she moved among the wild, laughing children, Maureen felt like a diver moving through schools of darting, colorful fish. She felt invisible to them, which, she figured, was a good thing. On the best of nights, when the party went most smoothly, the police on the parade route were as much a part of the background as the peanut vendors and the bead hunters.

This was not, however, she reminded herself, the best of nights.

"What're you having?" Hardin asked as they approached the corner of St. Charles and Sixth, where a local grocery and po'boy shop, called, inventively enough, the Grocery, sold hot and cold food and drinks and shots and cigarettes through an open window.

Outside the front door, a man sat on a barstool collecting a three-dollar cash fee to use the roped-off Porta-John on the sidewalk behind him. He had a large stack of bills in his hand. He nodded at Maureen and Hardin. The police got free access to the real restrooms in the back of the store. No business on the route minded having the police around, at least not during Mardi Gras, and offered what they could to help.

"Good gumbo, excellent Cubans. The muffalettas, too. They press 'em, serve 'em hot. We got a long way to go tonight."

"Oh, I know it," Maureen said. "I've been here before. I never got my coffee from Cordts. I could use one of those."

"I got you," Hardin said, tipping his cap to a group of stoned young women hustling away from the window, giggling and ripping open their bags of Zapps, the wine and weed stink hanging like an echo in the space they'd left behind. The jowly lady at the counter took a long drag on a long cigarette. She set it in a notch in a cracked plastic ashtray, and exhaled the smoke over her shoulder away from Hardin and into the kitchen.

"Dammit, Ma, I'm tryin'a quit!" somebody yelled from the kitchen.

"How you living, Madge?" Hardin asked.

Madge zipped up her red hoodie, smiling mischievously at Hardin. "Evenin', Sarge. I keep telling that boy there's no point quitting anything until Ash Wednesday. He don't listen."

"I'm guessing it's not the first time he hasn't taken his mother's advice," Hardin said.

"Ain't that the truth? If only." She leaned around Hardin to get a better look at Maureen. "Hey, sweetheart. You holding up okay?"

Maureen hesitated to answer. She hadn't yet adjusted to people recognizing her. But she'd worked in the neighborhood for months now, and had been out on the route for almost every parade. Even on regular duty, the Grocery was one of her regular stops for supplies. "I'm doing just fine, Madge. You making that money?"

"Always, dear. Always."

"Just two coffees for now," Hardin said.

Madge passed the small white cups through the window. Hardin stuffed a few singles into the tip jar. When she had first seen it there last week, Maureen had been amazed that Madge kept the tip jar, an old plastic mayonnaise jug, anywhere near the window. That was until Madge explained that the jug was nailed to the counter for the duration of the season. I should know better, Maureen had thought, than to question anyone who makes it through this craziness year after year with their sanity and their business intact. Everyone on the route, she remembered, whether it was for partying, policing, or doing parade route business, had a system. So much that looked like chaos wasn't. Which didn't mean there wasn't plenty of it to be had. She just had to learn which chaos was worth reacting to. Like jazz. Or porn.

"Is it true what I heard?" Madge asked Hardin. Maureen's ears perked up. She wanted to see how Hardin handled *this*. A line was forming behind them. She knew she wasn't the only one listening to Hardin's answer.

"Depends on what you heard," Hardin said, his tone light.

"I heard the gangs were going at it on the other side of St. Charles. That it was bad. That there was a dead kid on the route, right by here."

"That's an exaggeration," Hardin said, shaking his head. "A big one. No dead kids. You know better than to believe parade route gossip."

"It's every year now, Sarge," Madge said, "with the guns. And it's not just on the other side of the avenue. It's not just down by the Popeyes and the highway anymore. Now they come over this side. Fat Tuesday last year we had a shooting two blocks from here. On Fat Tuesday. You can't tell me I'm wrong. That's no gossip, that's fact."

"I'm not saying your concern is unfounded," Hardin said. "I worked that Fat Tuesday shooting last year." He paused. "We had a shooting, yes, I'm not gonna lie about that. You know me. No fatalities, though. No dead kids."

"Thank the Lord," Madge said, blessing herself.

"Indeed," Hardin said. "And the other guy the EMTs came for, he was an OD. Sad, but it had nothing to do with that other incident. Separate things. And the shooting looks like a random beef or something. I don't want you to worry. We're on it. We're handling it."

"Okay, if you say so," Madge said, shrugging, as if to let the doubt in her voice roll out her ear. "It's not like we have a choice. We can't afford to stay home. You *know* what this time of year means, Sarge. And we're just gettin' started. The big parades have hardly even got goin' yet. The weather sucks, and they sayin' it's not gettin' any better until Sunday for Bacchus. We can't have people havin' another reason to stay home this year."

Hardin reached into the service window, covered Madge's small, dry hand with his. "You're getting worked up for nothing."

"City says I have to put a new hood over my stove," Madge said. "This weekend is supposed to pay for that, long as people come out."

Hardin leaned down so he could meet Madge's eyes with his own. "We got this. The parades will keep rolling. Everyone will make their money. I promise you. We got it. If I can find a fix for the weather, I'll do that, too." He picked up a coffee cup in each hand. "We pull it off every year, don't we? This year's no different. Now keep doing what you do." He tilted his head toward the man on the barstool by the Porta-John. "And tell your husband if he's gonna concealed-carry he better have that permit like it oughtta be. I can't let that go. Not on the route. Speaking of guns. You know how we are about that."

Madge's face clouded over for a brief moment. "We're not the ones . . ." She let the rest of her comment trail off. "He's good. He's okay. He has it with him. I made him promise me."

Hardin smiled. He raised his coffee at Madge's husband then turned back to the window. "I never had any doubt. I'm just sayin'. Let's keep cool and have a good time. We're all family out here." He handed a coffee to Maureen. "Come with me, Officer."

Maureen took her coffee. She turned to say thanks to Madge, but the woman was already back to business, taking an order from the next set of customers.

# 23

Maureen peeled back the lid on her coffee cup and, sipping the hot liquid, hustled after Hardin, who strode ahead of her down Sixth Street, away from the parade and toward the relative dark and quiet of Prytania Street, the next street parallel to St. Charles, a different world entirely from the circus on the avenue.

They stopped at the corner of Sixth and Prytania, where a yellow wooden barrier closed the street to traffic. Across Prytania Street the white brick wall of the Lafayette Cemetery ran the length of the block. Here I am, Maureen thought, a carnival raging at my back, the city of the dead ahead of me, while I stand on the corner under the stars and the crepe myrtles drinking hot coffee. If only my mother could see me now.

"This is your chance," Hardin said to her, "to tell me your side of the story." The casual jovial tone he'd employed with Madge was gone. "There's no one else around to hear it, so I want it straight."

Maureen set her coffee on the curb. It was flavorless, but it was hot. She lit a cigarette. "All due respect, Sarge, and I'm not trying to change the subject,

I swear, but we caught that kid, the shooting suspect. We have him hooked up in a unit. I know him. I know his name. Todd Goodwin Curtis. Don't you want to talk about that instead? A lot of good work went into that."

"Not right now," Hardin said.

"But why don't—"

"Coughlin. Leave it."

"Yes, sir." She paused. "Okay, my story. That boy came running through the crowd. I saw him coming, there was some chatter on the radio, too. We knew about him. I tried to intercept him, and he threw himself on the hood of someone's car. A couple of rich kids, couple of jerk-offs. Anyway, I wanted to get them out of there. I was, *we* were, Cordts and I, trying to avoid a scene and keep traffic moving."

"Any info on the two kids in the car?" Hardin asked.

"I never took any," Maureen said. "The driver said they were going to the party on Delachaise. No one was hurt."

"We could use a statement from them," Hardin said, "about the condition and behavior of this John Doe."

"Yeah, I didn't really think about that," Maureen said. "I didn't figure I'd be in a position where I'd need witnesses on my behalf. I didn't think the kid was going to die."

"Ah, let's face it," Hardin said, shaking his head, he seemed so tired, "anything gathered at a Mardi Gras parade isn't worth much."

"I didn't tase that kid," Maureen said. "I'll turn my Taser in right now and you can check it. I haven't used it. I've never used it."

"I'm not worried about that," Hardin said. "Obviously, you didn't attack the kid. Nobody that matters believes that you did." He stepped closer to her. "But he died. And you made no effort, as far as I can ascertain, to get him medical attention before that happened."

"We were working on getting him help when we heard the gunshots, Sarge," Maureen said. "Gunshots. We're not supposed to respond to that?"

Hardin gestured for her to stop talking. "I know, I know. But when we figure out who this John Doe is and find his people, the police department is going to have to answer for how he was treated."

"I'm not afraid to talk to whoever wants to ask me questions."

"See, we don't want it coming to that," Hardin said. "That would be bad. *I'm* going to have to answer for you and Cordts, for the decisions that y'all made. I want to be able to do that."

Maureen felt the moisture leave her mouth. "Okay, I never thought, from the moment I first saw him running up the street, that his life was in danger. I prioritized managing his encounter with the car. I made sure no one got hurt. The safety of everyone involved was paramount to me, including that kid. He didn't make it easy, either. He tried to bite my face.

"I don't know what happened after we left him, I can't speak to that, but I never, ever thought that he was in any danger. We're taught what an OD looks like, a serious, he's-gonna-die OD, and I'm telling you, this thing didn't look like it. I don't know what this was.

"And even still, we were trying to help him, and to get him out of the street. That's what we were doing when we heard the gunshots. Cordts called EMS. They wouldn't come. You can't tell me, Sarge, that we did the wrong thing running after the shots instead of playing this kid's game about being passed out."

She sucked her cigarette down to the filter, pacing. "I'm sorry he's dead. Obviously. I'd rather he hadn't died, for him and his people as well as for us. I'm not without sympathy. But it was bad choices on his part, and bad timing in general that did him in, not bad police work. I can't say I'd do any of it different. And, due respect, Sarge, I don't think you would've done anything different, either, had you been there."

Hardin stared into the dark trees hanging over the cemetery. He was quiet for a long time. "One big question," he finally said. "Will Cordts tell me the same story that you did?"

Maureen wanted to cross her fingers behind her back. Who knew what the fuck Cordts would say anymore? "I guarantee it."

# 24

They both turned at the sound of footsteps approaching from the direction of the parade. Laine was walking up to them, but without the rest of her crew.

"Something I can help you with?" Hardin asked.

"The kid who died on the route," Laine said. "It was one of my crew who found him."

"And we're grateful for how promptly y'all reported that to us," Hardin said. "And for your discretion and respect for the deceased. We'll want to speak with Donna before too long, by the way. We're going to do a full report on his death, try and find out what happened to him."

"Any idea when you'll want to speak with her?" Laine asked. "I want to make her available, but we're going to be working pretty hard these next few days. There's a story here. Bigger than you might think."

"There's money here," Maureen said. "That's what's here. Exposure.

Attention. Not truth and justice. Violence and money. That's what you're here for, and a very bad day for a whole bunch of people is suddenly a very good day for you. Like a true vulture."

"I told you," Laine said, "we're here for the real Mardi Gras, the real New Orleans. It's not my fault it decided to show itself tonight. We didn't make it happen."

"If you're really interested in the real New Orleans," Maureen said, "then go film the families having a good time together, go film the kids from different neighborhoods playing on the parade route. Or are the kids in this city only interesting to you when they're shooting each other and dropping dead?"

"You don't know me," Laine said, "you don't know what I'm about. You google somebody and you think you know who you're dealing with. Who said you get to decide what's really New Orleans and what isn't? According to Officer Wilburn, you just got here."

Maureen waved her hand over her uniform. "And as you may have noticed I plan on staying and doing something worthwhile with my time here, not running off to the next party where someone's got their tits hanging out so I can throw it up on the Internet and call myself a journalist."

"What's next?" Laine asked. "You gonna call me a carpetbagger? Spoken like a true newbie."

"Do you even have a home?" Maureen asked. "A place that you actually care about? Or is it all one big video shoot to you?"

"Enough, enough," Hardin said. "This does nobody any good." He turned to Laine. "You'll forgive me if I prioritize my people's work over yours. Having cameras pointed at my officers the whole time that they're working a case doesn't help them any. It doesn't make the parades any safer. We're trying to prevent more violence. That's bigger than anything you're trying to do. If you have any experience reporting on a city, you know how fast these things can escalate."

"With respect," Laine said, "maybe Officer Coughlin is overstating her complaints about what I consider worthy content. I know for a fact you have a shooting suspect detained in the back of a police car, with no immediate plans to afford him due process. I saw it happen. I have a fair bit of it on camera. That gives me a very good opportunity to make the NOPD look bad if that's what I want, and I don't need anybody's permission to do that. No one would blame me. A lot of people would think me pretty heroic. And yet, my camera crew is here with me on the parade route filming a twenty-foot-tall light-up red shoe, instead of watching a teenage suspect get babysat by a cop twice his size who would clearly like to break him in half. What does that tell you?"

Hardin looked at Maureen. "Cordts is there, too," she told him. "Everything was copacetic when I left them."

"What do you want?" Hardin asked.

"I need to talk to you about the OD," Laine said.

"We haven't confirmed that's what it was," Maureen said. "The EMTs left with the body minutes ago, practically. There's been no statement from the coroner's officer. Don't put words in our mouths. There'll be nothing official until after the weekend at least."

"We don't have information on that incident to share at this time," Hardin said. "Other than to confirm there was a nonviolent fatality on the parade route tonight. Officer Coughlin is correct, there will be no news beyond that anytime soon."

"An official statement is not what I'm looking for," Laine said. "We're not the nightly news. Actually, I'm here because I have information to share with you. About what may have happened to that kid." She smirked and nodded at Maureen. "Off the record, of course."

"Depending on what you tell us," Hardin said. "We're talking about criminal activity. I'm not sure you get the final decision on what's off the record."

"We're all ears," Maureen said.

"I think I know how that boy died. I think I know what killed him."

"Really?" Maureen asked. "Did you see something happen after we left?"

"No," Laine said. "Donna found him in the street after she left that bar by the scene of the shooting. Look, I haven't been entirely honest about why we're here in New Orleans, why we're filming here now."

"I'm not sure I want to hear this," Hardin said.

"The Mardi Gras story is cover," Laine said. "Or more like a backup plan. I'm trying to make an on-the-fly, real-time documentary about flakka."

"Who?" Maureen asked.

"Not who," Laine said, "but *what*. It's a street drug, a brand-new synthetic cathinone, a superamphetamine. Alpha-PVP is the more official name. This shit is completely warping people. Like the bath salts that turned people into zombies, remember that? Only times ten. Times fifty. It's five bucks a hit and it's got people facedown in their driveways, naked, chewing concrete until they've ripped their own teeth out. People stay up eight, nine days in a row bingeing on it. They lose everything in weeks, if not days. It makes crack look like amateur hour. It's going be a bigger problem, and a bigger story, than meth and *no one* is on it yet. No one is seeing the pattern, seeing the sickness move, but me."

Maureen glanced at Hardin, shaking her head. "How have we not heard of this? Sounds like that 'mojo' shit."

"Sounds much worse," Hardin said.

"Right now," Laine said, "it's mostly rural whites taking it. Small towns, poor folks. Nothing sexy. No glamour. So who gives a fuck? Not national news, that's for sure. And not national law enforcement like the FBI or the DEA. But I've got interviews with a bunch of small-town Florida cops—Florida is where it started—who are *terrified* of this shit. And I did those interviews months ago. Since then it's moved north and west from Florida. It's creeping into the cities surrounding the Appalachians and it's moving along the Gulf Coast, too. They've had cases. And I think it's in New Orleans now."

"Why did you lie about reporting on it?" Maureen asked. "If it's such a big deal?"

"I needed a cover story," Laine said, "because how else am I going to

THE DEVIL'S MUSE 151

get the NOPD media relations to treat me halfway decent about talking to cops during Mardi Gras? I can't very well say I'm coming here to expose a brand-new drug problem moving into New Orleans that your police department isn't fighting because it doesn't know fuck-all about it."

"What better camouflage than another out-of-town hustler looking to cash in on Mardi Gras? That was the first thing *you* thought. Plus, if I don't get the flakka story here, I put up the Mardi Gras show on the YouTube channel and we get another half a million hits and my investors pay for me to chase this shit to Baton Rouge or Lafayette, maybe all the way to Houston, and the show goes on."

"You have investors?" Maureen asked. "In a YouTube channel?"

"We crowd-source," Laine said. "And Donna has fans in Silicon Valley. The Internet is a funny place."

"She's got silicon, all right."

"I nail this story, though," Laine said, "I don't need to go begging for cash or monetize Donna's tits. A story like this, I can get real money behind me again. A serious production company. Sell it to HBO. Showtime. Netflix. Cable news. I can really get my career restarted. For real this time. No more running from town to town, hiring kids off of Craigslist."

"And you think flakka's what killed this kid?" Hardin asked, all business. "You said you have interviews, but do you have real experience with this? You sure it's here?"

"I've never *taken* it," Laine said, "if that's what you mean by experience, my gonzo days are over, but I've been tailing it across the Gulf Coast. Florida, in the panhandle. Then Alabama? Mississippi? New Orleans *has* to be next. It's the biggest market between Pensacola and Houston, and it's fucking Mardi Gras. What better time, what better place to be pushing a new product that makes people absolutely crazy? You got people driving in, blending in, from a hundred small towns around the south. Some of them are carrying this shit. I promise you. "

"First it makes them crazy," Maureen said. "And then it kills them."

"I mean, the death rate isn't one hundred percent, obviously, but it's pretty lethal. And it's not just ODs. It's accidents that are killing people, too. Extreme violence. One woman tried jumping from an overpass onto an eighteen-wheeler passing underneath her. Naked. She missed. People jump off rooftops, stagger into traffic, throw themselves through plate-glass windows. I talked to a cop outside Mobile, he took down a kid running naked through the park stabbing trees with a butcher knife. That cop used the same word over and over again. 'Zombie.' Every cop I talk to, they use that word. No one could talk the kid down, no one could talk to him or reach him in any way. It was like he'd been beamed down to Earth deaf and blind from another planet."

"That sounds familiar," Maureen said, turning to Hardin. "This kid who died on the route was almost naked. And he was crazy enough, and violent."

"And covered in sweat, right?" Laine asked.

Maureen nodded.

"The flakka spikes your body temperature," Laine said. "The disrobing and the rampage that this kid went on, that's two of the main giveaways. I have footage of other people doing the same thing. I have eight cops in six different towns telling me the same stories."

Hardin pinched the bridge of his nose. Suddenly, his shoulders slumped and he seemed exhausted. "Is anything ever enough? Any drug, any high, any amount of money? There's always something new, something more, something *worse* coming right at us. Why not, what'd you call it, bath salts times fifty? A zombie drug? Why the fuck not? Why the fuck not? And this is New Orleans, when was the last time a plague passed us by?"

"Go ask the coroner about recent drug-related deaths," Laine said. "Check with the other police districts here in New Orleans about incidents like this guy's last rampage. I've been in town with my crew for a week and I've already uncovered two other possible cases, one in the CBD and one in the Quarter.

"The guy from the CBD is in a coma, unlikely to wake up. His body temp spiked so bad he cooked his brain. That's the usual cause of death, brain and massive organ failure from the crazy high body temp. He single-handedly destroyed the dining room of the Renaissance Hotel before collapsing on the sidewalk outside Lucy's bar. The guy from the Quarter is dead. He drowned in the river. He was fished out from under the *Creole Queen*. His body was caught in the paddle wheel."

"I heard about that one," Maureen said. "I heard he was a gutter punk, that he went swimming with his buddies in the river late at night and the currents got him." She looked at Hardin. "Right?"

"Happens once or twice a year," he said with a shrug. "Kids get fucked up on God knows what. River at night looks peaceful, looks calm. A drowning like that is nothing that draws special attention or points to anything out of the ordinary, I'll tell you that."

"I interviewed the drowned guy's swimming buddy," Laine said. "Keith, I think his name was. I wondered what they were doing swimming in the river in January. Keith said he and his friend took something they had never tried before. A guy passing through the Quarter gave it to them for free. Told them to pass it around, to share it, but I think they took everything he gave them.

"Keith said it was so powerful that it made them feel like they were cooking from the inside out, that they'd been tricked into swallowing charcoal briquettes and were trying to stop themselves from cooking so they wouldn't be cannibalized. He thought maybe that was why they jumped in the river. That they were afraid the guy who dosed them was going to hunt them down and eat them."

"Now that sounds like a story that would've made the rounds," Maureen said. She looked at Hardin. "'Cannibals in the Quarter'? How did that story not make it uptown?"

"I'm sure Keith told me more than he told the police," Laine said. "Does what he said sound like a story that a street kid would tell a cop?"

"No, it doesn't," Maureen said with a snort. "It sounds like a story a street kid would tell a lady with a camera and cash in her pocket."

"Well, as far as I could find out," Laine said, "the cops down in the Quarter didn't really ask for any info besides the basics. If they even asked for that."

"What else is there besides the basics?" Maureen asked. "The bottom line is that Keith and that other kid got fucked up and went in the river, at night, in the cold. Like the sergeant said, it happens. It was a thing before this new drug came to town. And since you're breaking this news to us about flakka tonight, why would those other cops think to ask this Keith about anything out of the ordinary, when everything else they were dealing with wasn't abnormal?"

"I'm trying to pass along what I learned," Laine said. "I don't want anyone else to die tonight, either. From flakka or from gunshots."

"I'm guessing," Maureen said, "that your pal Keith didn't offer up any good info on this mystery benefactor who provided the drug that killed his friend."

Laine shrugged. "Real tall but skinny. Super, super skinny, Keith said. Bald. Looked like he was made of chalk. Had a buddy. A short, skinny bald kid, boy or girl, he couldn't tell, with a big tattoo on their head."

"Sweet Jesus," Maureen said.

"What?" Hardin asked.

"Never mind," Maureen said. "Sounds like a pair even the supremely fucked up would remember."

"Sounds made up to me," Hardin said. "He's probably some short, fat guy with a dog. Haven't these guys literally fried their brains? We're gonna trust what they say?"

"Check with the hospitals about other ODs and drug casualties coming in," Laine said. "I guarantee you'll see a pattern. The sweats, the rage, the sudden collapse."

"And if we do that, when we put these stories together," Maureen said, "we should tell you about it for your movie, of course. You get great footage. You get your legwork done for you. Nice deal for you."

"I'd love an interview," Laine said, "with you, with you, Sergeant Hardin, or anyone else who'd be moved to contribute to the project. There's no rule that says we can't be on the same side here. I didn't have to tip you guys off to any of this. Any legwork done on this flakka story is work that I did. Yes, I'm trying to revive my career, but exposing this drug is also a public service. Why can't everybody win? Where's the law against that? I help you, you help me. Your whole department benefits. Every time a new drug hits the streets, the federal money starts flowing again, for the new equipment, for the task force and the overtime and the lab work. And, *and* you get a leg up on the next monster in the war on drugs. How can all that be bad?"

Maureen raised her hands. "You want to talk to the coroner and stuff, I can't stop you. But I'm not a detective, and I can't help you with any of this. I promise you no police officer in this city has time to go looking for Keith and his chalk-monster drug dealer. Good luck getting to the coroner, to be honest. We're all busy twenty-four seven for the next week."

"And I already said I'm inclined to believe you about this problem," Hardin said, "but I got an extra hundred thousand people in my neighborhood tonight, and tomorrow night, and the next four days after that. I got one shooting already and I'm scrambling to prevent the next one. I got no time to help you get your movie together. We won't get in your way, and if anybody from my district wants to help when this is over, Officer Coughlin or anyone else, I'm probably okay with that. But I'm asking you nicely one time not to distract my officers with your project. I need my people on point. Forget the zombies; I promise you that as we speak I got twenty to thirty live armed kids stalking the neighborhood wondering who shot who and why, and if they're gonna be the next target or the next shooter. *That* plague is real, and is already entrenched and killing people. I can't have anyone dying from it this weekend. The zombies will have to wait until Mardi Gras is over."

"I'm afraid more people are going to die this weekend from this drug," Laine said. "That's why I came forward with this."

"More people are going to die tonight," Hardin said, "if I don't find out the story behind that shooting on the other side of St. Charles. We're done here, Ms. Daniels."

# 25

After Laine had disappeared into the crowd, Maureen and Hardin made their way back up Sixth Street at a slow stroll.

"You buying this, Sarge?" Maureen asked. "About this new drug?"

"There's always a new drug," Hardin said. "What she's right about is that we haven't heard jack shit about flakka. I heard about that kid in the CBD who trashed the hotel. That's the Eighth District, where Wiggins took over for me when I transferred up here. We talk. He told me about it, as a joke. He had to punch the kid out in the back of an ambulance. I'm not telling Laine that, especially since the kid's in a coma now. The medics couldn't sedate him because they didn't know what drug he was on, so Wiggins had to do it the old-fashioned way.

"But Wiggins said the EMTs were freaked the fuck out. Even strapped to the gurney the guy did serious damage to the back of the ambulance anyway, thrashing around so hard. We won't get a tox report on that kid who died tonight for weeks. I'll bet anything no one even asked for one on the kid who got pulled out of the river. I don't know if we can get one on him now. I doubt it. I'm sure that body is gone."

"Maybe that kid comes out of his coma and can point us to the chalk monster," Maureen said. She sipped her coffee, which had gone from steaming hot to lukewarm. "I can't believe that sentence came out of my mouth."

"I hope he recovers, and I hope it's not before Ash Wednesday." Hardin massaged his bald dome with one gloved hand. "Because we don't fucking need this right now. I can't take this on right now. I can't. We're too thin to do what we have to do already."

"Speaking of," Maureen said, "what are we going to do about tonight? Morello has that Todd Curtis kid just sitting there. He wouldn't let me arrest him. In theory, they were waiting on Drayton to do that and question him before he goes in the system. But it's been a while now and nothing seems to be happening. Do we know where Drayton is?"

"You got this kid out from under the house?" Hardin asked.

"Well, no. I chased him under there. Canine got him out."

"But you were there when they cuffed him," Hardin said.

"I was. I started cuffing him myself, started his Miranda, but then Morello stopped me."

"You said earlier that you knew him," Hardin said.

"He's a neighborhood hard case," Maureen said. "He was part of that whole thing with those kids, Marques Greer and Mike-Mike. He'd split for Baton Rouge, but now he's back. His uncle was a dealer and a gunrunner."

"You think he's back in town working for his uncle?"

"His uncle's dead," Maureen said.

"Why am I not surprised?" Hardin said. "Who killed him?"

"We did. His uncle was Bobby Scales."

"Well, wherever he is," Hardin said, "I'm sure Mr. Scales is happy his legacy endures. Was his uncle Three-N-G?"

"No," Maureen said. "Scales was J-Street crew. That was his whole thing, trying to bring back J-Street after the feds took so many of them down in that big racketeering case after the storm."

"You think Goody's back in town trying to rebuild his uncle's business?"

"I don't know what he's up to," Maureen said. "If he's the latest neighborhood kid trying to resurrect the J-Street crew, why's he yelling about Three-N-G? For that matter, why the fuck is he shooting a middle school music teacher? And he won't even admit to being who he is, never mind admitting to the shooting."

"Would you?" Hardin said, suppressing a laugh. "When Goody came out from under the house, did he show any indication he was high on this flakka shit? Any chance of a connection between our OD and the shooting?"

"I doubt it, Sarge," Maureen said. "He came out from under the house stinkin' of something, but I think it was stray cats. He was sweaty and agitated, but we'd been chasing him for blocks." She paused, comparing the kid in the pink tights and the shooting suspect in her mind. "I don't see it. He was belligerent, but in the ordinary way. He wasn't violent. He was manageable. He could walk and talk and function. Having dealt with both him and the John Doe, they were too different."

"All right," Hardin said, "we need to prioritize. Forget the flakka for now. First thing we do, we need to make sure any contagion this shooting has released has been squashed. We can't have it infecting the whole route. So far we're hanging in there. I need you to go down by Erato and St. Charles, check with our people at the Wendy's, the Popeyes. Most years, when shit pops off the worst, that's where it happens. Any Three-N-G that's out at the parade, that's where they'll be. The tactical squads have that segment of the route. Ask around. See what the reaction is to the shooting, what the ripple effect is. Talk to them down there and report back to me."

"Ten-four," Maureen said.

"I'll get you a ride," Hardin said, grabbing his mic.

"Thanks. That's a long walk." Maureen's phone buzzed in her pocket. Not a number she recognized. She answered anyway. "Coughlin."

"Officer? This is Dakota. The bartender from Verret's."

"I remember. Is Susan okay?"

"She's sleeping it off on my air mattress," Dakota said. "I've got my eye on her. But listen, that's not why I'm calling. There's a man here, a detective. His name is Drayton."

"He's a tool," Maureen said, "but he's going to be investigating the case. Just help him out however you can. You might have to wake up Susan so he can talk to her. I'm afraid that can't wait."

"He hasn't even asked about Susan," Dakota said. "He seems more interested in my breasts than any crime that happened on this corner." That was Drayton, all right. "The only time he talked to me was to order a drink. He's a lousy fucking tipper, by the way."

"I'm sorry," Maureen said. "He is literally our only option tonight."

"I'm calling you," Dakota said, "because you seem like a decent person and I don't want you getting in trouble."

"Excuse me?"

"He is extremely pissed off," Dakota said. "Those other two cops? The two who did the yellow tape or whatever? They've been hanging around since the rest of you took off. Drayton is screaming at them. And I've heard your name more than once. I thought you'd want to know. You and the others, you seem to give a shit about Cordell and the other people who got shot; this guy, though: fuck him."

Maureen glanced at Hardin. He was a few feet away, talking with a group of kids who'd staggered out of a nearby house party. "Do you have any idea," Maureen asked Dakota, "what he's so angry about?"

"Is there or is there not a suspect in custody?" Dakota said. "That's what he keeps yelling. And why doesn't anyone at the scene know what's going on? He's demanding to know where you are, and where the other two cops who first worked the scene went. That's what he kept yelling about. That and the weather. I take it he's not a fan of leaving the office. He seems to think y'all caught the shooter." Maureen heard her light a cigarette. "Did y'all catch someone? That was quick. If you did, people around here will be relieved. I can tell Susan when she wakes up."

# THE DEVIL'S MUSE 161

"Speaking of Susan," Maureen said. "Do you think you can get to her phone?"

"I guess," Dakota said. "But I don't know if I can unlock it. I can wake her up. You want her to call you?"

"I need a picture of Cordell," Maureen said. "One where we can see his face real well."

"I can send you that," Dakota said. "I have that on my phone. A crew of teachers from Dell's school comes in almost every Friday for happy hour. I took pictures for the bar's Facebook page. I'll pick out the best and send it to you."

"Thanks, Dakota," Maureen said. "And thank you for the heads-up on Detective Drayton. When Susan wants to go see Dell, he's at UMC. She can go whenever she wakes up. If Drayton wants to ignore you, let him. He's not worth the trouble." She glanced at Hardin. "And do me one more favor."

"If I can," Dakota said.

"Don't bother telling Drayton that we talked, or about the picture."

"Not speaking to him is the easiest part of my night," Dakota said. "Have a good night."

After Dakota had disconnected, Maureen studied her phone for a long moment before she slipped it back into her pocket. Faye and Kornegay were either lying to Drayton or they didn't know the suspect had been apprehended. She tried to remember what she had heard over the radio about the bust. There'd been the original announcement that had sent her running, the radio chatter as they tracked Goody through the neighborhood, the call for the K-9 unit. But after that? She couldn't remember. She'd announced nothing on the radio.

Morrison had packed up her dogs and left once they'd got Goody out from under the house. Maureen had assumed Morello had put something out over the radio about that development, but she couldn't be positive. She hadn't heard it. Morello had said he'd called Drayton on the phone to update him on the situation, but Maureen hadn't heard him make that call.

Now, with an ignorant Drayton rampaging around the bar, Morello had obviously lied to her about calling the detective. Why was Morello hiding from Drayton the fact that they'd caught someone? Like Dakota had said, people would be relieved to know the police had the shooter in custody. It was good news. Why hide having Goody in cuffs?

She took out her phone, looked at it. She tapped it against her thigh. If her coworkers involved in this case were not talking about catching someone, they didn't want her talking about it. She sipped her cold coffee. Everything went cold so fast out here, she thought.

She put her phone back in her pocket and walked over to Hardin. "Excuse me, Sarge. I need a minute."

Hardin dismissed the drunk boys he'd been talking to. "Y'all be care- ful, fellas. Behave. No driving." He turned to Maureen. "What's the prob- lem, Officer?"

"Why doesn't Drayton know we caught somebody?" Maureen asked. "That bartender just called me. She said Drayton's at the scene of the shooting, and he's ripping Faye and Kornegay a new asshole trying to find out what's going on with the case."

Hardin waved a dismissive hand. "They can handle his abuse. You're new to him, but the rest of us, we've been dealing with his shit for years. Don't worry about them. They're big boys."

"She said he mentioned my name, too. And he's looking for Wilburn and Cordts."

"It's not hard to find out who worked the scene," Hardin said.

"It wasn't in a positive context."

"Don't worry about him," Hardin said, slower, obviously trying to make an impression. "Like I said before, I will handle Drayton."

Maureen's phone buzzed. She checked the screen. Drayton. She showed it to Hardin. "It's him."

"Don't answer it," Hardin said. "Ignore him. Stick with me on this. That's the best move. That's what Cordts and Wilburn are doing, I promise you."

"Morello never called him, did he?" Maureen asked. "He called you, not Drayton, when we got Goody out from under the house. You're running this thing."

"I'm the sergeant. Until someone gets a promotion, I'm the lieutenant, too. So it's my job to run things."

Hardin raised his chin at something over her shoulder. Maureen turned and looked. A patrol car waited for her at the end of Sixth Street, blue lights flashing. Her ride.

"Why would we not tell him we caught someone?" she asked.

"Officer, your ride is here," Hardin said. "Unless you want to walk that mile in the rain?"

Maureen wondered now if this reconnaissance mission Hardin had assigned her was meant to get her out of the way. Did Hardin, Morello, Wilburn, and Cordts have plans for Goody they didn't want her knowing about? She was new; they all knew one another. She'd seen her fellow officers take matters into their own hands. She'd done it herself, almost losing more than her career in the process. So she'd promised herself she wasn't going to participate in any more of that bloody business. But was looking away from it, she asked herself, any better, any less corrupt, than not participating?

Everybody knew Mardi Gras had its own rules and requirements, and that they existed for the safety of the greater good. What she didn't know, she realized, because she simply hadn't been in New Orleans long enough, was what those special rules and requirements were. And if she blew it today, she'd never get the chance to learn.

Fuck me running, she thought. I *hate* being the fucking new girl. Nobody trusts me. And I, she thought, don't trust them very much.

"What's the plan here, Sarge?" Maureen asked. "Why would we not tell *anyone* we caught a suspect? Isn't that good news? Just tell me what to do here. You can trust me. You have to know that by now."

"Look at me, Coughlin. You have your orders. Go down to Erato Street and get me a report. That's the plan. That's your role in the plan. The master plan, before you ask, is for you to follow my goddamn orders."

"Ten-four. Yes, sir. If anybody over there asks about an arrest, what do I say?"

"You tell them the truth," Hardin said, his patience gone. "That you don't know a fucking thing." He wasn't pissed at her alone, Maureen could tell. He was mad that Drayton had turned up so soon asking questions. Someone who mattered had lit a fire under him and now the detective was in the way, a nagging monkey wrench in Hardin's plan, whatever it was.

"Let me put it this way," he said, calmer now, "I'm sending you down there to ask questions, not to answer them. Now, go."

Maureen went.

She was climbing into the patrol car when she heard Hardin shouting her name. He sounded even less happy with her than he'd been only moments ago.

"Gimme another minute," she said to the officer behind the wheel.

"Take your time. I got all night. Better you than me."

She met Hardin on the street corner. He was squeezing his phone in his massive hand.

"What's up, Sarge?"

Hardin, his chest heaving, took a moment to calm himself, then he said, "I got a call. The superintendent of the NOPD and the commander of the Sixth District are on their way to the scene of the shooting, where they are very much looking forward to joining Detective Drayton in announcing an arrest to the press. At the mayor's direct insistence. This is happening in an hour."

Maureen pulled her knit hat down over her eyes. "Oh, my." Well, now they knew who was prodding Drayton into action. Even he jumped when the mayor called.

"Did you know about this?" he asked.

"The press conference?"

"Do not fuck with me, Officer. Now is not the time. Did you know that word had gotten out? Did you leak that we had a suspect in custody?"

"I have no idea what is going on right now," Maureen said. "That is the absolute truth. I swear to you. I was here, with you, while whatever happened was happening. I spent the last ten minutes demonstrating my ignorance to you. Maybe Morrison let something slip?"

"I talked to Morrison." Hardin wiped his hand down his wet face. "She said nothing. She knows better." Maureen couldn't tell if it was rain or sweat running down his cheeks. He held up his phone. "I've got orders. I have to meet DC Skinner at the crime scene within the hour to give him a full report about the shooting investigation so he can brief the mayor and the superintendent before making his arrest announcement in front of the news cameras. I can't tell Skinner there's no arrest."

"Maybe Skinner *doesn't* know about Goody," Maureen said. "Maybe he's hearing rumors and *assuming* we caught somebody. Or maybe this is his way of pressuring us into working faster. Maybe he wants you to lie to him? Who would know that we didn't catch someone if we said we did? Right?"

"But we *did* catch somebody," Hardin said. "And there's a good chance he's the guy who did it. I can't send my boss to his boss empty-handed when we do have someone in custody. I can't tell that lie. Word would get out after the fact. I'd be toast. We'd all be toast, everyone involved. Me, you, Wilburn, Cordts, Morello. That dick Drayton would be the only one left standing."

"Fuck that," Maureen said. "I still don't get why we haven't told Drayton about Goody. We didn't make the formal arrest because then the kid can invoke Miranda, which, considering his record, he'll know to do. I get that. But why not let Drayton question him without arresting him while he's detained in the car? Isn't that the next logical step? And it's not like we never do that. The way things are now, Goody's sitting in the backseat of the cruiser giving us nothing."

"It's like this," Hardin said. "The minute Drayton catches up to Goody, he'll arrest him."

"Why would he do that?" Maureen asked. "He knows Goody will dummy up when he gets arrested and we'll get nothing useful about preventing the next shooting."

"Drayton doesn't care about the next shooting," Hardin said. "That's the problem. That's why we're hiding Goody from him. The second Drayton makes this arrest, the investigation ends. All he cares about is clearing to-night's case, getting his attaboys from the brass and the press, and going back to watching porn with his shoes off. Once he makes it official with Goody, we have to take him to the jail wagon. Goody then goes to lockup, Drayton goes back to district, and our best lead on any other violence going down tonight and maybe for the next five days disappears into the system. None of us will have the time or the opportunity to go get him before Ash Wednesday.

"And what about making sure no one else gets shot this weekend?" Maureen asked. "What about that?"

"That's up to us," Hardin said. "Not Drayton, not Skinner, not the mayor. Us, out here working the parade. Now go *get* me some good news for the bosses, and good intelligence for us. Because of this press conference, we have to let Drayton make his arrest very soon. We're going to lose Goody as a resource within the hour. Go find out for me if we can safely do that. We're in an even bigger hurry now than we were before."

# 26

Maureen's ride dropped her off at Prytania and Erato Streets, in a neighborhood called the Lower Garden District, where most of the streets were named after muses or saints.

Though the parade was in full swing again, she had an easy time navigating her way across St. Charles to the lake side of the avenue. The Lower Garden parade-goers were for the most part a younger and funkier and grungier and more diverse lot than their more monied compatriots farther uptown on the other side of Jackson Avenue. Many people down here attended the parades in costume, the outfits often homemade. Maureen felt more at home in the LGD than she did in the heart of the Garden District. The people of the Lower Garden reminded her of her neighbors in the Irish Channel. Fewer doctors, lawyers, oilmen, former Saints, and current mayors, and more service-industry vets, shop owners, tattoo artists, electrical contractors, and ironworkers. They drank more, and drank stronger stuff, but they were older and they held it better than the fearless and brainless teenagers like Rob and Don farther uptown. The policing was different at this end of the route, as well.

While there were fewer parade-goers on the route in the LGD, there were more cops per block than up by where Maureen had been stationed earlier that night. They worked in larger teams, too. Where on her part of the route the cops worked in twos and threes, down here they stationed themselves in groups of six or seven. They hung almost exclusively on the back side of the route, keeping nearer the bars and drugstores and fast-food joints along that part of St. Charles than they stood to the parade. Maureen knew only the best officers worked this part of the route. This year, the two tactical squads and the gang task force were among the other experienced officers back in their blues and taking their turn with the lower part of the Uptown half of the route. Pairs of mounted officers sat atop their horses on every other block. The reasoning behind the differing personnel and strategy was simple.

While a shooting on Maureen's part of the route was an anomaly, a shooting along this section of the parade route had become an annual event, almost every shooting the result of a petty fight that had started somewhere else at some other time—back in this neighborhood, on the streets of another neighborhood, at school. Most everyone involved in the violence was a teenager or not much older. On a parade night, the guy you were beefing with was in that crowd somewhere, most likely on the back side of the route among the saints and the muses. Not only was the route a good place to make your move, it was a good place to make a statement.

Some of the fighting was rooted in school rivalries. Some of it was the result of neighborhood beefs. A lot of it was gang-related. Alcohol fueled some of it; drugs drove more. Hormones played a part, too. Knowing the players was valuable intelligence, which was why tactical and gangs got stationed here. They knew what faces to look for, and they knew the chatter on the streets. They had the best eyes for who had come to make trouble, and who had come to enjoy the festivities. They confiscated guns and made arrests on a regular basis. Hardin was smart to look for intelligence down here. Maureen hoped she could deliver it.

Once she made it to the back side of the route, it didn't take her long to find a familiar face. Half a dozen male cops leaned against a battered cruiser. With their ripped muscles and zero-body-fat frames, their flattops and their tattoos, they looked like Special Forces costuming as beat cops for the holiday. One of them was a tactical officer named Sansone. Maureen had met him when they served a warrant together once. Since then they had crossed paths on occasion around the district and most recently in the aftermath of a bloody standoff at the Tchoupitoulas Walmart.

He spotted her, slapped a buddy in the chest with the back of his hand, and pointed to her. The buddy grinned, but didn't look her way, focusing instead on the phone in his hands. As she approached the cruiser, which was parked on St. Charles in front of the Wendy's, she watched the men watch the crowd. Unless you looked at them closely, knew how to *watch* them watch the crowd, they didn't appear to be paying attention to anything beyond their phones and each other. But better examination proved that no two sets of eyes looked in the same direction. None of the officers, as far as she could tell, watched the parade.

They were like wolves, she thought. To the untrained eye they idled relaxed and at rest as they stood together in a loose pack, their breath making white clouds around their faces, but in truth they remained hyper-aware of everything around them, reading not just sights, but the sounds and the smells, the vibrations in the air. She figured Sansone had seen her long before she saw him notice her approach. They all had, and they all wondered what she was doing on their turf. She stopped in her tracks a few yards away from the group when three officers broke away from the pack and started walking at a steady but unhurried pace, shoulder to shoulder, to the neutral ground.

The three of them, somehow, created a wall, exuding a force field that extended ten feet in every direction. Maureen watched them step in between two groups of teenagers that she hadn't seen converge. The center officer shook his head and raised his arm straight up, rotating his pointed finger, telling one group to turn around and walk away. There was chatter from the group, some dissent, but the kids did what they were told. Then the other group, without being told, turned and walked away in the opposite direction. The officers watched both groups for a few moments then made their way back to their comrades at the car.

Maureen thought of Morello, of his threats and histrionics, of his cultivated air of menace and violence. Just now, the officers she had watched had been working while outnumbered three-to-one. Nobody had put a hand on anyone. No one had argued with anyone. No one had raised his voice. No one made threats. Not the cops, or the kids. No violence. No drama. Only results.

That right there, Maureen thought as she approached her fellow officers, is what I need to learn how to do. And while making it appear so effortless. That was power.

"Look at this," Sansone shouted, stepping away from the car and meeting her in the street. "The OC, down here with the riffraff." He walked toward her, his hand extended. "All the action is up your way tonight. What the fuck are y'all doing up there? Lock your shit down, rookie, or we're gonna have to do it for you."

Maureen shook his hand. She felt foolish in her coat, gloves, and knit hat while Sansone worked in the cold and rain in his shirtsleeves, and, of course, his luminous yellow vest. No one got away with not wearing one of those. Not even the rock stars like Sansone.

"So the word down this way," Sansone said, "is that you took somebody out, and that he croaked on you later, surrounded by nothing but civilians. That true?"

"He was alive," Maureen said, "when Cordts and I left him to see about the gunshots."

She wanted to explain herself, but remembered Hardin's admonitions about answering questions. She figured it applied to the entire night's events. "He's an OD, we think. Hardin probably doesn't want me talking about it. No offense."

"If Hardin's got your back," Sansone said, waving a dismissive hand, "you're good. I wouldn't worry. Trust me." He adjusted his vest. "You'd think they'd figure out how to size these fucking things. We use them all the fucking time. Nobody's got one that fits. Nobody."

"What's going on with y'all?" Maureen asked. "Hardin is curious."

"Quiet," Sansone said. "But we're watching. It's early yet for us down here."

"Those kids y'all separated?"

"That's nothing," Sansone said. "They're sticking out their chins at each other, posturing, both groups waiting for us to break it up before they have to do anything. You know, like kids in the school yard waiting for the teacher to separate them before they have to start swinging and hurt themselves. So we oblige them. May as well. We only need one of them to have one too many shots of Crown and make a mistake. Guys start throwing fists, then, next thing you know, somebody's got a gun out. Then someone *else* has a gun out. Before you can blink twice—we got bodies. That shit goes on all night. We take turns." His tone was that of someone describing kids spilling each other's soda at a birthday party. Sansone bumped her with his elbow and smiled at her. "Hardin really send you down here or you hiding out from Drayton? You in trouble again?"

Maureen shrugged, trying not to grin. "You think I'm this far from my route assignment," she asked, "without Hardin's permission?"

She looked away from Sansone, experimenting with trying to absorb the scene while projecting the outward impression she was uninterested and looking at nothing. She'd developed moderate experience with the skill, with absorbing the room, as it were, when she'd worked New York barrooms as a waitress. She'd worked to cultivate it since joining the police force. This parade business, though, was its own kind of science. It required her senses and her powers of observation to operate at a whole new level, one she hadn't hit yet. She knew that. The jump would come with practice. She lit a cigarette, offering one to Sansone. He took it and they stood together smoking, watching everything and nothing at the same time.

She didn't know Sansone very well, but he was becoming one of her favorite coworkers. It wasn't the athlete's body covered in rock star tattoos or the movie star smile, though those things didn't hurt. Here was the cop, Maureen thought, that Laine needed to put in front of her camera. No, it wasn't his looks that mattered to her. From the jump, Sansone had treated her like an equal. He loved being a cop. He loved other cops. He was natural with her, and without affect or agenda, and though she suspected it was part of his considerable charm, he treated her at times like she was cooler than him, like she was the more admirable individual of the two. While being Officer Coughlin could be a constant trial to her, she felt that being Officer Sansone was effortless, and she envied him his ease in his skin. She hoped that ease would rub off on her.

"I heard Drayton on the radio," Sansone said. "He's fucking *hot*. The prick. He's hollering for Wilburn and Cordts, too, who aren't answering him, either, by the way, but I heard him ranting and I thought, he's got *that* tone, that's gotta be Cogs. Tell me it's you. C'mon, tell me."

"Hardin sent me here," Maureen said, "for intel. He can handle Drayton."

"So where's Cordts and Wilburn then?" Sansone asked, smiling.

"I don't know where Wilburn is," Maureen said. "I think he got stuck chaperoning some amateur camera crew. Last I saw Cordts, he was baby-sitting the perp with Morello."

"So we did catch someone," Sansone said. "I had a feeling. Things had gotten awful quiet."

Shit, Maureen thought. Probably shouldn't have mentioned that. She was tempted, now that she'd given the secret away, to brag a little on being the one to run Goody down. She decided against it. "No comment."

Sansone barked out a laugh. "No comment? What the fuck does that mean?" He considered her for a few seconds. "Relax, we all know how it goes. You're hiding the perp from Drayton to protect your access to him. That's what I would do. Fucking Hardin. He hides it, but he can be a jokester. I promise you, he's got you, Wilburn, and Cordts spread all across Uptown just to fucking annoy Drayton."

"Hardin did send me here to talk to y'all," Maureen said. "At first glance, at least, it looks like it's gang business behind this shooting. He was wondering what was happening on that front down here."

"Who's the gangbangers? Victims or shooter or everybody?"

"Shooter," Maureen said. "We had multiple vics, one we specifically think was the target. The others are collateral damage. We think the shooter panicked when it came time to pull the trigger."

"A kid, then?" Sansone said. "These spray jobs that catch the bystanders, if they're not drive-bys, they're kids who can't handle themselves. What're we working with? A baby gangbanger making his bones?"

"He goes by Goody on the street," Maureen said, nodding, deciding on the spot to trust Sansone, or more to the point, that Hardin would. "He's fifteen, but was already J-Street by way of family, so I don't think he needed an audition. The main victim is a middle school music teacher. Two people who know him told me he's got no gang connection. Not by past association or family. Which makes me think he was chosen at random. Or that it was a mistake, that the shooter thought he was hitting someone else. But the teacher was shot at close range, and the shooter yelled 'Three-N-G' before he pulled the trigger. So we're wondering what that was about."

"If your shooter is part of the J-Street family, then he's trying to get *us* going after Three-N-G by calling out their name," Sansone said. "That's my first guess. They like to think they're clever. Some of them are, most of them not so much."

Sansone raised his chin at the crowd gathered on the neutral ground. "We got Three-N-G out here tonight. This is a prime spot for them. They're out here every night. Maybe we can make something happen, get them to give us some info."

Maureen looked at the cluster of young men Sansone had pointed out to her.

She noticed for the first time that many of the kids, the ones standing in groups back from the crowds, weren't watching the parades, either. They wore no beads or funny hats or blinking souvenirs. They had no stuffed animals or plastic cups jammed into their coat pockets. They watched, Maureen noticed after a moment, only one another, and their focus was intense, though they pretended not to be paying attention to anything in particular. Their attitude and affect wasn't very different from that of the police officers watching them.

Sansone and his coworkers watched the groups of kids watch one another. Everyone stood around for hours, posturing and gesturing and waiting to see what would happen next, or if anything would happen at all. The parade was the reason they were gathered together on St. Charles Avenue instead of going about their separate nights in their different pockets of the city, but the Muses parade itself held no interest for any of them.

"You're sure your suspect is J-Street?" Sansone asked.

"I know him, from another thing I did over the summer," Maureen said. "He was straight J-Street then. His uncle was in."

"You said the uncle *was* J-Street? As in past tense."

"Bobby Scales."

Sansone rocked back on his heels. "Oh, that dude. Yes, he is in fact dead. Man, he wasn't even twenty-five. And how old is the nephew?"

"Fifteen."

Sansone shook his head. "Fucking figures. Kids, it's always kids in the middle of this shit these days. I'd spend less time chasing teenagers if I coached high school football like my brother."

He gestured at another cluster of seven teenage boys. They stood maybe ten yards from the 3NG crew. "We got J-Street out here, too. Everybody's out every night there's a parade." He sighed. "We got Fourth Ward boys out here. We got some Harvey Hustlers from over the bridge. They're far from home, but it is Mardi Gras. That might be trouble, we'll have to see. Those guys over there? That's Young Melph Mafia. We got one-tenners, or one-tenner wannabes at least, I'm not sure, under the overpass bugging the homeless people. Them and another few dozen kids from across the city. They're still at that age where the boys and girls chase each other around. It's like a fucking middle school field day over there. Kids everywhere."

Maureen gestured at a group of tall young men in matching gray tracksuits standing close together, laughing. Each held a plastic water bottle.

One of them wore a small drawstring bag on his back that bulged with a bottle of liquor. "What about them? Who're those guys?"

Sansone laughed. "Them? That's the Edna Karr basketball team. Maybe some of them are track. The Karr marching band is in the parade. They come out to watch their buddies in the band, to flirt with the cheerleaders and the flag twirlers."

"I don't know my schools yet," Maureen said. "Not all of them."

"You a cheerleader in high school, Cogs?" Sansone asked with a smile. "You wave a flag for the band?"

"What do you think?" Maureen asked. "I ran track. I didn't wave anybody's flag."

"Too right," Sansone said. "We watch them, too, the good kids. If they leave in a hurry, that's a warning sign. Like how you know there's a hawk around when the other birds disappear."

"A warning sign?" Maureen said. "We've got half a dozen gangs in a six-block area. How much more warning do we need? Why don't we scatter them? Get them out of here?"

"Chase them where?" Sansone asked. "The next block up or down, where they're agitated and out of place and the next cop's problem? Back into the neighborhood, where we can't watch them?" He shrugged. "Besides. For now, everyone is behaving. Most of the time, everyone behaves themselves just enough for us to leave them be. There's no reason to upset that balance. They know the line, they're good at walking it, and the ones that don't, usually it's not us that have to teach them. Nobody wants that much of our attention. And believe me, *you* don't want to be the reason something starts out here.

"For the most part, even here, the route polices itself. Let it. We're here to relieve the pressure, not add to it. Simple physics. The balloon can stretch, as long as it doesn't pop. That's all we care about."

Maureen hitched up her gun belt. "So do you really think any of these guys are worth talking to?"

"About what happened up by you?" Sansone winced and shrugged. He sighed. He narrowed his eyes at the 3NG crew. "You want, I could get a couple of those characters over here, ask 'em a few questions."

"What're they gonna tell me?" Maureen asked.

"They're gonna tell you lies," Sansone said. She got the impression he was regretting his earlier offer to speak to one of them. She understood. If they had their shooter in custody, why excite the atoms he was responsible for? He added, "But it lets you get a look at them."

"I can see them from here," Maureen said. "And I don't want to upset your environment. Seems pretty mellow, actually."

"It is," Sansone said. "For now."

# 27

As he talked to her, Maureen watched Sansone focus on a young man in the 3NG group, eighteen or nineteen, talking to a group of half a dozen girls. Sansone threw a glance back at his fellow officers by the car, alerting them to what and whom he was watching. Maureen saw them notice. The pack loosened a tiny bit, each officer giving himself a clear running lane should they need to charge. She was convinced that were the scene played back on video, you'd never see any of them move a muscle.

"Yeah, honestly," Sansone said, as if he'd forgotten she was there for a minute. "I don't know if I see the point of talking. I know these guys, what they do, who they run with. They know I know, but they're not admitting to anything. Not without leverage, and we don't have any of that. We'll learn more letting them be. They'll tell us what's up." He held out a hand, trembled it. "There'd be a buzz in the air if something big was going down. That's why I don't know what to tell you. I'm not feeling it." He shrugged. "That's a good thing."

As she listened to Sansone, Maureen watched the same kid that he did. He stood out from the others, and it was clear to Maureen that he meant to. He wore diamonds in his ears bigger than any she'd ever own. They sparkled in the colored lights of the passing floats. He wore a small diamond cross around his neck, against his camel-colored cashmere sweater. Over that he wore a rust-colored down vest that had cost plenty more than the seventy-dollar fluorescent vest she wore. Baggy cords. Brand-new boots. Everything matched, and everything he and his friends wore looked fresh off the rack. They looked like they'd stepped out of a magazine or catalog shoot. The young man looked, Maureen had to admit, very good. They all did, his whole crew, but he shone brighter, and it wasn't jewelry that made the difference.

She noted that he wore a camouflage bandanna around his head, which marked him as 3NG, the knot tied in the front. His buddies wore bandannas, too, but theirs were tied around a wrist or an ankle, where it was semi-hidden by a pant leg or a shirtsleeve. It occurred to Maureen that Goody had not been wearing a camo bandanna. The 3NG shout, she decided in agreement with Sansone, had been a ruse, a diversion for the witnesses to send the cops in the wrong direction. Deciding what Goody wasn't, though, Maureen thought, didn't help much when trying to determine why he had done what he did, and what kind of retaliation his actions might inspire.

"What about the J-Street guys?" she asked. "Would any of them give something up? Considering we got one of their own in the back of a police car?"

"I'm not seeing it," Sansone said, distracted. "They'll disavow him, no matter if he's actually in with them or not." He turned to her. "He may not even be in with J-Street anymore, no matter who his uncle was. There's been leadership changes since Scales is gone. Goody might not be welcome anymore."

"Can we find any of this out?" Maureen asked.

"That's what I'm saying. They won't tell us, either way."

This kid here, Maureen thought, the one Sansone watched, noting the bandanna on his head again, was the only one with a crown. Maureen wondered for a moment why the king was the only one talking to any of the girls. He didn't seem to favor one of them in particular over the others. Then she saw the reason. His 3NG buddies were busy watching the J-Street guys watch him. Only the king has a harem, never the king's guard. Away from the castle, the king needed protecting.

And the girls? They knew everybody saw them, noticed them, and stared at them, the gangbangers and the regular boys, the basketball team, the cops, too, and they played their part to the hilt. Hips rocking, hair flipping, chests stuck out. They charged the air around them like downed wires in a puddle and they knew it. Dangerous. Fire starters. Sirens. Dragons. Maureen could feel the hormones shaking the ground under her feet like a passing drum line.

"You think these Three-N-G guys know about the shooting?" Maureen asked.

"Oh, I guarantee it," Sansone said. "Every one of them. I mean, they know that it happened. I don't know that they know who did it. I don't know that they care, especially since the guy who got shot didn't belong to any of them. I have not seen a ripple in the night's proceedings. Nobody's reacting to it. Not Three-N-G. Not J-Street. Not the others. I'm thinking your boy may have been freelancing, that this was a personal grudge."

"What do I tell Hardin?" Maureen asked, considering Sansone's suggestion of a grudge. "I don't want to go back to him with nothing. In less than an hour, he's got to prep the DC and the superintendent on the case. I don't want to tell him to give them the all clear if the violence isn't over."

"What you got by coming here is not nothing," Sansone said. "You ask me, no news is the best possible news there is. Tell Hardin that he's dealing with an isolated incident, a case of mistaken identity, probably, if you can't find a connection between Goody and the victim, and if you can, it's something personal, and that we caught the guy who did it and now it's over. Unless Goody's gonna confess, we don't need him anymore. Let Drayton lock him up and be done with it." He spread his hands. "Look, Cogs. There was a shooting, and we caught the guy. Enjoy it. Bask in it. Fuck, dude. Good work."

"Except for the OD John Doe I let die in the street," Maureen said.

"Can't win 'em all," Sansone said.

"C'mon," Maureen said, "that's harsh. Even for you. That's like, Morello harsh."

"I'm just saying, that little girl, that teacher, that grandmother, all they were doing was going to the parade. That guy in the street, he did it to himself. It's a shame, but it's not on you, that one. Let it go. Don't carry him around with you."

# 28

"Before I go back to my route assignment," Maureen said to Sansone, "I want to ask you about something, while I've got you and the other tactical and gang guys here."

"Go for it."

"So there's this TV crew out on the route," Maureen said, "well, video or Internet or whatever, it's a long story."

"Nobody takes their tits out up here," Sansone said. "They hafta go to the Quarter for that bullshit, you told them that, right?"

"They're not looking for that kind of material so much," Maureen said. "It's a documentary on a new kind of drug. Something called flakka."

"Never heard of it," Sansone said.

"It's like bath salts," Maureen said. "Or mojo. But ten times worse."

"Damn. And it's here? Of course it's here. Why wouldn't it be here?"

"The producer on the film crew," Maureen said, "she's telling me this drug may be what killed the kid on the route."

"I thought Hardin didn't want you talking about it."

"Hear me out," Maureen said. "This producer woman, Laine Daniels, she thinks we're looking at a big problem with this thing. You guys spend a lot of time on the gangs, kicking in doors. Have you heard anything about it?"

"Okay, okay," Sansone said. "You know what . . ." Maureen could tell something was coming together in his head. "We heard the radio calls while that guy was running around freaking out, trashing shit and hitting people and whatever. We're listening, we're laughing, except for Achee over there." He gestured to a tall officer with salt-and-pepper hair leaning against the cruiser. "He's tuned in to the details. Turns out, the whole thing sounds familiar to him. Something about an eviction he was in on or something." Sansone straightened up. "He can tell you better. Yo! Henry! C'mere."

Henry Achee walked over, taking his time, looking around. The officers on this part of the route, Maureen noticed, had their own pace, their own speed. Not quite languid, but deliberate. It wasn't tiredness, and it certainly wasn't laziness. They didn't want to miss anything that mattered while rushing to deal with something that didn't. Achee nodded at Maureen. She didn't recognize him.

"Achee," Sansone said, "Officer Maureen Coughlin. She works the Sixth. She's new. Kinda. Cogs, Officer Henry Achee." He and Maureen shook hands. "What was the story with that crazy drug casualty you had the other week?"

Maureen saw the recognition flash across Achee's face. "That was you," he said, "that handled the OD up the route."

"That was me," Maureen said. "He died."

"I heard," Achee said. "Rotten fucking luck."

"You were saying earlier," Sansone said, "that what happened with him sounded like something you had. Tell Coughlin about it."

"Fucked up," Achee said, shaking his head, "is what it was."

"Can you elaborate, please?" Sansone said. "We know it was fucked up."

"Last week, we were backing up the sheriff on a problem eviction. In the Upper Nine. Really out of the way. Somebody said something about weapons in the house, so we went with. Anyway, there was nothing to that, but there was this couple, and they were bat-shit insane. This is at, like, six in the morning. They'd barricaded the front door with the fridge, drug it from the kitchen, but they forgot about the back door, so we went in that way. Wasn't even locked. They never heard us coming, and we made noise. Both of them are stark naked, and fucking emaciated, the two of them. Covered in this greasy sweat. The house fucking stank.

"When they finally realized we were really there, that we weren't hallucinations, they literally started trying to climb the walls. Afraid of us not like we're cops, but like we're *monsters*. The girl, she was like someone had stuck a live wire up a wet cat's ass. All nails and teeth and we couldn't get her calmed down. The dude just threw himself through the front window, which was closed, of course. Cut himself to shreds. We thought he might bleed out in the street. I couldn't believe he got enough force to get through the glass. The girl, we finally had to tase her. Fucking embarrassing." Achee shook his head. "Hitting a naked, ninety-pound woman with a Taser. But she grabbed some scissors, started threatening to jab her own eyes out, and we needed to end it before shit got worse. Took six people to get the bleeding guy into the ambulance. Six. When we were done, there was blood on the walls, literally."

"Did anyone ever find out," Maureen asked, "what they were high on?"

Achee shrugged. "She went in one ambulance, he went in another, and off they went. We didn't do a search of the place. It wasn't a drug bust. We were the backup, the muscle. Evictions are sheriff's department business. You *know* they didn't follow up on anything. I didn't think much about it until today, when I heard about your guy up the way. You think it was the same shit? Sounds like it to me."

"Could be," Maureen said. She pulled her phone from her pocket. She found Wilburn's number and sent him a text: *Are you with the camera crew? I need a photo of the John Doe.*

"That makes four of these cases in the past couple of weeks," she said. "The Quarter, the CBD, the Upper Nine, and now, if you count tonight's John Doe, up here on the parade route. That sounds like a problem." Wilburn's answer came. *One sec.* "Bear with me a minute."

"We're here all night," Achee said.

Less than a minute later Maureen got a message from a number she didn't know with an area code that wasn't New Orleans. In the message was a clear photo of the John Doe's face. Except for the feverish sheen of sweat on his face, he looked for all the world like he was fast asleep. The words under the photo read: *You're welcome, L.*

Maureen enlarged the photo. "You guys work with the gang unit, you know all the big players, right?"

"Big and small," Sansone said.

She passed her phone to him. "We got nothing on this kid. I'm hoping he's local. We'd like to find his people and we need a place to start looking. He look familiar to you? Anything you can give us?"

Sansone's eyebrows jumped up his forehead. "Well, shit." He touched the screen, enlarging the face again. He turned the phone to Achee. "Who's that look like to you?"

"It *looks* like Benji Allen," Achee said. He shook his head. "If Benji starved himself for a couple weeks."

Sansone checked the picture again, and something settled in his face this time. "But look at that, Henry, that weird mole on his left temple. That's Benji fucking Allen. Fuck." He handed Maureen back her phone. "We've been wondering what happened to him." He directed a stare at the 3NG crew. "So have they. He was one of theirs." He pointed at the J-Street crew. "They been wondering, too, and waiting for Three-N-G to blame them. So have we, to tell you the truth. Cogs, you solvin' mysteries left and right tonight."

"Here's a mystery for you," Maureen said. "Now what do we fucking do? Should we tell these guys that their missing member is dead, and that it wasn't the other gang that killed him?"

"That's heavy news for Mardi Gras time," Sansone said. "Maybe we let that go."

"Think of the next of kin, too," Achee said. "They should hear about this from us."

Maureen took out her notebook. "Speaking of. I'll bring this back to

Hardin." The department would send someone to tell the family tomor-row morning. "You guys know the next of kin? Any of the family?"

Both men were quiet for a long moment. Sansone spoke up. "Yeah, actually. We do know some family of his. We went to them not long ago asking after Benji. We wanted to find him or find out what happened to him before Mardi Gras, didn't want any extra fuel to burn down here on the route with these guys out here on top of one another." He glanced at Achee.

"I guess they were telling us the truth when they said they had no idea what happened to him. Go figure." He turned back to Maureen. "He's got a sister, and an older brother. The sister had a kid maybe a year ago, a little less, maybe. I don't know who the father is, but I don't think he's around much. The girl, Alisha, I think, moved in with the brother. They live a little farther uptown, on Harmony Street, above St. Charles. Brother drives a tow truck for the city, I think. I forget the house number, but I can get it."

"No need," Maureen said. "I know the place you're talking about. Alisha was the one who gave us the shooter."

Sansone shook his head. "This flakka shit you're talking about killed him in, what, ten days, two weeks? What the fuck?"

# 29

"Alisha and her brother must know the shooter," Achee said, "if he went to their house on Harmony Street after to try and hide out."

"But Alisha and her brother wanted no part of him," Maureen said. "They dimed him to us, in fact."

"So they *really* don't like him," Sansone said.

"And you say the shooter is this young cat, Goody Curtis," said Achee, "who you pulled out from under the house. Where does the teacher fit in?"

"I don't think he does," Maureen said. "Based on info I got at the scene from his girlfriend and other witnesses, I think he's a stranger to that whole crew. I'm convinced he was a mistake."

"What else do you know about this flakka?" Sansone asked.

"Not much," Maureen said. "I'm only hearing about it for the first time tonight. It got started in Florida. The film crew I was telling you about, their producer, she's my source on this. She said it's coming this way along the Gulf Coast, though it looks like we've been dealing with it already."

"You got a picture of the teacher on that phone, too?" Sansone asked.

"His name is Cordell," Maureen said. "He lives in the neighborhood around where he got shot. The bartender at Verret's knows him." She searched her messages for the photo that Dakota had sent. She pulled it up, showed it to Sansone. "You recognize him?"

"Nope," Sansone said after a beat. "But I would've said different had you not told me who he was first. I have an idea. Can I borrow your phone for a sec?"

"Yeah, of course," Maureen said. She handed it to him.

Sansone took a couple of steps toward the 3NG crew. "Kenny," he called out.

The kid with the bandanna on his head didn't look over, but he stopped talking. The girls looked at the ground. Kenny's boys didn't move. "Kenny Polite, come here for a minute."

Sansone held up Maureen's phone for Kenny to see. "I need you to settle a bet for me. It'll just take a second. One quick question. I'll owe you a favor, a small one."

Kenny relaxed. He smiled, touched his top lip with the knuckle of his index finger. He gazed at the girls from under his perfect eyebrows. They watched him, asking without any words what he intended to do about this cop who was interrupting their flirting. Kenny turned on his heel and eased himself loose-limbed in Sansone's direction, his hand fixed under his nose.

Maureen watched Sansone, who smiled as Kenny went through his motions, and Achee, who did not smile at anything as he watched everyone else.

"Sansone, man," Kenny said, "you see what I got happening over here. You know how I do. You got no one else you can ask this question?"

"You love it," Sansone said, with a smile as always. "Don't bullshit me. You love looking important to the Five-Oh in front of those girls. I'm doing your situation a favor." He turned and gestured at Maureen. "This is Officer Coughlin. Y'all should get acquainted. She's going to be running the Sixth District in no time flat."

Kenny nodded in deference to Maureen, lowering his eyes. She said nothing, did nothing to return the gesture. Kenny certainly didn't expect anything from her. But he was a good diplomat, she figured. Don't make a new enemy if it can be avoided, which it could, for now.

"Officer Coughlin and I have a wager," Sansone said, "and we need your knowledge of the neighborhood celebrities to settle it." He brought up the picture of Cordell on the phone and turned the device so Kenny could see it. "Who is that?"

Kenny laughed at the sight of the picture then leaned in closer for a better look at it. He stroked his chin. "Looks like Dee Harris to me. Not the best picture." His forehead furrowed, though his voice stayed jovial. "How you get a picture of that m'fucker in a *tie*, though? Looks like he in court, with that tie on, and that nice shirt, that's a good color, but Dee never been to court. Never been arrested even." He smiled at Sansone widely, teeth as white as Sansone's or Laine's. Here was another guy who'd do well in front of Laine's camera. "Not that y'all ain't tried." He looked at Maureen. "Y'all always after Dee, y'all think he's a bad man, but Dee ain't like that."

"We know how he do," Sansone said. "We'll leave it at that."

"Does Dee teach middle school?" Maureen asked.

Kenny barked out a laugh. "She *is* new, ain't she?" he said to Sansone. "Dee ain't no teacher, that's for damn sure."

"Answer me this," Maureen said, "does Dee have a white girlfriend?"

"Now how the fuck you know that?" Kenny asked.

"'Bout my height, brown hair?" Maureen asked.

"Who the fuck *are* you?" Kenny asked, gawking at Maureen. He turned to Sansone. "The fuck she's new."

Maureen watched the realization of what was happening dawn across Kenny's handsome, unlined face. "Let me see that picture again. Yeah, yeah, the haircut ain't exactly right, but damn, if this ain't Dee, then it look a lot like him." He tapped the screen with the finger he'd been holding under his nose. "A lot." The playfulness he'd exuded since Sansone had called his name had left him. "That's who got shot tonight, isn't it? Up on Washington. Y'all think they was after Dee and they got this teacher instead. That's why you showing Dee's picture around."

"We said nothing of the sort," Maureen said. "But why don't you tell us why you think someone would be out gunning for Dee?"

"*I'm* not telling you that," Kenny said. "Y'all are telling *me* that, showing this picture, asking these questions. I didn't know a thing about anyone gunnin' for Dee. Until now, that is."

Sansone stepped close to Kenny. Maureen saw his boys tense, but they didn't move. She couldn't imagine they'd try anything against Sansone, not with her and Achee standing right there and five other cops across the street watching their every move. Not without the okay from Kenny.

"I need you to pay attention to what I'm saying," Sansone told Kenny, his voice lower than it had been. He was done playing, too. Kenny had picked up on the change. He lowered his head to listen, his lips pursed, his hands clasped behind his back.

Maureen marveled at Sansone's composure, at how well he handled Kenny, doing and saying nothing to embarrass him or intimidate him in front of the girls, or his crew, or the other police officers. As a result, he had Kenny's patience and respect, which in turn gave Sansone a shot at getting through to him, at least for tonight.

"The guy who shot the teacher," Sansone said, "we got him. We picked him up a while ago. So there's no reason to go out looking for him. Dee is in no danger tonight, not from that guy. And while I'm not going to discuss the details of a police matter with you, I will tell you, as a courtesy to you being Dee's friend, that we don't think anybody else put him up to it. So I don't want you to worry. I don't want you to feel like you or your friends need to do anything to protect Dee. That's what I'm telling you. If you hear about somebody gunning for Dee, they're not. It's old news. It's *already* over. You understand?"

Kenny nodded, lips pressed together, his expression serious.

"I need to know you understand," Sansone said. "Peace on the route is priority number one. Everyone needs to have a nice, calm, fun Mardi Gras. You hear me? You know how *we* do. The regular folk need to be able to enjoy their holiday."

"I hear you," Kenny said. "I do. I mean, I don't know what you want *me* to do, I'm just me, one person, you know. But I hear you."

"I want you," Sansone said, "to keep doing exactly what you been doing. Hang with your boys, talk to those girls, have a drink, enjoy the parades, give the J-Street boys their space. Keep doing what you been doing is what I'm asking from you."

"I can do that," Kenny said. "I can."

"I know you can," Sansone said. "Off with you. Those girls are getting bored."

Kenny gave Maureen a last, long glance, committing her face to memory, and headed back to his friends.

"There you go," Sansone said, turning to Maureen. "Goody thought Cordell was Dee, a Three-N-G soldier, and tried to take him out. Shot the wrong guy."

"Shot a bunch of the wrong people," Maureen said.

Sansone nodded. "Roger that."

Maureen giggled to herself. Sansone was shocked to hear it. "What the fuck was that? I've never heard you make *that* noise."

"Lack of sleep. Lack of food. Really, I can't believe how well this is working out. I'm so relieved. We got motive and everything."

"We got motive up to a point," Sansone said, cautioning her. "We know Goody shot Cordell because he thought he was shooting Dee Harris. But we don't know why Goody wanted to kill Dee Harris in the first place."

"Of course, of course," Maureen said. "Wow. I was really happy for a few seconds there." She sighed. "But that can wait, right? For tonight, Harris is safe from Goody. Goody is safe from revenge and he's not doing any more shooting tonight. Kenny will listen to you and keep everyone cool. No more violence, right?"

"Not from this situation here," Sansone said, waving his hand over the scene in front of him. "No, I wouldn't think so. But I can't, like, promise you no one else gets hurt tonight. That's impossible."

"But you'd be surprised?" Maureen said.

"Yeah, I would. This just doesn't feel like one of those nights."

"So I'm not making a mistake going back to Hardin with the full package—an arrest, a partial motive, moves to prevent further violence and escalation—in time for his press conference."

Sansone took a few seconds to think about it. "I think you're good doing that. I would, if I were you. I'd feel pretty okay with doing that."

Maureen clapped her hands. "And on top of it all we did the good work while Drayton is spinning his fucking wheels. I love it. I love Mardi Gras." She felt her phone buzzing her pocket. Probably Hardin, she thought. She *was* cutting it close with the press conference. She answered. "Sarge, I got good news."

"I am walking now to the press conference," Hardin said, "and I don't know what I'm telling Skinner. What've you got?"

"Looks like the shooting was an isolated incident, a mistaken identity. Cordell looks a lot like a local player named Dee Harris. We think he was Goody's target. Looks like Cordell, even has a white girlfriend that looks like Susan."

"And what's the beef between Harris and Goody?" Hardin asked. "Do we have that?"

"That we haven't figured out," Maureen said. Dispatch came over the radio, so she turned the volume down to better hear Hardin. "But with Goody in custody, that puts an end to it until after Mardi Gras, at the very least. Probably for much longer, considering Goody's record. He may have seen the last of the streets. I've been talking to Sansone, and he's talked to the neighborhood representatives, you could say. He's got a good feeling about things."

From the corner of her eye, Maureen could see Sansone moving away from her with his head down, listening to his radio. She tried to watch him, but he moved into her blind spot.

"I got a name on the OD, too," Maureen said. "Benji Allen." She waited for Hardin's reaction. She was pretty proud of herself for getting that info, too, and wanted Hardin's praise. But Hardin said nothing. "Allen was J-Street, too, like Goody. He went missing a couple of weeks ago." She waited again. Nothing. Was Hardin even listening to her? "Warrant squad was looking for him. It was Allen's sister who called in Goody from Harmony Street. Dee Harris is Three-N-G, but this shooting, according to the reaction Sansone isn't seeing on the route, appears to be more a personal thing than gang business. Goody may have been trying to start one, but there's no J-Street and Three-N-G war. Not tonight, anyway."

"All right, that's good for now," Hardin said, distracted. "Good work, Coughlin. I'll let Drayton make the arrest so he can jerk off to himself on TV at the press conference. I owe him that favor. We've got half a parade to go yet. Get back on your route assignment. I'll have Drayton send Cordts to meet you there. Let's try to get back to normal, such as it is, and finish out the night strong."

"Ten-four," Maureen said, but she could tell Hardin had already hung up. She frowned at her phone. "What was that, Sarge? I got everything you wanted and more."

Sansone tugged hard at her vest. "What the fuck?" she snapped, jerking away from him.

"We got shit to do," Sansone said.

"Hardin wants me back at my spot," Maureen said.

She watched two mounted officers gallop past, down St. Charles toward the I-10 overpass. A few people in the crowd turned away from the parade to watch them. She watched Sansone's crew drop their heads to better hear their radios.

"We got to go, Cogs," Sansone said. "We got a ten fifty-five under the Ten. Gotta let the air out of it before it becomes a thing. New mission. I'm sure Hardin will understand."

"Fuck me," Maureen said. A 10-55 was an officer in need of assistance.

"Let's not overreact," Sansone said. "It's Code One, so it's not life-threatening." He frowned, shaking his head. "Something's not right."

"What?" Maureen asked.

"I think it's Wilburn who put out the fifty-five," Sansone said. "Didn't you say something about him and a camera crew? I think they're getting robbed under the overpass. That's according to the original nine-one-one call, but now he's saying something else. All right, what I hear is something approaching clusterfuck status. Let's go sort it out, you and me. Stay close. Do what I do. We're about to be outnumbered, by a lot. We don't want things getting explosive if we can help it."

# 30

Maureen jogged with Sansone to the intersection of St. Charles Avenue and Calliope Street, a few more officers now striding along several yards behind them, traffic running over the six lanes of the highway echoing above their heads as they moved under the overpass.

As the parade rolled under the highway, the surrounding concrete scrambled the sounds of it into a disorienting and blurry echo: the rumble of the tractors pulling the floats, the screaming of the crowd, and the distorted, booming pop music combined into a vibrating cloud Maureen could feel in her chest. She couldn't imagine what a full-throated drum line would sound like under here. The air was sticky, and it stank of cigarettes and corner-store cigars, of clothes wet with rainwater and sweat, of spilled rotgut alcohol and filthy tractor exhaust. Cologne. Perfume. Hair spray. The crowd was huge, young, and rowdy. Partying teenagers surrounded her. Maureen felt like she had crashed a party at a giant club. None of the partiers cared that a sizable group of police officers had come running. It wasn't for them that the police had come, and they knew it. It wasn't out of the ordinary for the police to be around while they were try-ing to have a good time. This intersection wasn't where the trouble was happening.

Maureen stepped up onto a curb beside Sansone and looked around, searching for an anomaly in the crowd, a glitch like she had seen when Benji Allen had come sprinting her way up St. Charles Avenue earlier that night, punching bystanders as he ran.

Under the highway in both directions was a series of parking lots. The city had long-standing plans to fence them in and turn them into pay lots, but that hadn't come close to happening yet. So, in recent years, the lots had become a long-term homeless encampment complete with dirty tents and scrounged furniture. The campers stood at every traffic light along both sides of Calliope Street, asking with cardboard signs for money and prayers and help. Before the holiday got into full swing, which meant before the tourists arrived in droves for the street parties and parades, the city sent charity and health workers and then the police department to clear out the campers and haul whatever they left behind to the dump.

With the encampments broken up and the homeless scattered into the nearby neighborhoods on parade nights, the parking lots closest to St. Charles were filled with parade-goers and their folding chairs and makeshift bars and barbecue grills. The lots behind those were a free-for-all, herds of kids stampeding across them like bison on the Great Plains. Mau-reen and Sansone now stood on the edge of this sea of kids, all of them laughing and running at and away from one another, many of them hold-ing phones at their ears. The vibrations that Sansone had talked about radiated from them. Simple physics, he had called it. Maureen felt as if she were watching two hundred bouncing atoms, powerfully attracted to and forcibly repelled from one another. The charge they created in the air was tangible, undeniable. She could feel it on her skin. Sansone seemed to be reading her mind.

"Yeah," he said, "I don't like the feel of it either. It's not them that's the problem, though, these kids. They're just reacting to what's in the air. They hardly even know what they're doing."

"Those other guys will follow us into the crowd, right?" Maureen asked. "There are four of them."

"So that would make six among two hundred," Sansone said. "What's the difference, numbers like this? The more cops we bring into the crowd, the more danger and trouble we're communicating to the crowd. What those four can do is watch our backs."

"If something happens to us deep in that crowd," Maureen said, "they won't get to us in time."

"But *they* can," Sansone said, pointing at the mounted officers.

The mounted officers had stayed outside the crowd, watching everything from Calliope Street, from the wings of the big show, seated high and upright atop their saddles. Maureen had figured they'd go riding through the crowd ahead of everyone else, cutting a wide swath to the endangered officer, like the cavalry. It was a powerful image to think about, but it was a dumb idea to put into action, she realized. The reality, the end result of that ride would be a dozen trampled seventh graders, which was exactly the kind of damage that no one wanted.

Right now, the true advantage of the mounted officers, Maureen realized, was that high up on those horses they could see everything, the edges of the crowd and everything that was happening deep within it. One of the officers, a short, thick-thighed woman, keyed her radio mic and spoke. Maureen listened as the report came over the radio.

It was indeed Wilburn who had called in the 10-55. From the tone of the mounted officer's voice, though, she felt his report had been a touch hasty. She described an ongoing incident involving a homeless person, a bunch of teenagers, a couple of women, Wilburn, and what looked like a camera crew. One person was now down on the pavement and that person was not Officer Wilburn. Other than some arguing, as far as she could see, not much else was happening. The main problem seemed to be the teens' refusal to disperse. And the flood of kids was creeping closer to the incident, in which case Wilburn could be overrun if something set them off.

The camera crew was the problem, Maureen thought. There'd be no getting rid of the crowd of kids as long as they thought a TV camera was pointed at them.

She listened as the dispatch officer advised the others on foot to proceed with caution. The mounted officers would track their progress through the crowd. They'd advise and assist as necessary.

"Before we go into the crowd," Sansone said, "a few things to remember. First, they're *kids*. So they're going to be stupid and annoying. Plus, it's a parade and there's way more of them than us so they're feeling pretty full of themselves already, and whatever happened back there with Wilburn has them even more fired up. We don't care about any of that. None of it. You're gonna hear a stream of shit from them, about being a cop, about being a woman, about being white, and various combinations of the three. Ignore it. All of it.

"What we cannot have is an additional incident. We cannot have escalation. *You* do not want to end up in the middle of something that could have been avoided, where your fellow officers have to come to your rescue, using force and putting everyone around us in danger. We can't be down here guns drawn because you couldn't take hearing 'Suck my dick, white bitch' from a drunk fourteen-year-old."

"Like it would be the first time," Maureen said.

"That's the Mardi Gras spirit," Sansone said.

"Just one thing," Maureen said. "I have to ask. Why don't we go around them instead of through?"

"And cede territory?" Sansone said. "Nonsense. We can't send that kind of message. Believe me, they would notice. We can't give them *too* much permission, either. We're the police. We go where we want, when we want, and they get out of the way."

"Gotcha," Maureen said.

"Hands at your sides," Sansone said. "Eyes front."

"Yes, indeed."

"Shall we, then?"

"I thought you'd never ask," Maureen said.

# 31

It wasn't every day, Maureen thought as they moved through the crowd, that she heard "Fuck the police" from someone whose voice hadn't changed yet, or "Drop dead, white bitch" from someone who was obviously a young girl.

But it didn't take Maureen long to realize that the catcalls and insults were not really for her. The kids were talking to, were performing for, the other kids, like birds chirping their boasts and claims to territory. As if the cops were cats who couldn't climb trees, Maureen and Sansone didn't concern them; they didn't expect or even want a reaction. They were showing off for one another. The boys trying to impress the girls with their consequence-free braggadocio, the girls proving that they could be as tough and fearless, as daring and profane, as the boys. The groups of kids even moved in murmurations like starlings in flight—swirling, twisting, and gliding this way and that, the flock changing direction simultaneously as if of one mind as they ran out of the path of the slow-walking police officers who clearly had no intention of chasing them. All the time chirping and chattering, shrieking and shouting and laughing.

They found Wilburn in a heated but respectful discussion with two well-dressed teenagers, the three of them bathed in the white light of Cortez's camera, a microphone on a pole nearby. The situation didn't appear to be an argument as much as the teenagers were vigorously complaining and Wilburn, arms crossed, was marshaling his last reserves of patience as he listened to them. He was, Maureen thought, observing the same rules of parade police physics that Sansone had mentioned. He was letting the pressure release rather than adding to it in defense of his own ego.

Laine observed the scene from a few feet away. Donna sat on a curb across the parking lot, her long legs splayed out in front of her, leather jacket zipped to her neck, smoking a long white cigarette and looking away from the action, dejected. A shopping cart piled high with clothes, newspapers, aluminum cans, and God knows what else sat off to the other side. A yellow boa that had been wrapped loosely around the handle drooped to the ground. Alone on a curb, as distant from the center group as Donna was, hands cuffed behind his back, sat a shirtless, long-haired homeless man. Maureen knew it was impossible, but, the way they were sitting, Donna and the homeless man looked quite a lot like a sparring couple that had been separated by cooler-headed friends.

"This could be fucking anything," Sansone said.

"Could be a lot worse," Maureen said. "No blood, no bullets."

"Let me call it in, I guess."

"Doesn't look like anyone's hurt," Maureen said, as Sansone told Dispatch that the scene was under control. She felt disappointment as she watched the mounted officers trot away. She wasn't sure what she felt she had missed, or what she had wanted them to do. Something about seeing horses, maybe just the sheer strangeness of the sight on city streets excited her.

"I like Wilburn," Sansone said, clipping his mic back on his shoulder. "But a fifty-five for this?"

"Do any of us show up if he calls in anything else?" Maureen asked.

"That's a good point," Sansone said. He scratched at the stubble on his chin.

"This the camera crew you were telling me about?" Sansone asked.

"It is indeed," Maureen said. "That's the producer, the redhead behind the camera crew. The guys filming, they're local. It's an Internet documentary of some sort. About what I'm not exactly sure. It's a long story."

To Maureen's surprise, Sansone said, "Cool."

"Do you recognize the guys Wilburn is talking to?" she asked. "I don't know them from the neighborhood."

One of them, the taller one, wore an oversize purple polo shirt and low-slung jeans with fat white stitching and a white belt. He had thick-framed glasses, white, and long braids that he wore tied up in loose bunches at the back of his head. His friend, a light-eyed Creole kid in a flat-brimmed Saints cap, wore black tracksuit bottoms and a tight long-sleeved T-shirt, muscles rippling under the gray fabric. He had a thick hooded sweatshirt tied around his waist.

"Those boys? You mean do I recognize them from the gang detail?" He shook his head. "They don't bang, those two. No way."

"I didn't think so," Maureen said.

He spied Donna. "She part of this? She looks very L.A. to me."

"She's the, uh, she's the on-camera talent, I guess," Maureen said. "She does the interviews."

"Well, we're here, right?" Sansone said, hitching up his gun belt. "Let's see what's up. Maybe the TV people will make us famous."

As they headed Wilburn's way, an NOPD Explorer rolled up, pulling into the parking lot from Calliope Street and parking on the far side of where everyone stood, light bar pulsing.

Morello climbed out of the car, raising his hand in salute as he limped, though less severely than he had earlier, in Wilburn's direction.

"Him, too?" Sansone asked. He shook his head, nudged Maureen with his elbow. "It's almost as if he waited until he heard the all clear before he came over."

THE DEVIL'S MUSE   201

"He was in the neighborhood," Maureen said.

His presence told her that Drayton had made the arrest, releasing Morello and Cordts from their duties babysitting Goody. With Wilburn the one supposedly in trouble, though, she was surprised Cordts hadn't come along to check things out. He'd probably had his fill of Morello and followed Hardin's order to get back to his original route assignment, which was something Maureen realized she was quite looking forward to. After the overdoses, shootings, foot chases, fornicating couples, irate neighbors, citizen journalists, zombie stories, and gangland parleys, she was perfectly okay being bored for the last few hours of her shift.

As she approached Wilburn, though, the two young men who'd been venting at him became unnerved at the arrival of three more cops. She remembered what Sansone had told her about avoiding officer-instigated incidents. She did not want another chase, or to call for the dogs, or try to get ambulances across and around the parade again. Morello and Sansone, she realized, looked like enforcers, and these guys were worried now that Wilburn had pretended to listen to them and had kept them talking only while he waited for reinforcements to better take care of them.

"Do me a favor, Sansone," she said. "Hang back a bit. You and Morello are scaring these two guys."

"Roger that, Cogs. Good call." He produced his cigarettes. "I'll be close by if you need me. But let's see if we can't put this mess to bed with a quickness, please. We should all of us be back on the route. And I could use something to eat."

"I got you," Maureen said.

She walked up to Wilburn, determined to ignore the camera, which continued to roll. The teens had stopped talking at her approach. They couldn't decide, she figured, whether the small white woman cop arriving first made things better or worse for them.

"Officer Wilburn," Maureen said. "Everything copacetic?"

"I think so," Wilburn said, eyeing the young men. "I think everyone has made themselves clear."

"Officer," the one with the glasses said, turning to Maureen, eager to press his case to a new audience, reading her name tag. "Officer Coughlin, we didn't do a thing. Not a thing. We came to *help* the camera guy. The homeless guy attacked him. We could've watched, like those two white ladies who stood there doing nothing, but we came to help."

"One of them did *something*," the other guy said, acid in his voice. Maureen didn't have to ask which women he was talking about; had to be Donna and Laine.

"Wils?" Maureen asked.

"More or less," he said.

"Can we *go*?" the young man in the hat asked. He turned to his friend. "I'm telling you, we're gonna get nowhere with this."

"Gentlemen," Maureen said. "Your names, please."

"I told you," the Hat said, disgusted at her question. "I *told* you. Now *we're* going to get in trouble. Why else would this guy call for more cops? I told you."

Maureen raised her hands. "No one is getting in trouble. I want to know what to call you while we have this conversation." She looked at the Hat. "It's called manners. Y'all don't have name tags like we do."

"Don't need 'em," Hat said. "We're all the same to y'all anyway."

"I'm Malik," the young man in glasses said, "and this is Albert."

"What can we do for you?" Maureen asked.

"I want to know where to get paperwork on this incident," Malik said, "and Officer Wilburn won't tell me that. I want to see the police report when it's done, and get a copy of it." He held up a tablet with a big crack across its screen, shook the device at Maureen and Wilburn. "I want to be reimbursed for this. This wasn't cheap." He pointed at the camera with the broken tablet, yelling to Laine, "Y'all owe me. We have the same rights to do our work as y'all do."

"Fellas, give me one more minute," Maureen said. "Hang out for one more minute. Let me talk to my fellow officer here."

She and Wilburn walked a few feet away.

"Are these kids serious?" Wilburn asked. "I'm gonna have to write on this so they can have some goddamn paperwork for their computer insurance or whatever? I'm sorry, I feel bad for them. They seem like good guys. It's a shitty break, but fuck that. I'm going home after work tonight. I'm not writing a police report for a broke iPad. What do they expect, bringing that iPad to a fucking parade. If it's so valuable, leave it home."

Violent retching echoed under the overpass. Maureen and Wilburn turned to see the homeless guy vomiting dark liquid between his legs.

"I am not holding his hair back," Wilburn said. "Fuck him, too. Man, I'm fucking tired. And we got five more days of this shit."

"Is this guy cuffed for a reason?" Maureen asked.

"It's not necessary anymore, I guess," Wilburn said. "It calmed him down." He circled around the man's back. "Sir, if I release you, will you remain calm?" The man heaved and gagged again, hacking and spitting. "I'll take that as a yes," Wilburn said. He unlocked the cuffs and freed the man's hands.

Maureen and Wilburn backed away from him slowly as the puking continued, though less violently. The man didn't hold his hair back, either. He had consumed quite a lot of something that was deep purple and was returning most of it to the world. To her relief, Maureen saw that the liquid was too dark to be blood. From the smell of it, wine was more like it.

"Do we call in a medical for him?" she asked.

"If he keels over, yes," Wilburn said. "If he can get up and make it to his cart I figure he's good to go. I think he's pretty experienced at this stuff. Not his first rodeo. We'll keep an eye on him."

"What is this, Wils?" Maureen asked as they moved away from the man. "What're we doing here?"

Wilburn stood with his mouth hanging open for a moment as he thought of where to start.

"Okay, I was bringing Laine and those guys through the neighborhood. They wanted shots of Lee Circle. We were taking the backstreets to get there instead of dealing with the route. We saw this guy heading this way pushing his shopping cart. He was half-dressed and shouting nonsense and thrashing around so I guess those guys thought, hey, maybe some good footage. More 'real New Orleans' shit. Laine, especially, got all excited. It was obvious to me that he was plain old living-under-the-highway crazy, these guys are a dime a dozen, and that what he was doing really had nothing to do with Mardi Gras. I tried telling them that, but . . ." He shrugged.

"Anyway, they chase him under here, and I follow them. He parks his cart, and Donna walks up, trying to interview the guy. About 'the real Mardi Gras.' She thinks she's discovered this angle that no one's ever taken, you know, homeless Mardi Gras or whatever, like do they celebrate it or do they feel left out, when, suddenly, Whizzly Adams over there turns on her, pushes her to the ground. Starts snarling. Donna gets up and runs, screaming. Cortez and Larry, God love 'em, they have no idea if they're supposed to keep shooting or help Donna get away, so they stand there and do nothing and crazy pants goes after *them*. He starts grabbing at the camera, chasing them around, roaring like an animal. They start screaming. That's when the younger kids started noticing and I started getting a little nervous.

"Still, it's pretty hilarious, to tell the truth, and no one's really getting hurt, when Albert and Malik come running over. They're both of them premed at Xavier, and they're filming the whole shebang on their iPad, 'cause they're making a documentary about out-of-town people exploiting the real Mardi Gras with their 'real Mardi Gras' documentaries about it—and this is just too perfect—when hairy man finally gets a good grip on the camera and it looks like he's going to get it away from Cortez and Larry. They run to help Cortez, but Donna turns out to be a racist bitch who calls nine-one-one while I'm fucking standing right here because she thinks the med students are trying to steal the camera from Cortez and Larry while they're distracted by the homeless guy. That's why she's in time-out. Tits and boots or not, I can't deal with her act anymore.

"I was able to call off the nine-one-one, but . . ." He hesitated, taking a breath. He was clearly still furious with Donna. "With the running around and yelling we were starting to get more and more attention from that mob of kids over there. They look over and see a couple of black kids struggling with a bunch of white folks, including a white cop. I thought they might bum-rush this circus back here and I didn't know how much backup I was going to need to get everybody out of here, including them, and me, in one piece. I decided to err on the side of caution and call it in."

"So, to be clear," Maureen said, "we're not detaining anyone, no one is hurt. No one is being arrested or charged. Nobody actually stole anything."

"No," Wilburn said. "Really, I've kept everyone here because I want Laine to make Donna pay for that fucking busted iPad but Laine's having none of it and the students, they're not letting it go." He shook his head. "So here we are. At an impasse, as they say. Like we got nothing fucking else going on tonight. If there was a way to arrest Donna for this ridiculousness, I wish I could."

"Do those guys know what Laine is doing with her camera crew?" Maureen asked. "Do they know about her series on YouTube?"

"I don't know," Wilburn said. "I doubt it. She won't give them her name. They keep yelling at me now because I won't let them go over there after her, or Donna, and settle things themselves. I can't have tempers getting out of control."

"So tell them who Laine is," Maureen said, thinking of Philippa and her accountability crusade. "Tell Malik and Albert everything we know about Laine and the *On Fire* series. Then they can get on their Facebook pages and Twitter feeds and *her* YouTube channel and whatever else is out there and call her out on this whole mess. Her shit pay for her crew. Her racist on-air host. Her exploitation of violence, drug addiction, mental illness, and homelessness for crowd-sourcing dollars."

"Well, damn, Coughlin," Wilburn said, smiling, leaning back. "That's a great idea. I didn't think you understood the Internet like that. You're mean."

"I don't understand jack shit about the Internet," Maureen said, "but I know plenty about getting even. Tell the med students what I told you. Either they get reimbursed or they get even. That way they don't leave here with nothing. Go talk to them. If they're savvy they can put Laine out of business by morning and she knows they can. They can make her a villain real quick. I'll go talk to Laine, woman to woman, redhead to redhead, and get her to see reason."

Maureen and Wilburn watched as the homeless man struggled to his feet and staggered to his shopping cart. He unwound the boa from the cart's handle and wrapped the feathers around his neck, wiping his mouth with one end of the boa before proceeding. If he had any recollection that he'd recently been handcuffed or violently ill, or that there were other human beings in his immediate vicinity, he gave no indication.

"Wils," Maureen said, "looks like our boy is going to make it."

"That's a real New Orleanian right there," Wilburn said, watching the man push his cart across the parking lot, away from the parade. He pulled a broken strand of beads from his wagon and tossed them into the middle of Calliope Street.

"The parade goes on," Maureen said, admiration in her voice.

"We're a resilient city," Wilburn said.

"He gets to go?" Albert complained, walking over to them. "He assaulted that cameraman and he gets to go and we have to stay here?"

"I never said y'all had to stay here," Wilburn said. "Y'all can go whenever. Staying was your idea. Don't make this something it's not."

"I thought you wanted to get reimbursed for the broken tablet?" Maureen said. "One of you should take a few pictures of it. Create a record, for your own personal use. Officer Wilburn here will give you some ideas on what to do from here. Discuss it with him."

The students hesitated, Albert looking over his shoulder at Laine. "Don't let her leave." He pointed at Wilburn while speaking to Maureen.

"While he handles us, you let them get out of here. Don't do that to us. They already treated us like criminals. Don't you treat us like we're stupid."

"Her name is Laine Daniels," Maureen said. "She slips away from me, you google that name. But she won't leave. Give your information to Officer Wilburn, please, and we can all get out of here with everybody moderately happy. Can you do that for me?"

The students nodded. "But we got y'all's names, too," Albert said.

"Yes, you do," Maureen said. "But you're not getting my phone number. We good here?"

"We're good," Wilburn said. "Gentlemen, come this way with me. The air's turned sour over here."

Keep everyone moving, Maureen thought, good idea, watching Wilburn lead the students away from her. Keep everyone separate. Nothing coagulates. Don't let pressure or tension build up.

She walked over to Cortez and Larry, her hand in the air to get Morello's attention. "Shut it down," she said to them. "Shut it down now."

Cortez lowered the camera and Larry lowered the microphone, seemingly only too happy to obey. Morello stood right behind them, and they knew he was there, but Maureen didn't think the large police officer at their side had inspired their ready compliance. They looked very tired, and ready to commit the remainder of their night to packed bowls and fried chicken and waffles. The boys looked as if they'd only be too happy to go along should Maureen tell them to lay their equipment on the pavement and walk away. She was tempted to give the order. Everyone else would feel better without the camera watching them, and Laine would be pissed that her project had stalled. Win-win, as far as Maureen was concerned.

"Officer Morello," she said, "would you help these young men keep an eye on this expensive gear?"

"Why the fuck not?" Morello said. "We meet again, fellas. How you liking the Muses parade?"

Maureen walked away, knowing Laine would follow her.

"You don't think I see what you're doing?" Laine said. "Siccing that big cop on those two poor kids. That's state terrorism. That's abuse of power."

"Please," Maureen said. "It's giving two tired, overworked, and underpaid local kids a perfect excuse to ignore their domineering boss. Look, Laine, don't you think it's time to pack it in for the night? Give those two, and the rest of us, a break. There will be more drug abuse and violence tomorrow, I promise."

"Mardi Gras is a public event that happens on public streets," Laine said. "That's part of the point, and one of its biggest selling points. You can't manage what parts of it the world gets to see. You can't control it. Give me a break, it's like a stripper saying I'll take the money but don't look at my stretch marks. If you put your shit on worldwide display then you can't complain when everyone looks. That's not how the world works."

"And you," Maureen said, "are creating a public nuisance tonight. And I am *this* close to fucking arresting you for it. Enough. Enough of this shit. You know what else Mardi Gras means? It means the ordinary rules go out the window. One parking lot away I've got two hundred kids hopped up on sugar, energy drinks, liquor, hormones, a full night of parades, and who knows what else, and they're all wondering what's going on down here with a bunch of cops, a camera, and a couple of other black kids. I don't need their attention. I don't want their attention. I want it back on each other and their phones and the last half of this parade."

Laine put her face in her hands. "You don't know how much pressure I'm under."

Maureen's first impulse was to laugh, but she choked it back. Pressure? she thought. Have you been paying *any* attention to what my coworkers and I have been dealing with tonight? But she didn't say that, either. She didn't much care whether Laine understood her job or not. She just wanted the camera out of the way so she could keep doing it.

"Here's what I can do for you," Maureen finally said. She raised her arm and waved at Sansone. He waved back. "You see that very handsome tattooed hunk over there?"

"I'm a lesbian," Laine said.

"Congratulations," Maureen said. "That's not what I'm offering." She laughed. "Jesus, I'm not a pimp."

Laine couldn't help a laugh, either. "Gotcha."

"My *point*," Maureen said, "is that Officer Sansone over there is with the Special Tactics squad. He's done the warrants task force. He's done gang work. I know for a fact he's got a buddy who's almost as good-looking as he is who's got a great flakka story."

Laine frowned.

"C'mon," Maureen said. "Would you rather spend the rest of the night talking to Sansone or chasing homeless guys with a camera, hoping they turn into drug-crazed zombies?"

"It's not that. This is too good an offer. I don't trust you."

"You make Albert and Malik whole over their iPad," Maureen said, "and I'll set you up with Sansone. He knows cops *and* criminals across the city. He can get you in with a lot of people you could never otherwise talk to."

"Those two kids?" Laine said, rolling her eyes. "A friggin' iPad doesn't make them journalists, or filmmakers, or whatever they're calling themselves. I don't want to hear about their 'project.' They saw something cool that they could record and throw up on YouTube for a few laughs. What're they even doing out here with that? What kind of video are they going to get in this light? And the sound, forget it. What kind of postproduction were they planning on doing?"

"I didn't ask," Maureen said. "Who put you in charge of who gets to be legit? What happened to all that DIY First Amendment and public space stuff?"

"If I give them my contact info," Laine said, "then I can't get rid of them. They'll be pestering me for jobs on my crew. They'll want my advice on their work."

"I don't think they're that interested in working with you. Certainly not in working with Donna. I promise you that."

"You don't understand how so-called new media works," Laine said.

"They're all about disrupting everything and doing something new until they think someone on the inside of Hollywood or New York might offer them a job, then they're reading you their résumé."

"Hollywood?" Maureen asked. "In case you haven't noticed, you're standing under a highway overpass in a parking lot that smells like piss and puke with a stoner duo you found on the Internet for a crew. I don't know how Hollywood works, but you want the real Mardi Gras, you need friends on the inside. You want friends like that, you need to take care of the locals. And not with the bullshit and pennies you're offering Cortez and Larry."

"You're an officer of the law," Laine said. "Making me pay those kids is extortion."

"It's media relations," Maureen said. "It's neighborly. C'mon, what's screen repair for one of those things cost? Sansone's got a smile that's worth ten thousand hits on its own."

"You'll vouch for me," Laine said. "With him." Maureen could see the hit counter turning in her head. "You'll do more than just tell him my name."

"I can't *make* him do anything," Maureen said. "But I will encourage him to help you, yes. He's a good guy. He loves the job. He loves talking about being a cop." She borrowed one of his moves and bumped Laine with her elbow. "You can't tell me that he and his tattooed muscle-boy buddies won't look fantastic on camera."

"You've got a deal," Laine said. "I'm trusting you with my project. You know how important it is to me." She dug into her shoulder bag. She found her wallet and pulled out two crisp hundreds. "This is most of my cash for the weekend." She extended the bills to Maureen. "Give those guys this two hundred cash and tell them we're even for the iPad."

"Excuse me?" Maureen said. "I look like a bagman to you? Give them the money yourself. That's part of the point here. Acknowledge them. That's Malik with the glasses, and his friend's name is Albert. And bring Donna with you when you go over to them, and she apologizes for calling the cops on them. Then we have a deal."

"Changing the terms already," Laine said, tucking her wallet back in her shoulder bag. "You sure you don't know anything about Hollywood?"

"Fuck Hollywood," Maureen said. "Welcome to New Orleans."

"Yeah, well, I'm not staying," Laine said. "Enjoy yourselves." She called Donna's name then she walked away, her head held high, her money clutched tightly in her hand.

# 32

Maureen lit a cigarette, taking a deep satisfying drag as she watched Laine and Donna talk to Malik and Albert. The students seemed satisfied with the deal and the apology. After Malik had pocketed the cash, Donna walked away, head hung low. Maureen saw Laine straighten her shoulders and arch her back. She took a deep breath, readying herself to launch into a lesson for the boys about journalism or ethics in media or something of the sort. Albert and Malik didn't listen. They walked away from Laine in mid-sentence and made a beeline for Cortez and Larry. The four of them set to discussing the camera Cortez was using.

Maureen watched Laine watch them, and for a moment felt an empathetic pang of loneliness for Laine, who always seemed, once the drama had been resolved, to end up standing by herself off to the side of things. Sansone and Morello conferred, and after a brief conversation walked over to Donna, who cocked a hip at their arrival, threw her hair back, and tried to smile, but even at a distance she'd been drained of an essential animating energy. Maureen could tell, from yards away, that despite the selfish, uninterested pout she put on for the world, Donna felt awful about assuming the two black kids who had come running to help her coworkers were thieves instead. She'd bounce back, Maureen thought. She was too deeply selfish not to, and the attentions of Morello and Sansone made for a fine consolation prize.

Locating Wilburn took her a minute.

She finally spotted him, away from everyone, leaning against a concrete pillar with his phone held to one ear and his hand pressed flat against the other. A band was now marching under the overpass, and even at their distance, the blare of the brass section was prodigious. He did not look very happy. Maureen walked over to him. He finished his call and watched her approach, slipping his phone into the pocket of his coat. He seemed ready to say something to her, but then something else caught his attention. Another NOPD Explorer turned off Calliope and into the parking lot.

Maureen stood beside Wilburn and watched the approaching vehicle. "Do we know who that is?"

"Your phone been buzzing?" Wilburn asked.

Maureen checked it. "Nope."

"When you were a teenager," Wilburn said, "you ever go to one of those house parties your best friend threw only to have the parents come home early and walk in on a shit show?"

"I guess," Maureen said. The vehicle parked a few yards away from her and Wilburn. Hardin was driving. There was no mistaking that enormous form. "I've seen it in the movies, at least."

"It's, like, you're not the one who fucked up, technically, but you're going to get a ration of shit anyway."

"Oh, for sure I know *that* feeling," Maureen said. "Yes, indeed."

Sergeant Hardin got out of the truck. He waited for his passenger, who Maureen also knew.

"That's how I feel right now," Wilburn said. "And I don't like it any more now than I did then."

A short, thick-bodied man in a long, expensive fawn-colored wool coat disembarked from the passenger seat of the Explorer, stooping to comb his wavy gray hair in the car's side mirror. He left the door open when he was done using the mirror like he was used to someone being there to close his car doors for him. Drayton. He and Hardin riding together, she thought. That can't be good. They are not here to congratulate us on a job well done, she thought. The door alarm on the Explorer started beeping. Drayton turned and slammed it closed. Maureen could see Hardin roll his eyes from where she stood. His jaw was tight. His whole body was locked up with tension.

She turned at the sound of a loud whistle from across the parking lot. Morello. He stood next to a confused-looking Sansone, his hands in the air. He didn't know what Hardin was doing there, either, or why he had brought Drayton with him. Maureen half expected the two of them to bolt for Morello's unit and make a quick escape.

"Don't worry about them," Hardin said, walking up. "Worry about me."

Drayton stood at the front of the Explorer. He smoothed the front of his open coat with his fat hands. He had quite the wardrobe, Maureen thought, and one hell of a nice watch, for an NOPD homicide detective. None of the other detectives she had met wore clothes like him. He spared no expense on the cologne or the hair product, either. He had a fleshy reddish face and thick purplish lips, black eyebrows like dead caterpillars stuck above his eyes. He spread his feet and crossed his hands at his shiny belt buckle, waiting, Maureen figured, for everything in the world to come to him like it was his due. He wore a gold pinkie ring with a large black stone. Drayton was always gross and cheesy, she thought, but this meeting in a dirty, dimly lit parking lot had him turning the act up a notch. He'd struck a pose, she realized, like he was a B-movie mafioso making a late-night deal, with Hardin as his hired muscle. For real. This wasn't even a Mardi Gras costume. This was how Drayton was in real life.

Despite how she felt about Drayton, and despite her skepticism of Laine's project, Maureen would not have blamed the woman for trying to capture this scene on camera. Drayton was something to behold, that was for sure.

Hardin waved for Morello and Sansone to join them at the car. Heads lowered, the two men hurried over. Maureen watched from the corner of her eye as Cortez discreetly raised the camera to his shoulder and started filming. Malik tilted the tablet back and forth, trying to see through the cracks and swiping at the broken screen with his finger. Albert was texting away on his phone. Cortez, Albert, Malik, and Larry had the look of a team. Laine had not moved a muscle; she simply watched. Donna kept her distance from everyone.

"What're y'all doing here, Sarge?" Maureen asked. "That press conference has got to be starting soon."

"It most certainly is," Hardin said. "It most certainly is."

Wilburn's phone started ringing. He pulled it from his pocket, frowned at the number.

"Is that Officer Cordts?" Hardin asked.

Wilburn looked up, licking his lips. "What? No. No, it's not."

"Then you're free to not answer that," Hardin said. "We're having a very important meeting right now. For you, especially."

Morello and Sansone arrived.

"Hey, Sarge," Sansone said, no smile. Morello said nothing.

"Officer Sansone," Hardin said. "I want you to take this camera crew far away from here. Take them back to the route. Let them shoot whatever they want, keep them entertained, just get them the hell away from here. You're a charming motherfucker. Think you can handle that? I think you can."

"Ten-four, Sarge," Sansone said, raising his eyebrows at Maureen and mouthing "good luck" at her, clearly happy to be excluded from future proceedings. He headed in Laine's direction to relay Hardin's message. If the woman had any sense of how to read other people, Maureen thought, she would know this was not the time to raise a stink with Hardin.

"You want me to help him with that?" Morello asked, already turning to make his escape.

"I want you to stay here and tell me," Hardin said, "why you left Officer Cordts alone with our suspect?"

Oh, fuck, Maureen thought. Cordts, what did you do? She turned to Wilburn, who she saw had turned as ashen as death. "What happened to Cordts?" she asked.

A loud banging startled them. Drayton was beating his thick fist on the hood of the Explorer. "What *the fuck* happened to my fucking suspect?"

His face approached the color of an eggplant, the flush brought on by the effort of the histrionics, Maureen figured, and not from rage or frustration. Maureen watched his gray eyes flick for an instant in the direction of the film crew. She turned and saw they were walking away now, a smiling, spotlit, gesticulating Sansone leading them back to the parade route like the Pied Piper. If the Pied Piper had been a gorgeous Navy SEAL.

"Fuck Cordts," Drayton said, his disappointment audible as he, too, watched the camera crew leave the scene. "I don't care about that loser."

"You should," Wilburn said.

"Where is my suspect?" demanded Drayton.

"What happened?" Maureen asked. "Me and Wils, we're missing crucial info here."

"Coughlin, you told me," Hardin said, "that I could send Drayton to arrest Goody Curtis?"

"I did."

"I trusted you, so I did what you said."

"And?" Maureen asked.

"And no one was there when Drayton arrived," Hardin said.

"What do you mean, no one?"

"Fucking no one," Drayton said. "What part of 'no one' is hard to understand, Coughlin? No. Body. Nobody but that bitchy hotel maid who owns the house that you supposedly caught this kid hiding under."

"She supervises housekeeping for the Canal Street Marriott," Morello said with a shrug. "It's a big staff." Maureen looked at him. "We got to talking. There was nothing else to do."

"I give a fuck?" Drayton said. "About any of this? A boss maid is still a maid, that's not the point."

"Supposedly caught?" Maureen asked. "What the hell is that supposed to mean?"

Drayton wagged his finger at her. "I don't know about you, Officer. Who's to say you caught anybody? This is not the first time one of your"—he made air quotes with his fat fingers—"suspects went missing."

"She caught him, Drayton," Wilburn said. "I was there when he came out from under the house."

"Me, too," Morello said. "You're being ridiculous."

"Hey, you know what," Drayton said. "Three guys go out fishing in the Gulf. Boat comes back, all three guys says one of them caught a big-ass shark. So let me see it, I say. But when I look in the boat, no fucking shark." He paused, letting the story's wisdom soak over them. "You know what I think when that happens? I think the buddies are a bunch of liars looking out for themselves and fuck everybody else."

"What's that got to do with anything?" Maureen asked.

"We don't have time for this," Wilburn said.

"Sweetheart, you *say* you caught him," Drayton said, his ire still focused on Maureen, "but I ain't got him, so as far as I'm concerned, you didn't catch jack shit. If he's not in the boat, he's not caught."

"What's this have to do with Cordts?" Wilburn asked.

"When the detective arrived at the scene to effect the arrest," Hardin said, "both Officer Cordts and the suspect were gone."

"They were there when I left on the fifty-five," Morello said. "Everything was copacetic. I made sure." He glanced from Wilburn to Hardin and back. "I know how Cordts is."

"He's worse tonight," Wilburn said. "Bad as I've seen him."

"I know," Morello said. "That's why I checked him before I left him. I swear. Goody was hooked up in the backseat, and Cordts was sitting on the hood of the unit, chain-smoking cigarettes, looking at a little red sneaker. He had those black wings open on the dashboard."

"Jesus, Morello," Wilburn said, "and that's 'okay' to you? That's copacetic?"

"Hey, I'm not the one who called in a bullshit fifty-five," Morello said. "You handle your shit and I don't have to leave Cordts alone with the suspect."

"Do you have any idea, any of you," Hardin asked, raising his voice to kill the argument, "where Cordts could have taken Goody?"

"Maybe Cordts got tired of standing around waiting for the detective," Maureen said. "Maybe he made the arrest himself, like we should have from the get-go."

"We checked the jail wagon," Drayton said. "No dice. They're both in the wind, and I am pissed."

"If Cordts was driving around doing police work," Hardin asked, "why would he not be on the radio about it? Why would he not answer his phone? Why would he go dark?"

"No reason that I can think of," Maureen said. "None at all. I'm sorry. I wish I had something to offer."

"So do I," Drayton said. "I'm unimpressed with the lot of you so far."

"Wilburn?" Hardin asked, ignoring Drayton's derision. "You need to talk to me. You're covering for him. I appreciate that, but now is not that time."

Wilburn didn't seem to hear. His phone was buzzing again. He held it in his hand and stared at the screen.

"I swear to Christ, Officer," Hardin said, "if you don't silence that phone and get your priorities in order, there are going to be consequences."

Wilburn looked up from the screen, blinking at Hardin.

"Where is Officer Cordts?" asked Hardin.

Wilburn turned the phone so that the screen faced Hardin. "He's here."

"Ed Gallagher," Hardin said, squinting at the screen. "That name means nothing to me. Get serious, Wilburn."

"Shit," Wilburn said, thumbing the screen. "I meant to show you the text, not the phone call. Ed runs the Dublin House, over on St. Charles and Melpomene. He's the one who keeps calling me. He's an old friend of me and Cordts, from back in the day. We march in the St. Pat's parade together. He got sick of me not answering his calls, and sent me a text. Cordts is at the Dublin House; he's got Goody with him. And they are not there for the fish and chips. Cordts asked Eddie to keep the dining room clear. To lock them in." Wilburn reread the message, unleashed a long sigh. He swallowed hard. "Fuck. Eddie says Cordts looks ready to paint the walls with this kid."

"So Cordts has locked himself in the Dublin House with Goody and this guy Eddie?" Maureen said. "We're now dealing with a hostage situation, during the night's big parade."

"We keep fucking around here," Wilburn said, "and I'm worried we're gonna be dealing with a homicide situation."

"I cannot believe how y'all have fucked this up," Drayton said. "Unreal."

"The *only* thing I want to hear anybody talking about," Hardin said, "is how we're getting Cordts and Goody out of the Dublin House in one piece." He turned his full size on Drayton. "That includes you, Detective. Everyone in the car. We're rolling."

# 33

Maureen sat in the back of the Explorer with Wilburn. Hardin and Drayton sat in the front, Hardin in the driver's seat. The sergeant had the engine running and the heat on. The windows were fogged and the inside of the car was humid. Everyone's clothes were damp from working outside all night in the mist and drizzle, except, of course, for Drayton the house cat's pricey coat and expensive suit. The cloying spice of his cologne cut through the vaguely locker-room-smelling atmosphere in the truck and tickled the back of Maureen's throat, gagging her. Hardin had shut him down when he'd tried firing up a cigar.

The Explorer was parked at the intersection of Melpomene on the lake side of St. Charles, which put them on the back side of the parade. There was no reason to try driving the car across the parade route with Muses rolling. They could much more easily walk to the Dublin House from where they were parked.

"Has Cordts answered you yet?" Hardin asked from the driver's seat.

Wilburn checked his phone. "He hasn't, and I don't think he will, Sarge. Why would he start now?"

"But he knows we're out here," Maureen said.

"I guess so," Wilburn said. "I texted him. I told Eddie we're out here, too. He'll meet us at the front door and bring us back to Cordts, whenever we're ready. He's offered to clear out his staff."

"We don't want to do that just yet," Hardin said.

"I need to make this arrest," Drayton said. "I don't give a shit about Eddie and his fucking bar. He's got plenty more nights to make up the business he's losing tonight."

"That's not the point," Hardin said. "We're on the parade route. We send the staff out onto the route, how long before word gets out there's a police standoff happening at the Dublin House? That doesn't do anybody any good. No panic. No escalation. We're going to handle this ourselves." He looked at Wilburn in the rearview. "Are we sure the staff is safe?"

"As far as I can tell," Wilburn said. "They don't do much inside business during the parades. They have the outdoor bars and tables and the Porta-Johns. That's where the business is. They don't serve food inside during the parades. That's what Eddie told me."

"Well, we can't keep waiting him out," Drayton said. "We don't have the time for that. The DC is already texting me. This whole section of the route is covered by the two tactical squads. You're telling me we can't get four or five of those guys together on the fly and put an end to this? There's nobody in that dining room but Eddie, Cordts, and that kid, right? The people in this car outnumber them."

"You really want me to run a SWAT operation in the middle of a parade?" Hardin said. "Is that what you're telling me? Have you lost your mind?"

"Not like a formal, official operation," Drayton said. "Geez, relax. Just a handful of guys. Make it a black-ops kind of thing. They do this shit all the time. They love it. Maybe just that tattooed gym rat from under the overpass. He looks like he can handle himself. Keep the customers and the staff outside—I'm not an animal—and roll in one canister of tear gas. One. How much damage could it really do? Cordts'll be fine in an hour."

"Gas a fellow cop?" Wilburn said. "What is wrong with you?"

"Roll tear gas into a restaurant?" Maureen asked. "During Mardi Gras? Are you serious? Not to mention, like Wilburn said, we shouldn't have to point out to you, that's one of our own in there."

"Not as far as I'm concerned," Drayton said. "Not right now. The way he's fucking things up, the way he's fucking *me* and messing with my arrest by pulling this drama ahead of my press conference? Fuck him. He's asking for this shit. He knows better. I don't know what side he's on but it's not mine. Not tonight." He turned in his seat, looking at Maureen and Wilburn. "He knows I'm out here, right? You told him I was out here."

"Oh, he knows you're here," Wilburn said. "Everybody knows where you are, Drayton."

Maureen couldn't stop staring at Drayton's pinkie ring. She wanted to snap that fat fucking finger right off his hand.

"You had to get the kid out from under that house, right?" Drayton said. "With the dogs?"

"Detective," Hardin said. "Stop. You're not helping."

"What?" Drayton said, glancing at everyone, as if he couldn't believe they weren't all thinking the same thing. "I mean, we wouldn't send them after Cordts, please, give me some credit. Just have them drag the kid out. They're trained. They're smart. Dogs can't see color but they can tell the difference between black and white, right?"

Maureen felt her jaw drop. She'd always thought that was just a hyperbolic expression, but there she was, her mouth hanging open in paralyzing disbelief. "They let you carry a gun?"

"It was a joke," Drayton said. "To lighten the mood. Christ, you people. Whose side are you on?"

"Holy shit," Wilburn said. "I can't believe you're a real person."

Drayton frowned at Wilburn a long time. He started to say something else, but thought better of it and stopped when Wilburn leaned forward in his seat. This is great, Maureen thought, watching Wilburn fume at the back of Drayton's head. Cordts has already come apart, that's why we're here. Who knew what he was thinking? Wilburn can't lose it, too, she thought, and make things worse. But the longer they sat here doing nothing, the greater the tension in the car was going to get. It needed releasing. Maureen knew she needed to put more space between the vibrating atoms trapped together in the warm, smelly car.

"It stinks in here," she said, and she opened the door, getting out.

As she had hoped he would, Wilburn got out, too.

"Who the fuck does that guy think he is?" Wilburn asked. "It's like he thinks he's Serpico and Sonny Corleone at the same time. He's unstable."

"He's not even worth discussing," Maureen said, jamming her hands in her coat pockets. "Wils, what are we going to do about Cordts? This is bad. Goody's no fucking prize but we can't let Cordts take him as a hostage. We can't let him hurt this kid. What the fuck is he doing in there? Is he really not responding to your messages?"

Wilburn held out his phone. "You want to see for yourself? He's not answering anything I send him. The only way I know he's still in there is 'cause Eddie's telling me he is."

"Why the Dublin House?" Maureen asked. "What's he thinking?"

"You're assuming Cordts *is* thinking," Wilburn said.

"He is," Maureen said. "He totally is. That's the key. Cordts knows he's not acting right. He wanted us to find him, and without it taking too long." She took a deep breath, let out a long sigh. "He wants us to stop him from hurting Goody. 'Cause he wants to, he's wanted to hurt someone all night, and he wants us to stop him. We can walk right in there. He's been waiting for us to show up."

"Yeah, yeah. I think we can do that," Wilburn said, nodding. "We can get as far as the front door, at least, and take it from there."

"Okay, good," Maureen said. "Text Eddie, tell him me and you are coming to the door, that we're coming in for a talk with Cordts. I'll tell Hardin."

She left Wilburn to his phone and walked around the vehicle to the driver's-side window. She knocked. The window rolled down.

"You have good news?" Hardin asked.

"I'm sick of their stalling," Drayton said.

She looked past Hardin. "Anytime you wanna get out of the car and handle this situation yourself, you go right ahead, tough guy."

Drayton looked away, muttered "cunt" under his breath. Maureen thought of the middle schoolers in the parking lot. They'd at least had the nerve to shout it at the top of their lungs.

"Talk to me," Hardin said. "And only to me."

"Wilburn and I are going in," Maureen said.

"Tell me why," Hardin said.

"Cordts chose the Dublin House," Maureen said, "because he's looking for a controlled environment. Someplace quiet, where he can make the rules. He knows the manager, who he knew would reach out to Wilburn, and so we'd be able to find him there. He knew the restaurant would be mostly empty, keeping the civilian danger to a minimum. He's trying to get away from the chaos and the noise both in his head and on the streets. There's something he's trying to figure out how to do."

"And you don't think that something is how to hurt or kill Goody?"

"He couldn't have set himself up worse to do that," Maureen said. "If we'd really lost him, he would've killed Goody already. Cordts has the whole city at his disposal. Practically the entire department is spread out along the parade route. He had a car. He could've taken Goody anywhere, done anything he wanted with him, and he stayed in the neighborhood. Because he wanted to be found. He wants us to help him."

Hardin thought for a moment, staring through the windshield into the parade crowd. "You want me to go in with you?"

"I don't," Maureen said. She raised her chin at Drayton, who was playing a video game on his phone. "If you go, he'll want to go. More important, if things go wrong in there, we're going to need someone out here with their shit together to pull us out of the fire."

"As soon as you guys get inside," Hardin said, "I'll get in position on the sidewalk. Let's keep everything as smooth and as cool as we can. Safety first, but if we can pull this off without making a scene and causing a panic on the route, that's the optimal outcome."

Wilburn came around the side of the car. "Eddie's ready when we are. I think the longer we wait, the more likely Cordts's head gets tangled up again."

Hardin looked into each of their faces. "Make your move."

# 34

Eddie met Maureen and Wilburn at the front door of the restaurant. He was a stocky, dark-haired guy with a thin goatee and huge bags under his eyes. He wore all black: jeans, a polo shirt, a ball cap with the Irish tricolor on the front. Those bags under Eddie's eyes, Maureen thought: Dakota had them, so did her bar back; Ms. Cleo, who worked at the hotel; and Madge, who worked the window at the Grocery. Maureen knew she had them, too, as did most of the people she worked with. They're like a tattoo or brand identifying their wearers as part of the same society: the Mystic Krewe of Somebody's Got to Throw This Fucking Party for the Rest of You.

Eddie stepped aside as he let Maureen and Wilburn inside the Dublin House. His obvious exhaustion made it hard for her to tell how nervous he was about what was happening in his place.

"Eddie Gallagher," Wilburn said, "Officer Maureen Coughlin."

They exchanged nods. This wasn't the kind of meeting, Maureen thought, that called for handshakes and the exchange of pleasantries. Eddie took off his hat, wiped his brow with the back of his hand. It was warm

inside the restaurant. The windows were mostly fogged. Despite everything going on, she felt a wave of sleepiness that wobbled her knees. She
unzipped her coat, pulled off her knit hat for the first time that night.
She had no doubt Eddie had coffee on somewhere in this place.

Maureen had always meant to check out the Dublin House, but had
never got around to it. It seemed too attractive an establishment, with its
long mahogany bar, golden, magic-hour lighting, and plush leather booths,
to visit alone. Well, she was here now, and she had company with her.
This wasn't how she'd pictured her first trip to the place. She looked across
the wide dining room at Cordts, who sat, of course, facing the door. He'd
taken the booth in the far right corner of the restaurant. There he could keep
his back to the wall and keep everything that happened in the restaurant in
front of him. Like an outlaw in the old West, Maureen thought.

She could see the back of Goody's head. She was relieved to see him
in one piece. Nothing had happened yet, she thought, that couldn't be
undone, and that couldn't be forgiven for having happened under the
umbrella of temporary Mardi Gras madness.

Cordts said nothing, didn't wave, didn't give any indication of what he
wanted or expected her and Wilburn to do. He did not seem surprised to see
them, fortifying Maureen's belief that they were doing exactly what Cordts
wanted them to do. He sat there, tranquil as death, staring at them. A large
Guinness mirror hung on the wall behind him. In the mirror Maureen
could see the tabletop that was otherwise blocked by the back of the bench.

A basket of ketchup-drenched fries was in front of Goody, who sat upright with his hands on the table. He was no longer cuffed. That observation told Maureen that fear was holding the boy in place. She saw why. In
the center of the table Cordts had positioned Lyla's red sneaker and her
black fairy wings. In front of him on his side of the table there were messy
plates of food, a pint glass half full of lager, and, resting by his right hand,
the gun he'd recovered at the shooting.

"He hasn't been here very long," Eddie said. "I called you right away,
as soon as I realized he planned on staying."

"Christ, it's hot in here," Maureen said.

"Heat's busted," Eddie said, shrugging. "Stuck at eighty. Wasn't so bad until we had to close the place up when he got here. Can't get anybody out here to work on it before tomorrow morning."

"Cordts say anything to you?" Wilburn asked.

"Just that I should keep the dining room and the bar clear," Eddie said. "He didn't say for how long."

"What's the situation with your staff?" Maureen asked.

"I got a couple guys in the kitchen," Eddie said, "prepping stuff for the grill outside. They can stay in there. They can get out the back door. My people cooking outside can get what they need through the kitchen. Thankfully, we don't seat the dining room during the parades. We do all of our bar and food and bev service from the outside stations. So I have no floor staff on. We even have bathrooms out there, so it's not that hard keeping people out of the building. Though the shitty weather doesn't help.

"Everyone is so busy right now they're not asking questions, but Muses is almost over. I can lock the customers out, but the staff, they're gonna want to come in and get warm, count their tips and get checked out, and go out or go home. Then they're going to ask questions about why they have to hang around outside, and why the cops are inside."

Maureen turned her back to Eddie and to the room so Cordts couldn't see her face. She spoke as low as she could. "He has a gun out. It's on the table."

Wilburn nodded, trying to keep his face expressionless. "Eddie, do me a favor and check on your people outside. And stay out there if you can."

"What do I tell them about what's happening in here?" Eddie asked. "They saw y'all arrive. They know I'm in here talking to you. Everybody knows people got shot just off the route earlier. I don't want my people getting nervous."

"It's Mardi Gras," Wilburn said. "The weather sucks, we're borrowing the room for a little while, for a special detail, is what you tell them. Something boring. Nothing's happening. This has nothing to do with that shooting."

"But it does, though, right?" Eddie asked.

"As far as you're concerned," Wilburn said, "it has less than nothing to do with that. Don't even bring it up to deny it."

"And as best you can," Maureen said, "keep them off their phones. We don't need rumors getting around. We don't need people showing up here trying to get a look through the windows or get pictures of whatever. We want to put a quiet, peaceful end to this."

Eddie lifted skeptical eyebrows and then his cap, scratching his scalp. He grabbed a black jacket from the rack on the wall and pulled it on. "A peaceful end would be great. I plan on doing a lot of business this week-end. Good luck. I got my phone if you need me. I'll lock the front door behind me."

After Eddie had gone, Maureen said, watching Cordts, "He's just sit-ting there, staring at us. Goody hasn't moved a muscle since we came in."

"How do we play this?" Wilburn asked.

"Text Hardin and tell him we're inside," Maureen said. "And that we have eyes on Cordts and Goody and they both seem okay. The more we keep Hardin in the loop, the more he'll let us work this ourselves."

"Which is what we want," Wilburn said, nodding, speaking as much to himself as to Maureen.

"Here's what I think," Maureen said. "I'll approach alone."

"I don't like it already," Wilburn said, shaking his head. "I've known the guy for years. I can talk to him better."

"You know Cordts better than I do," Maureen said, "but I know both him and Goody, and I think that'll help." She was thinking about the mounted officers and the others on foot who had backed her and Sansone under the overpass. She wanted backup at hand, but with room to maneu-ver if trouble popped off at the table.

"I want you positioned somewhere in the middle of the room," Maureen said, "at a table, or over at the bar would even work. From there, you can see us, you can block anyone coming in from outside, and you can inter-cept Goody if he tries to make a run for it, should it come to that. You can report to Hardin while I talk to Cordts, and if things go badly, you can call for more backup and bail me out, or escape."

"I'm not leaving you in here," Wilburn said.

"No sense both of us being trapped in that booth."

"Do me a favor," Wilburn said. "Don't let it come to that."

She and Wilburn turned and faced Cordts's table. He kept right on staring at them. They waited a moment, letting Cordts pick up on the fact that they were going to cross the room to him and Goody, giving him an opportunity to protest. Or to get up and walk to them.

They took their first steps. Cordts placed his hand over the gun. They stopped.

Maureen watched Cordts in the mirror. She didn't reach for her weapon. Wilburn didn't either. Cordts's movements were deliberate; he meant them to see what he was doing. He wasn't drawing on them. He was asserting authority, his control over the situation.

After another long, silent moment, Maureen and Wilburn continued their approach, their hands raised slightly at their sides. Though he never took his eyes off them, Maureen could see his shoulders relax a touch. Good, she thought. They were off to a good start. No panic. Do. Not. Escalate. No bullets, no blood in the Dublin House tonight.

When Maureen and Wilburn had made it halfway across the room, she saw Cordts straighten and stiffen in his seat. They stopped walking.

# 35

"I'm gonna come sit with you," Maureen said from a few feet away. "Just so we don't have to yell at each other. Wils is going to give us some space." She tried to smile. "We can send him to the bar for us."

Cordts did not smile back. "You can come over. Give your weapon to Wilburn first."

"Seriously?" Maureen asked. Already a request she hadn't expected and did not like. "I don't think that's necessary. It's me, Cogs."

"I know who you are," Cordts said. "Don't talk to me like I'm some neighborhood goon. Do it, please. Give it."

"This is a meeting," Maureen said. "A conversation. It's not a showdown."

"Then you don't need your weapon," Cordts said. "Be glad I'm not asking you to give it to me."

"You're asking another officer to give up her weapon?" Maureen asked. "You realize what you're doing? You're disarming a police officer with a weapon in your hand."

Cordts rolled his eyes. "Do I look concerned with breaking the rules?

Wilburn will give it back when this is over. It's temporary." He closed his hand over the weapon on the table. "Humor me."

It wasn't too late, Maureen thought, to turn around, walk outside, and turn this mess over to someone else. To people with more authority and experience. She rubbed her burning eyes. She was so tired. She couldn't stop sweating. She could hear a dance troupe going by outside. "Mardi Gras Mambo," one more time. What a fucking night. But she was here now, she thought. Only a few feet away from Cordts and talking to him. She reached for her hip and unbuckled her weapon. She had to keep things moving; she couldn't let the momentum stall.

"You are so going to owe me for this, Cordts," Maureen said. "Like season-tickets-for-the-Saints owe me. This is that big."

She did not like doing it, but she pulled her gun from her holster, double-checked that the safety was on, and surrendered it to Wilburn handle-first. He took it, set it on a table, and sat at that table, Maureen's gun close to his hand, within easy reach. He let out a long sigh, slumping in the chair.

"That's it. Just make yourself comfortable, Wils," Cordts said.

"I can't believe what I'm hearing," Wilburn said. "This is fucking surreal."

Maureen couldn't believe Cordts let Wilburn keep the gun that close at hand. Was that part of the plan? she wondered. Was Cordts going to force Wilburn to make a very bad choice?

"Coughlin," Cordts said. "Grab a chair. Sit over here at the end of the booth. Near me."

Maureen hesitated. She'd thought they'd entered the bar on a rescue mission. Now she wasn't so sure Cordts hadn't set them up for something much worse. Was he using them to get himself out of the bar, or to make sure he died here? Don't do it, she thought. Don't make one of us kill you, Cordts.

"Cogs," Cordts said, waving her over, "come sit with me."

Maureen did as she was told. What choice did she have?

Cordts relaxed and, after a quick glance at Goody, smiled for the first time at Maureen. He folded his hands on the table. "Now, what shall we talk about?"

"You tell me," Maureen said.

"You bring Drayton with you?"

"He brought us, really," Maureen said. "We were working something and he and Hardin caught up to us there. Couldn't be avoided."

Cordts grinned. "I imagine he's pretty pissed."

"He wants the collar," Maureen said. "More than that, you know him, you're messing with his chance to show off in front of a camera."

"The press conference. Ah."

"About fifteen minutes from now," Maureen said. "But fuck Drayton, it's Hardin you're really putting on the spot with this decision. He's got to report to Skinner so the commander knows what to tell the chief and what to say to the press. The mayor's waiting for an update, too. They're going to be looking at him."

"Fuck the brass and fuck the mayor," Cordts said. "They're as bad as Drayton, no help to any of us."

"I'm with you," Maureen said. She leaned her elbow on the table. "I'm going to ask the obvious question first. How about the three of us walk Goody outta here, hand him over to Drayton, and get on with our night?"

"Not likely. We're not all gonna make it."

"What can we do to change that?" Maureen asked.

Cordts lifted his beer glass and drank a few big gulps. "Fucking warm." He set the glass down carefully, turned it atop a coaster that featured a map of divided Ireland. "I want to know why." He raised his glass, gestured with it at Goody, drank down the rest of his warm beer, and set the glass back down. "I want to know why he did it."

"I didn't do nothin'," Goody said. "I don't know what the fuck I'm doing here."

Maureen turned to look at him. "We got the gun."

"What gun?" Goody asked.

"That gun right in front of you," Maureen said. "The gun you used to shoot those people, we found it at the scene."

"Fuck y'all and your bullshit planted gun," Goody said. "Don't matter to me."

Cordts slammed the glass on the table. "I fucking found it myself."

The pint glass had cracked up the side, knicking his fingertip. Cordts watched a pearl of dark blood forming there. He reached across the table and pressed his bloody fingertip into Goody's forehead, pushing the boy's head back against the padding of the bench.

"In case you don't make it to Ash Wednesday," Cordts said, returning his hand to his weapon. Maureen swallowed hard as she watched Cordts bleed onto the grip of the gun.

*Now* Goody was scared. The kid wasn't dumb. He knew that a crazy cop pretty much destroyed any case against him in court, but he had to survive the encounter first. Maureen could see Goody losing confidence in his survival chances. She saw no reason to change his perspective.

"Everything okay over there?" Wilburn asked.

"We're good," Cordts said. He picked up the gun, wiped his nose with the back of his hand, set the gun back on the table. "*You* all right, Wils? That fifty-five was you, right? Sorry, I didn't think to ask right away."

"I'm fine," Wilburn said. "I'm good. No problem. I had plenty of help. Long story, I'll tell you later. We're here for you, Cordts. You could avail yourself of this assistance? We walk through those doors, me, you, Cogs, the perp here, even. We'll tell the world whatever story you want them to hear. You tell us what to say and we'll say it."

Cordts ignored him. He stared down Goody instead. "Even if I kill you, we'll still prove you did it. We'll do a residue test on your hands, anyway, and run your prints. And I know you're in the system. So, since we got the gun, we've got you. So this 'I didn't do nothing' bullshit is over. Stop it. We've moved on to bigger issues. We have the gun you used, we have witnesses who saw you use it, and we'll have video of the whole goddamn circus by sunup. Own it, like a man. Because that's how you'll be tried, and that's how you'll jail, like a grown man, with all the other grown men."

Goody looked at Maureen, beads of sweat making tracks through Cordt's bloody fingerprint. "You heard that. He said I gotta confess or he'll kill me."

"What I heard," Maureen said, "is calm, quality advice from a man who's running out of patience."

"A man who's lost his fucking mind," Goody said.

"You and I," Cordts said to Goody, "after tonight, one way or another, we'll never see each other again. So I need answers from you tonight, because I won't get another chance to ask you. Why? What made you think you had the *right* to open fire on a crowded street? What were you *thinking?*"

Goody was breathing heavily. His eyes cast about as if someone might walk in and save him, or yell "surprise" and reveal this whole night to have been one big joke. Maureen imagined the way his mind was turning. Cops like these had killed his uncle. Part of him, a small part, the youngest part, continued to think that he could get away with what he'd done if he kept denying he'd done it, continued to believe that he could wear them down with stubbornness. And these cops would lie, he was thinking, about finding a gun, because they were cops. They did that shit constantly. Kill black people they didn't like, frame them. But a bigger part of Goody, Maureen thought, a part of him that was growing stronger by the second, was getting more and more concerned with walking out of that restaurant alive, and if that had to happen in cuffs, so be it. He could beat the rap later. His case would probably never even make it to court, he was thinking, crazy as this thing had gotten. But he had to get out of this room alive first.

Goody rolled his shoulders, slumping a tiny bit deeper into the bench, trying to affect a more relaxed posture, as if that would make him seem less defiant. That move was a welcome sign. When suspects did that, Maureen thought, it was like they were trying to physically, literally loosen their tongues. Goody looked at her when he spoke.

"He make it sound like a different thing than it was," Goody said. "I ain't saying what happened was anything I did"—Cordts slapped the table, hard, and Goody threw his hands up—"or that it wasn't, I'm just sayin' it didn't happen the way this man said it did."

"Why don't you tell us, then," Maureen asked, "how it happened?"

Quick as a rattlesnake strike, Cordts reached across the table and grabbed Goody's face. The palm of his hand crushed Goody's nose. The boy's eyes, wide and terrified, stared out from between Cordts's fingers. Maureen could hear his wet, frantic mouth-breathing against Cordts's hand.

"I had a little girl once," Cordts said, leaning across the table, his fingers white with the pressure they applied to Goody's skull. "A little girl I'd love to dress up in feather wings and little red shoes. For almost six months, she was mine. I never saw her open her eyes. I never saw her take a breath in the world, never felt her breath on my skin. But I heard her heartbeat. I listened to it every night. Until it stopped. Just. Stopped. No one could ever tell us why. For a long time after she died, even after my wife left me and left New Orleans and I started to forget *her* voice, if I could get the house real quiet, I could close my eyes and hear *that* tiny heartbeat again. Out of the darkness like a drum."

Cordts paused, releasing his grip on Goody, grabbing the gun off the table. He held it loosely and dug in his pockets with his other hand. Maureen feared he could pull out anything, from a human heart to a hand grenade.

Instead he produced orange prescription bottles, stood them on the table. Three of them. Empty. "Cymbalta. Klonopin. Xanax. Tried them all. I stopped when I couldn't hear that drum anymore."

He turned to Maureen. "You know what I've been thinking about all night tonight? Those times you thought I couldn't hear you? I was trying to imagine her weight on my shoulders. My daughter. She'd be Lyla's age. She'd look just like her if she'd lived. I know it. I saw it when that girl was lying in my arms."

Cordts softly touched the sneaker, then the fairy wings, adjusting them ever so slightly, as if they were charms on an altar.

"We fucking know how tonight happened, don't we?" Cordts said. "All of us. We all know." Cordts raised the gun, still held it loosely, gesturing at Goody with it. Wilburn shouted for him to put the gun down. Just above a whisper, Maureen said, "Cordts, the gun. Be careful."

"Like this *stupid* motherfucker?" Cordts asked. "This stupid *child*, who ran into the middle of a crowded intersection, blocks from a fucking Mardi Gras parade, and started throwing bullets? What I want to know is why should *I* be careful? He shot a little girl just like mine. These wings are hers. She should be on her father's shoulders, wearing her wings on her back, the colored lights in her eyes and her hair, catching beads from a float. Instead, she's in fucking *surgery*." He turned to Goody. "You shot a little girl, a grandmother, and a middle school teacher. What the fuck is wrong with you?"

Goody raised his hands, shaking his head. "Man, fuck that. Fuck this. You gonna let him do this to me? I don't know what y'all are talking about. Shot a teacher? Somebody's grandma? I don't know nothing about any of that. I don't know nothin' about no wings, no dead girls. None of it." He was close to tears. "Y'all are trying to kill me."

"Nobody's trying to kill you," Maureen said. "We're just trying to question you. To understand you."

Cordts tapped the gun on the table. "But I don't feel like I'm getting through to you."

"You don't understand," Goody said. "Y'all can't do me like this." He looked right at Cordts. "I got a little girl, too."

Of course, Maureen thought. The little girl in Alisha's arms, at the house on Harmony Street. Cordts set the gun down and went very still. Maureen jumped on the moment.

"Dee Harris," she said. "We know everyone else was an accident. But Goody, why were you out to kill Dee Harris tonight?"

"Man, anyone would want to kill Dee Harris," Goody said. "You gotta ask me that? Like y'all don't know. He a dirty piece of shit. Nothing good about that man. Not in any way."

Maureen took out her phone. She found the picture of Cordell that Dakota had sent her, and showed it to Goody. Cordts leaned forward to get a look at the picture. He was letting Maureen play out her plan. A good sign, she thought. Something sane and logical remained at work inside him.

"That's the motherfucker right there," Goody said. "Man, fuck him *and* that tie. He ain't no businessman, he evil. Straight up."

"*Evil* is a strong word," Maureen said.

"Listen, Dee so devil he can't catch fire, you know what I'm sayin'?"

"He's Three-N-G though?" Maureen asked. She thumbed her way to the photo of Benji.

"What difference does that make?" Goody asked, trying to see what Maureen was doing with her phone. "I don't know if he is or isn't."

"You're J-Street," Maureen said, "he's Three-N-G. You see where I'm going with this."

"Alla y'all police with this J-Street this, J-Street that. There *ain't* no J-Street family no more. Not like it used to be." He tried to affect a steely-eyed glare. "Y'all made sure of that."

"We both know these things don't die with one person," Maureen said. "Somebody's running a J-Street posse. You know it. We know it."

"Maybe there is, maybe there isn't," Goody said. "But if there's a new J-Street thing going on, I ain't part of it. I been out of town, me, until a few weeks ago. So whatever mess y'all are chasing around, I'm not in on it. No way. I'm done with that shit. I been in Baton Rouge, learnin' some shit."

"You shot three people tonight," Cordts said, "but you're telling us now that you don't roll with a gang anymore? So you're a freelance assassin now? Is that it?" He laughed. "Well, let me tell you something, you fucking *suck* at it."

"Hey, Cordts," Maureen said, "I got this."

But he ignored her. "That guy you shot? That's not Dee Harris. That's a middle school music teacher. His name is Cordell and you're a fucking retard. You're a father? You're a stumblebum punk."

Fuck it, keep rolling forward, Maureen thought. She enlarged the photo she'd pulled up on her phone and showed it to Goody. "And who's that?"

For the first time that night, for an instant, Goody looked to her like the child, the teenage boy he was. A flash of sadness crossed his face, then maybe love, then straight rage erupted in his eyes and burned everything else away, setting his face back into the hard, blank mask Maureen had recognized at Ms. Cleo's house. He looked like, it made her sad to think, himself again.

"That's my boy Benji," Goody said. "Benji Allen." He looked closer at the photo, frowning, picking up the phone before Maureen could grab it away from him. "Look how fucked up he is. Nothing but skin and bones now. We been looking for him, me and a few other people, for weeks. Motherfucker up and disappeared on us. Y'all found him?"

"Do you know why he vanished?" Maureen asked.

"Who took this?" Goody asked, his distress growing as he continued studying the photo. "Why do you have a picture like this? Where is he?"

Maureen reached for her phone; Goody held it away from her. "He passed out in the street or something? His eyes are kind of open, that's weird." And then she saw it hit him. Just because Goody was fifteen years old didn't mean he hadn't seen people lying dead in the street. Maybe it had taken him a minute to remember it, but he knew what death looked like, knew the mask it laid over the face of people like him and like his friends. "He's dead."

Maureen held out her hand. "Return that phone to me."

Goody held the phone in the air away from her and Cordts, his face falling apart one section at a time, like a visage crumbling off a statue. The eyes welled and weakened first, then the cheeks sagged, then the jaw quivered. She could hear Wilburn's chair creak behind them.

We get this wrong, Maureen thought, we fuck up how we handle this, and Goody's going to get violent. Then we all get violent.

"He's dead," Goody said again.

"Return that phone to the officer," Cordts said. "Now."

Goody slammed the phone on the table, cracking the screen, bouncing the dirty plates. Cordts's cracked glass fell off the table and broke on the floor.

"He overdosed on the parade route," Maureen said. "We did everything we could for him."

"That's why that motherfucker Dee *had* to get got. That right there is why. Because he gonna do everyone like he done Benji. With that shit he slingin', that *evil* shit."

"Flakka," Maureen said.

"What?" Goody asked.

"That's what it's called. Flakka."

"TWD. That's what Dee call it," Goody said. "TWD."

"TWD?" Maureen asked.

"The Walking Dead," Wilburn said.

"What-fucking-ever," Cordts said. "So you're Goody the Do-Gooder now? You a vigilante, out cleaning up the streets? Give me a break. Who you're supposed to be is changing every other minute here."

"I told Dee not to bring that shit around our neighborhood," Goody said. "I went to him like a man and I told him straight-up not to bring it around Benji no more. That shit turned Benji into a *fiend* in like a *day*. No joke. And then other people are asking around about it, like it's this great new shit, and I'm like what the fuck? Look, I got nothing against a motherfucker trying to honest earn out here, I quit that mess but I don't judge, but that shit's like voodoo black magic. I don't want no part of that. I don't want my friends having no part of that. I told Benji, and I told Dee, shit like this? Only white people make up shit like this. White people in white coats in laboratories are behind this shit. That's how this shit happens. I told you I learned some things in Baton Rouge. There's white people behind this shit. I say, don't bring it into our 'hood. I got a kid here now. Not J-Street, not Three-N-G, not nobody should be touching this stuff. Let it keep killing white boys in the Quarter. Keep it there where it belongs."

Goody realized he'd begun crying as he talked. He wiped his hand down his face, wiped his tears and snot on his already filthy jeans. "Then it's a do-nothing motherfucker who look just like Dee that gets shot, and Dee right as rain out there working for the white man selling this evil to the rest of us. You telling me there ain't something fucking *wrong* going on with all that?"

"Fuck this," Cordts said. "Fuck this avenger sob-story bullshit. Cogs, you know this kid because he killed a friend of his, right? His own friend. A twelve-year-old."

"I didn't do Mike-Mike," Goody said. "I did not."

"So you just stuffed him in the trunk and helped burn the body, then," Cordts said.

Goody said nothing, seething as he gripped the edge of the table.

Maureen watched Goody's wet eyes flit to Cordts's gun and off to the side, to the gun and away, again and again. She knew Cordts saw it, too. She watched Goody's hands. Don't do it, Goody, Maureen thought. Don't do it. That was Goody's problem: that habit of reaching for the gun as a solution. She heard Wilburn's chair creak again as he stood. She glanced up at the Guinness mirror and saw Wilburn had his hand on his weapon.

"The house you ran to, Goody," Maureen said. "Not where you hid, not Ms. Cleo's, but the house on Harmony Street. Why did you go there?"

"The girl there, Alisha, she's Benji's sister."

"You wanted to tell her," Maureen said. "You wanted to tell her you'd killed Dee for her. And she turned on you."

"She knew me and Benji was tight," Goody said. "She called me all damn day, every day. Asking me where Benji at? Where Benji at? You his best friend, where my brother at? I mean she knew, but she didn't want to *know*. And I couldn't tell her nothin' good anyway, because I couldn't find the motherfucker, either."

"So, what, you wanted to impress her by killing someone?" Cordts asked. "No wonder she ratted out your punk ass."

"That baby girl Alisha was holding," Maureen said, "that's your daughter."

"She's mine and Alisha's," Goody said, nodding. "Alisha stay there with her brother and our baby girl. Big brother Will don't like me. I just wanted to tell her that Dee was gone. With Dee gone, I thought maybe we'd have a better chance of getting Benji back. I had to do *something*. Getting Dee was the only thing I could do for Benji. To protect him. If he couldn't get that shit no more, maybe he'd at least go back to Alisha and Will's house. They tight, that family. Except for Benji, they do right." He looked at Cordts. "I told you. I got my own little girl, yo. I got my own daughter."

Cordts said nothing.

"That little girl is why I came back to New Orleans from Baton Rouge," Goody said. "I didn't even know about her until a few weeks ago. I'da stayed there if not for her. Will didn't want her to tell me, but Benji did. I guess Benji talked Alisha into telling me, into going behind Will's back. Benji knew a baby girl would get me back to New Orleans.

"I was doing all right in Baton Rouge, you know?" Goody said. "Thinking about going to school and shit. Then Alisha call me, said, 'Come for Mardi Gras, I got something to tell you.'

"After I heard, I figured I got to man up, and stay in New Orleans, you know? I *got* to. It was like I knew already in Baton Rouge that I had to get my mind right. I told Alisha we could get a place, be a family. She laughed at me, said Will would never have that." He wiped his face again, looking at his dirty hand, wiped it on his shirt. "I thought if I could get Benji away from that TWD, get him home, Will, he might look different at me, you know? Because I proved I could do something for the family, do right for the whole neighborhood, getting rid of Dee."

Maureen put her face in her hands, took a deep breath. Her hands smelled like sweat and coffee and nicotine. Benji had died within minutes, she figured, of Goody pulling the trigger, and in the process throwing his own life away by shooting three innocent bystanders instead of one drug dealer who probably had it coming.

"Oh, for fuck's sake," Cordts said, tossing a cloth napkin across the table.

"And now here I am," Goody said, wiping his snotty hands on the napkin without picking it up. "In a fucking cracker bar with three fucking cops. Happy fucking Mardi Gras."

Maureen looked at Cordts, watched him absorb what Goody had said. He was as pale as she'd ever seen him. Milk pale. Almost chalk pale. He worked the tip of his tongue over his teeth, drummed his fingers on the table. What Goody had said about having a daughter, that fact *had* to matter to Cordts.

Nobody spoke for a long time. Maureen could hear Wilburn shifting in his seat behind them.

"You're fifteen," Cordts finally said, his voice cracking. The conversation had sapped his rage, reduced him to something spent and exhausted, like the papery shell of an exploded firework. "And because of what you did tonight, you'll be a grandfather before you get out of fucking jail. You'll watch the girl grow up through Plexiglas, if she ever knows you at all. And I'll get old and fat chasing your grandkids around New Orleans. It never fucking ends, does it? The madness. It just never ends. No matter what we do."

He slid to the end of the booth. He handed Maureen his gun, then handed her the gun he'd found in the street. "Make sure that girl gets her stuff back."

He peeled off his yellow vest, tossed it on top of the sneaker and the wings. "Fuck you. Fuck this. Fuck all y'all. Fuck Mardi Gras. Fuck New Orleans. I'm done. Have a nice fucking press conference. I'm going home and I'm going to sleep until Ash Wednesday." He took a deep breath. "Then I'm packing the car and driving to wherever the fuck I run out of gas and I'm staying there, like I shoulda done after the storm."

He looked at Wilburn. "Sorry, bro. I tried."

Cordts turned and walked away into the kitchen, making his way, Maureen guessed, out into the night through the back door.

"Do we stop him?" Maureen asked, rising to her feet, turning to Wilburn.

"So what now?" Goody asked, fixed in his seat. "Does this mean I can go?"

Wilburn looked into the empty space that Cordts had left behind. "You know what? Nobody but us knows what happened in this room tonight."

He glanced at Goody, then Maureen. "Whatever we say happened, that's what happened. That's the story. Just a thought."

"So we're not going after Cordts then," Maureen said. "We let him disappear?"

Wilburn turned in his chair and looked out the front window of the restaurant. His face was shiny with sweat. "Well, look at that. Parade's over."

# 36

"I need you to stand up, Goody," Maureen said, passing Cordts's service weapon to Wilburn before tucking the extra gun into the back of her pants, "and put your hands behind your back."

"Man, fuck this," Goody said. "I told y'all all that shit and y'all are gonna do me like this? Y'all really gonna arrest me after you kidnap me? Man, fuck the police."

"Do it," Wilburn said, jaws tight. "Fucking shut up and do it."

He was furious, Maureen could tell, about Cordts, and he was fighting hard not to blame Goody for Cordts's nightlong meltdown, a collapse that meant the end of Cordts's career and probably their friendship as well. She knew that in Wilburn's mind, what had happened to Cordts tonight had been triggered by Goody shooting up that intersection. He believed that had Cordts not held that bloody little girl in his arms, he might have made it through the night.

After a long moment, Goody slid out of the booth without a word. Maureen cuffed him and sat him in the chair she'd been using.

"Wils, call Hardin and tell him we're coming out with Goody and without Cordts, and that Cordts is fine and we'll explain later."

Maureen waited until Wilburn had started walking for the front door, phone at his ear, before she grabbed Goody by the arm and stood him up.

"I got a little girl," he said. "Why would I shoot one?"

"But you did," Maureen said. "Whether you meant to or not, you did. Her and two other people. That won't ever go away."

"Man, that other crazy cop," Goody said, "he straight-up kidnaps me, holds me hostage, and he gonna walk away from this shit like he didn't do nothing wrong and I go to jail. Ain't that some shit."

Maureen bit her tongue and marched Goody to the front of the restaurant, where Wilburn and Eddie waited at the door.

"Hardin was able to get the car across," Wilburn said, "now that the parade's over. He's right out front."

"Open it," Maureen said to Eddie. "Let's get this over with."

Eddie opened the door. As Maureen stepped through it, shoving Goody ahead of her, a bright light blinded her and she felt her prisoner torn from her hands. She saw a flash of a long coat and wavy gray hair. She shaded her eyes from the spotlight, yelling, "Goddamn it, Cortez!"

But before she got the name out, the light had moved away from her, following a stern-looking, made-for-TV Drayton as he loaded Goody into the NOPD Explorer, his fat pink hand pushing down on Goody's head. Donna shouted questions at him. Laine stood off to the side of the action. Maureen spied Hardin behind the wheel of the truck. He didn't look at her.

Drayton slammed the back door and climbed into the front seat beside Hardin. He rolled down the window so Cortez could continue to shoot him for as long as possible. Maureen shaded her eyes again as the roof rack erupted into a sapphire light show and the car pulled away.

Cortez and Larry hustled into the street, filming the Explorer as it bounced across the now-deserted, trash-strewn neutral ground, over the streetcar tracks, and hung a U-turn, racing, Maureen was sure, to the site of the press conference. Donna checked her makeup in the reflection afforded by the restaurant window. Laine held her position on the sidewalk, watching her Craigslist camera crew grab a last few seconds of dramatic footage.

Maureen and Wilburn stood alone on the sidewalk, empty plastic cups and torn plastic bags blowing around their feet and along the gutter like tumbleweed. They could still hear the parade as it rolled on without them.

The rain started falling again, coming down for the first time that night in big, heavy drops.

Maureen turned to Wilburn. "We got our man and I feel like shit. Absolute shit."

"You get used to it," Wilburn said. "Goody's survival chances weren't any better if we *didn't* catch him. Especially once word gets out he was gunning for Dee Harris. So there's that. And that's the best I have to offer right now."

Laine, her down vest pulled over her head for shelter from the rain, approached them. "You think we can get a ride to the press conference?"

Maureen and Wilburn laughed. "In what vehicle? We're as stranded as you are."

"Cogs," Wilburn asked. "You want a beer?"

"I'd love one," Maureen said.

They walked back to the Dublin House.

"First round is on me, Officers," Eddie said, holding the door open for them. "We've got a long way to go yet before we sleep."

Laine followed them to the door. "Oh, thank God. It's really starting to come down out here."

Maureen watched from inside the bar door as Eddie extended his arm to block the entrance in front of Laine. "Sorry," he said. "Parade's over. Bar's closed. But don't worry. We're doing it all over again tomorrow night."

"And the night after that," Wilburn said.

"And the night after that," Maureen said. "And again the night after that. You get the picture. Happy Mardi Gras. Remember, Laine, it's a marathon, not a sprint."

"Seriously?" Laine asked. "You're really doing this to me?"

Maureen hesitated. She looked at Eddie, who shrugged, then Wilburn, who said before he walked away, "Do whatcha wanna, I'll be at the bar."

"Eddie, go pour the man his beer," Maureen said, standing before Laine and her crew, bedraggled and pathetic, huddled in the doorway.

"You can walk over to the press conference in the rain, or you can come in here and have a beer. But the camera stays off. Those are your choices."

Nobody said anything as they filed into the bar.

"And a happy Mardi Gras to all of you, too," Maureen said.

# 37

Less than twenty-four hours after Benji Allen had come storming down St. Charles Avenue, raging through the last minutes of his short life, Maureen was back on the route for the Friday-night parades. Her back ached. It had started hurting nearly the minute she took her route assignment at Eighth and St. Charles. Her feet felt swollen in her shoes. She imagined that various aches and pains would remain a fact of life for most of the next week. She'd get by; she'd endured worse. A touch of her hangover remained, but the headache that came with it was, thankfully, fading. She'd had only one beer at the Dublin House. But after her shift, she and Wilburn had caught up with Sansone and his crew and their postparade bar crawl had kept Dakota and her crew hopping until the horizon had lightened. She'd had worse hangovers.

And it's dry out here tonight, Maureen thought, shifting her weight from one foot to the other and back again, looking, she knew, like a child stuck waiting outside an occupied restroom. The rain and mist of the night before had moved on, leaving a crisp and cool early evening. The dry air was supposed to last clear through the weekend and Fat Tuesday. No sniffles tonight. Weather-wise, she thought, the worst was over. For the most part, she felt pretty damn good.

She was surrounded for the moment by proud, strutting middle school majorettes wearing sleeveless, sparkling green-sequined uniforms and tasseled white boots. They were beautiful. And they knew it. High-stepping, chins up, smiles peeking through their discipline as the crowd cheered for them, batons spinning over their perfectly coiffed heads, the girls, every one of them three feet and change and nothing but muscle, they reminded Maureen of the kids she'd walked through under the overpass last night. She wondered how many of these girls ran in those wild flocks of kids. She thought of Lyla, not much younger and smaller than they were, maybe a future majorette herself, recovering from her gunshot wound in the hospital. She thought of Cordts's lost almost-daughter, who never got to be any of these girls.

She thought of Goody, who now sat in jail, and who was not much older than the majorettes. Alisha, the mother of his daughter, wasn't much older, either. It was kids like the ones surrounding her, like Goody and Alisha, too, and like those who had been carousing under the overpass and all up and down the parade route and who marched in every single Mardi Gras parade from beginning to end last night, who Cordell taught in school every day. He'd survived his wounds, guarded but stable with the ferocious Susan stationed at his bedside. But he wouldn't be back in the classroom for quite some time. Maureen didn't know the first thing about Cordell as a professional, or about teaching, or music, for that matter, but she had a feeling in her gut that Cordell would be missed where he worked.

Hands clasped behind her back, chin raised, Maureen stood her post, her eyes scanning the crowd.

The flag twirlers followed the majorettes, the band followed them, passing around Maureen like a river around a rock, drowning her in their thunderous version of Gary Glitter's "Rock and Roll, Part 2," the beating drums shaking her rib cage, vibrating her heart.

# 38

After the band had passed, carrying their thunder on down the avenue, a gap emerged in the parade. As parade-goers spilled into the street and awaited the next of the Krewe of Hermes's twenty-nine floats, Laine stepped out of the crowd and came her way, dodging wild children scrambling after beads and toys in the street. Maureen looked for the others, but Laine was alone. She wore her down vest like she had when she was working, but wasn't holding her clipboard. Instead she held a forty-ounce bottle. Around her neck she wore several long, colorful strands of beads, one that swung down to her knees. On her head, peeking inches above her wild red hair, she wore one of Hermes's most prized and popular throws: a pair of blinking wings.

She approached Maureen with a sly smile. "Evening, Officer. Good to see you again."

"Hey, Laine," Maureen said, feeling friendly and relieved not to have to fight off a camera. "I like your wings."

"I do, too," Laine said. Her eyes were a touch glassy and she spoke as if her lips were swollen. The half-drunk forty-ounce in her hand, Maureen thought, was clearly not her first of the night. "Appropriate, right? Hermes, the messenger. He might've been a journalist, in modern times, right? We're, what do you call it, simpatico, me and Hermes."

"Sure," Maureen said with a smile. "Why not?

"Right?" Laine rolled her eyes upward, as if trying to see the blinking wings on the crown of her head. "I might keep them on my desk. If I ever have a desk, or an office, again. Or a job. Ha! Where's the rest of your team?"

"Wilburn is around here somewhere," Maureen said. "Follow the smell of grilled chicken, you'll find him. Morello's on patrol in the Garden District, I think, making sure no one's breaking into the parked cars. He likes that gig. Hardin's supposedly moving around the route, pretending to keep an eye on us. He's probably over at the Grocery eating a Cuban and drinking coffee."

"I hope you don't mind me asking," Laine said, "but are you and Sansone, you know, a thing?"

Maureen shook her head. "We are not."

"Why the hell not?"

"I gave up shitting in my own nest," Maureen said, "when I took this job."

"So he's single?" Laine asked.

"Have at it, girlfriend."

"I just might. Happy Mardi Gras to me." After a long pull from her bottle, she leaned in close to Maureen's cheek, burping a fog of malt liquor into Maureen's face. "Is Cordts okay? He vanished last night. It was weird."

Maureen coughed into her fist, blinking until the air around her cleared. "He got a mental health day today. Hardin's orders. He'll be back on the route tomorrow for the day parades."

"And that's it?" Laine asked, leaning back, trying to take in Maureen's whole face, as if that full view might tell her more. "A day off? He got a day off for taking a hostage?"

"We need him," Maureen said, checking the time on her phone. By now, Cordts was already unpacking at the mental health clinic three parishes away, the only deal other than charges that Hardin was willing to offer, but Maureen wasn't telling that to anyone not on the job. "Look at how things turned out in the end. Nobody got hurt. As far as everyone's concerned, he stepped out of the weather for a while with a suspect in custody, and after some miscommunication with the detective, handed that suspect over." She straightened her shoulders. "It's not often we treat a shooter to a basket of fries at a friend's bar before he goes to jail. How mean can we be? I'd hardly call that hostage-taking."

"Wow," Laine said, shaking her head, "this city is a trip."

"Everything that needed to get done, got done," Maureen said. "Nobody else got shot last night. The press conference was a glorious success, the brass was happy, the mayor was happy, the late news and the morning papers put the panic to rest with the magic words *isolated incident*. What's not to love?" She waved her arm over the crowd, bigger than the previous night's by half and twice as boisterous. "The show must go on. That is the prime directive."

Of course, Maureen thought, the case against Goody for the shooting was a leaky shambles, even with witnesses and the gun. Any halfway decent public defender, and Goody might actually luck into one of those, would shred the conversation in the Dublin House. As for Cordts taking him there in the first place, the department's version of events wouldn't hold up under duress or under oath, and an ambitious private attorney might see a chance to make their name and sue the city on Goody's behalf. The chain of custody for the evidence and the preservation of the crime scene were both highly questionable, just as a result of the general, unavoidable chaos surrounding the shooting.

If you were committing a crime in New Orleans, Mardi Gras was a good time to do it.

Nobody had died in the shooting. Homicide changed everything. The lack of one meant the DA was a lot less likely to add Goody's case to an already overwhelming pile of gun crimes. After the holiday, hell, by Saturday, as long as there wasn't another significant incident—as long as there were no more, as Cordts would say, bullets and blood—the shock and anger over the shooting would fade in no time. Goody might be charged with lesser crimes as a way to keep him in jail as long as possible, most likely as a juvenile, but indictment was unlikely. He wasn't worth the effort.

None of that was Maureen's concern. Not until the next time she was putting Goody in handcuffs. She hoped to hell there wouldn't be a next time, but Goody had no one out there on the streets to help him stay out of trouble and out of jail. No way Alisha's brother would let him within a hundred yards of Alisha or that baby.

Maureen was a new cop but she was an old enough human being not to be naïve about her chances of making a real difference in Goody's path. She'd take her shot at it, should the opportunity arise, but the odds were poor. She was just another white cop. She wouldn't be the one to save him. Someone else would have to do that, or better yet, lead Goody to where he could save himself. That wasn't surrender or cynicism; it was fact.

"And good on you," Maureen said to Laine, "for being more the participant than observer tonight. We're a participatory city."

"Thank you." Laine took a slug from her bottle. "Why let everyone else have all the fun? Right? I thought of lugging that camera out here— I heard this is a gorgeous parade—but I couldn't work up the motivation. I forgot what a pain in the ass it is carrying around that equipment myself." She danced in a circle, wiggling her hips. "I feel so free."

"Where's the rest of *your* crew?" Maureen asked. "Gave them the night off? Or are you making them work while you play?"

"Gave them the rest of their lives off," Laine said. "That's what I did." She lowered her head, red curls falling over her face. "Well, no, no, no, to be honest, they *took* the rest of their lives off."

Too much real New Orleans for them, Maureen thought. "They quit on you? After the drama last night?"

"You could call it that," Laine said. "Larry and Cortez decided they'd rather work with Malik and Albert, so they bailed on me. For free, if you can believe that, though I think the four of them are plotting a Kickstarter or something. They'll make millions somehow, just watch. The fuckers, they'll go straight from shooting on an iPad to working for Showtime. Donna's at the airport, on the standby list for the next flight to L.A., probably blowing someone for an upgrade to first class." She shrugged and opened her arms, the malt liquor swishing in the bottle as she waved it around. "No great loss. She's not much for working in the field. She's more of a studio talent, or a hotel room, or a stadium bathroom, if you know what I mean." She sighed. "Those tits made money, though. I'll say that. They'll be tough to replace. Purely as assets."

"Well, I'm sorry to hear that," Maureen said. "I thought y'all might pull off something good."

And Maureen found that she *was* sorry that the band had broken up, so to speak. It was easy for her to see that Laine felt bereft without her work. It wasn't just the bottle of malt liquor she clutched that gave her away, or the slur in her speech, or the bitterness toward her ex-crew. Laine exuded the air of someone who'd suffered a death in the family. To Maureen, Laine seemed to weigh less, to be less substantial than she'd been the night before, as if she'd been hollowed out overnight.

Life isn't good, Maureen knew from experience, without good work to do.

"I know this flakka project was important to you," she said, "and that you'd put a bunch of time and effort into it. And money. It sucks that it crapped out."

"I have a lot of raw content on my laptop," Laine said, with a shrug. "I can probably piece something together to put up on the YouTube channel. Sansone and Achee said they would give me interviews, maybe connect me to other cops who worked what could be flakka cases, if I could wait until after Mardi Gras. I mean, that chalk monster giving this shit away in the Quarter sounds like something special, doesn't he?" She took a long pull from her bottle.

"I've got some money left, especially now that I'm not paying Donna anymore. Cortez can't be the only bargain-basement cameraman in New Orleans. Maybe the project can come back from the dead." She gave Maureen a lopsided grin. "You know, like a zombie."

"Will you hang around?" Maureen asked. An idea had sparked in her brain. "How long do you think you'll stay in town?"

"I don't know," Laine said. "Without a crew to help on this project, if I can't muster up a new one, and I don't much feel like doing that, I don't have much reason to be here. But I don't really have anyplace to go next. Lord knows I'm not going to Baton Rouge or Houston for the fucking fun of it. There's no point if there's no story in those places. And the apartment I rented here is paid through Ash Wednesday. No sense throwing *that* money away." She giggled. "I may just say fuck it and party for the next four days. I'm already here. There's nobody waiting for me anywhere, that's for sure. You got a cigarette?"

Maureen pulled her pack from her pocket. With it, she pulled out Philippa Marlowe's pink business card. She lit a smoke, gave it to Laine, and lit another for herself. She thought of the photo of Benji Allen that Laine had provided.

"You were helpful to us last night," Maureen said. "You did us a real solid. But I won't spread the word you helped the police. Bad for your reputation."

She passed the pink card to Laine.

"Who is this?" Laine asked. "This card is a horror. Is she a hairdresser?"

"Local woman," Maureen said. "Fancies herself a citizen-journalist. She's a character, but she pays attention to what's happening in the city, and she gives a shit. You two should meet. You'd like each other."

"I know the type," Laine said. "You think she'll give me an interview?"

"About anything," Maureen said. "Believe me." She took a long drag on her cigarette, considering her next words. "She doesn't have Donna's considerable Hollywood assets, but she loves New Orleans, I think she knows a thing or two about it, and she has personality to burn. I'm no talent scout, but she might work well in front of the camera."

"But does she know anything about the flakka stories?"

"What if you left that story behind?" Maureen asked. "I know that zombie drug is what brought you here, but there's no reason you can't adjust your, you know, journalistic mission. Especially now that you're starting over. Believe me, lots of people come to New Orleans for one reason and stay for another."

Laine frowned. "Who said anything about staying?"

"What about Goody's story?" Maureen asked. "Why don't you tell that? You want compelling stories? That kid is fifteen, already with a baby and maybe serious charges coming to him. He did what he did trying to save his daughter's uncle from the drug that killed him. When I first met him he had two best friends. One, named Mike-Mike, ended up dead in the trunk of a car that Goody helped burn. The other one, his name is Marques, he got out of the life and started his own brass band. How does that happen? How does it go so differently for three kids from the same 'hood? I'm trying to figure that out myself.

"Goody's got a record as long as his arm and a child with a neighborhood girl. What's her story? What's that baby's story gonna be? Nobody's asking about these kids. But you could. You came here to capture the real New Orleans? These kids are it. Every one of them. And not just them. Philippa. Sansone. Morello. Hardin. Malik and Albert. Ms. Cleo. Them, too. Even that jackass Drayton. There's this detective named Atkinson, she's the anti-Drayton. I want to be her when I grow up. I'll introduce you to the couple that owns the Grocery, on Sixth. I'll introduce you to a guy named Preacher. He was my training officer and my first duty sergeant. Taught me everything I know. No one else like him in the world. You won't believe he's real."

"That's an awful lot of work," Laine said. "Meeting all those people, learning about them. It's harder than jumping from place to place. A lot harder. That's a real commitment, telling those stories. That's serious work."

"It's a *life's* work," Maureen said. "But there are endless stories here for the taking, stories you can't get anywhere else, and you won't believe the crazy ways they connect with each other. You might run out of money, you might run out of brain cells, but you'll *never* run out of stories here. I promise you."

Laine took a long pull from her forty-ounce. "I'm intrigued. I admit it."

"But if you want to see this real New Orleans everyone keeps talking about," Maureen said, "if you want to be a part of it, if you want to live it and not watch it go by like an out-of-town parade, there's one thing you have to do."

"And what's that?" Laine asked, smiling at Maureen over the top of her forty-ounce. "Flash my boobs? Suck the head? Wear a Saints hat?"

Maureen laughed. She saw that the parade had started rolling again. She could hear the rumble of the tractor pulling the next glowing float toward them down St. Charles Avenue. She could see the thousands of hands rising into the air at once, the float swaying on its wheels, its riders on both sides hurling spinning strands of beads into the night air above the adoring crowd. She turned to Laine, who stared at the spectacle, arms loose at her sides, her mouth hanging slightly open.

"You have to give New Orleans your time," Maureen said. "You have to stay. Do that, and who knows what'll happen?"

## ACKNOWLEDGMENTS

Writing requires solitude, but suffers in isolation. None of this good stuff happens without the generous love, patience, and support of family and friends. I am grateful and indebted to all of you—no one more so than my most amazing and talented wife, my great love, AC Lambeth.

Much gratitude to my heroic agent, Barney Karpfinger, and everyone at the Karpfinger Agency whose hard work and prodigious talents keep me upright and sane.

Thanks also to my fabulous editor and publisher, Sarah Crichton, who always demands the best book I have in me, and who sees it in the pages even when I don't. Thanks also to Lottchen, Caroline, John, Abby, Rachel, Spenser, Elizabeth, and everyone at FSG and Picador for believing in me and working so hard to bring Maureen Coughlin and her New Orleans adventures to the world. Once again, thank you to Alex Merto for the spectacular cover. One reason I wrote a Mardi Gras book was to see what you would do with it.

Much of this book was written to live recordings of Oasis. Why that is or why it worked, I have no idea.

Other music important to this book includes but is not limited to: local artists Kelcy Mae, the Revivalists, the Rebirth Brass Band, Truth Universal, Soul Rebels Brass Band, Dr. John; as well as Juliana Hatfield, Sixx A.M., P!NK, Joan Jett, Mötley Crüe, Metric, the Dead Weather, the Tragically Hip.

Much love to booksellers and librarians everywhere. Without you my career literally would not exist. Thank you for always welcoming me with good coffee and open arms and for fighting the good fight.

Thank you, Joey K's and the Executive Tuesday Krewe. Stay in the game.

Thanks to the Bend Media and Production for making me look good.

Happy are They Whom the Muses Love. Find out more about the Krewe of Muses at kreweofmuses.org.

You can support marching band education and tradition in New Orleans. Check out the Roots of Music at therootsofmusic.org.

AC and I also support the brave and important work Steve Gleason and Team Gleason do on behalf of people with ALS and their families. Learn more at teamgleason.org.

## A NOTE ABOUT THE AUTHOR

Bill Loehfelm is the author of the critically acclaimed series about the New Orleans Police Department rookie Maureen Coughlin, as well as the stand-alone novels *Fresh Kills* and *Bloodroot*. His short fiction and nonfiction have appeared in several anthologies. He lives in New Orleans with his wife, AC Lambeth, a writer and yoga instructor, and their dog. He plays drums in a rock-'n-'roll band.